A Killing Kindness

A Killing
Kindness

Reginald Hill

FELONY & MAYHEM PRESS • NEW YORK

All the characters and events portrayed in this work are fictitious.

A KILLING KINDNESS

A Felony & Mayhem mystery

PRINTING HISTORY
First UK edition (Collins): 1980
First US edition (Pantheon): 1980
Felony & Mayhem edition: 2009

ISBN: 978-1-934609-38-5

Manufactured in the United States of America

Library of Congress Cataloging-in-Publication Data

Hill, Reginald.
   A killing kindness / Reginald Hill. -- Felony & Mayhem ed.
      p. cm.
   "A Felony & Mayhem mystery."
   ISBN 978-1-934609-38-5
   1. Dalziel, Andrew (Fictitious character)--Fiction.2. Pascoe, Peter
(Fictitious character)--Fiction. 3. Police--Fiction. 4. Yorkshire
(England)--Fiction. I. Title.
   PR6058.I448K5 2009
   823'.914--dc22
                                          2009027189

For Dan and Pat

The icon above says you're holding a book in the Felony & Mayhem "British" category. These books are set in or around the UK, and feature the highly literate, often witty prose that fans of British mystery demand.

For information about British titles or to learn more about Felony & Mayhem Press, please visit us online at:

www.FelonyAndMayhem.com

Or write to us at:

Felony and Mayhem Press
156 Waverly Place
New York, NY 10014

Other "British" titles from

FELONY&MAYHEM

MICHAEL DAVID ANTHONY
The Becket Factor
Midnight Come

ROBERT BARNARD
Death on the High C's
Out of the Blackout
Death and the Chaste Apprentice
The Skeleton in the Grass
Corpse in a Gilded Cage

PETER DICKINSON
King and Joker
The Old English Peep Show
Skin Deep
Sleep and His Brother

CAROLINE GRAHAM
The Killings at Badger's Drift
Death of a Hollow Man
Death in Disguise
Written in Blood
Murder at Madingley Grange

CYNTHIA HARROD-EAGLES
Orchestrated Death

REGINALD HILL
A Clubbable Woman
An Advancement of Learning
Ruling Passion
An April Shroud
Death of a Dormouse

ELIZABETH IRONSIDE
Death in the Garden
The Accomplice
A Very Private Enterprise
The Art of Deception

BARRY MAITLAND
The Marx Sisters

JOHN MALCOLM
A Back Room in Somers Town

JANET NEEL
Death's Bright Angel

SHEILA RADLEY
Death in the Morning
The Chief Inspector's Daughter
A Talent for Destruction
Fate Worse Than Death

L.C. TYLER
The Herring Seller's Apprentice

A Killing Kindness

The man that lays his hand upon a woman,
Save in the way of kindness, is a wretch
Whom 'twere gross flattery to name a coward.
—*John Tobin*
The Honeymoon

CHAPTER 1

...it was green, all green, all over me, choking, the water, then boiling at first, and roaring, and seething, till all settled down, cooling, clearing, and my sight up drifting with the few last bubbles, till through the glassy water I see the sky clearly, and the sun bright as a lemon, and birds with wings wide as a windmill's sails slowly drifting round it, and over the bank's rim small dark faces peering, timid as beasts at their watering, nostrils sniffing danger and shy eyes bright and wary, till a current turns me over, and I drift, and still am drifting, and...

What the hell's going on here! Stop it! This is sick...

Please. Oh God! Be careful you'll...

Jack! No!

Ohhhh...

See! Look. The lights...please

...fakery... I don't want

...lights! Mrs Stanhope, Mrs Stanhope, are you all right?

...auntie, are you OK? Please, auntie...

...thank you, love, I'm a bit...in a minute...did I get...

...vicious blackmailing cow and I'll see...

'...picking up lots of forget-me-nots. You make me...'

'Sorry,' said Sergeant Wield, switching off the pocket cassette recorder. 'That was on the tape before.'

'Pity. I thought she was proving that Sinatra really was dead,' said Pascoe putting down the sergeant's handwritten transcription of the first part of the recording. 'Did you switch off there, or what?'

'Or what, I think. I had the mike in my pocket, nice and inconspicuous. When I jumped up to grab at Sorby it must've fallen out and pulled the connection loose. I'm sorry about all this, sir!'

'Oh no, you're not,' said Pascoe. 'Not yet. When Mr Dalziel comes through that door with the *Evening Post* in his hand, that's when you're going to be sorry.'

Wield nodded gloomy agreement with the inspector, who now studied his report as if seeking some hidden meaning.

Like all Sergeant Wield's reports, it was pellucid in its clarity.

Calling on Mrs Winifred Sorby in pursuit of enquiries into the murder of her daughter, Brenda, he had found her in the company of her neighbour, Mrs Annie Duxbury. A short time later, Mrs Rosetta Stanhope and her niece, Pauline, had turned up. Mrs Stanhope was known to the sergeant by reputation as a self-professed clairvoyant and medium. It emerged that Mrs Sorby wished Mrs Stanhope to attempt to get in touch with her dead daughter. The sergeant had been pressed to stay and take part. Agreeing, he had excused himself to go out to his car where he had a small cassette recorder. Concealing this under his jacket, he had returned and joined the women round a table in the dead girl's darkened bedroom. After a while Mrs Stanhope had seemed to go into a trance and finally started talking in a voice completely different from her own. But only a few moments later the door had burst open and Mr Sorby, the dead girl's father, had entered angrily and brought the seance to an end.

His fury at his wife's stupidity had been redirected when he became aware of the sergeant's presence. He had rapidly found a sympathetic ear for his complaints in the local press and by the time a chastened Wield had returned to the station, Pascoe had already fielded several enquiries about the police decision to use clairvoyance in the Sorby case.

'His wife's always gone in for that kind of stuff,' explained Wield. 'Sorby's never approved. Naturally she wasn't expecting him back for a couple of hours.'

'Perhaps he's got second sight,' grunted Pascoe.

He was examining the transcript again. It had taken Wield nearly an hour of careful listening to sort out the confusion of overlapping voices.

'Let's get it straight,' said Pascoe. 'Mrs Stanhope in her trance voice. That's clear. Then Sorby arrives and starts shouting. OK?'

'Yes,' said Wield. 'Next—that's *"Please. Oh God"*, etc., is the niece, Pauline. *"Jack...no!"*—that's Mrs Sorby.'

'And this great yell?'

'Mrs Stanhope coming out of her trance. Then the niece again, Sorby going on about fakery, Mrs Sorby asking Mrs Stanhope if she's all right.'

'Which she is. Speaking in her normal voice again, right?'

'Right. And Sorby again. The niece had jumped up and put the light on. Sorby pushed her aside and looked as if he was going to assault Mrs Stanhope. That's when I got in on the act.'

'And the rest is silence,' said Pascoe. 'That's apt.'

'I wish it had all been bloody silence,' said Wield. He had one of the ugliest faces Pascoe had ever seen, the kind of ugliness which you didn't get used to but were taken aback by even if you met him after only half an hour's separation. The advantage of such an arrangement of features was that it normally blanked out tell-tale signs of emotion. But at the moment unease was printed clearly on the creased and leathery surface.

The phone rang.

It was the desk-sergeant.

'Mr Dalziel's just come in,' he said. 'He's on his way up.'

The door burst open as Pascoe replaced the receiver.

Detective-Superintendent Andrew Dalziel stood there. A long intermittently observed diet had done something to keep his bulging flesh in check, but now anger seemed to have inflated him till his eyes threatened to pop out of his grizzled bladder of a head and his muscles seemed on the point of ripping apart the dog-tooth twill of his suit.

Like the Incredible Hulk about to emerge, thought Pascoe.

'Hello, sir. Good meeting?' he said, half rising. Wield was standing to attention as if rigor mortis had set in.

'Champion, till I got off the train this end,' said Dalziel, raising a huge right hand which was attempting to squeeze the printing ink out of a rolled up copy of the local paper.

He pretended to notice Wield for the first time, went close to him and put his mouth next to his ear.

'Ah, Sergeant Wield,' he murmured. 'Any messages for me?'

'No sir,' said Wield. 'Not that I know of.'

'Not even from the other bloody side!' bellowed Dalziel. He looked as if he was about to thump the sergeant with the paper.

'It's all a mistake, sir,' interposed Pascoe hastily.

'Mistake? Certainly it's a bloody mistake. I go down to Birmingham for a conference. *Hello Andy*, they all say. *How's that Choker of yours?* they all say. *Fine*, I say. *All under control*, I say. *That* was the bloody mistake! You know what it says here in this rag?'

He unfolded the paper with some difficulty.

'*It has long been common practice among American police forces to call on the aid of clairvoyants when they are baffled*,' he read. 'I leave a normal English CID unit doing its job. I come back and suddenly it's the Mid-Yorkshire precinct and we're baffled! No wonder Kojak's bald.'

Pascoe risked a smile. Lots of things made Dalziel angry. Not having his jokes appreciated was one of them.

The fat man hooked a chair towards him with a size ten foot and sat down heavily.

'All right,' he said. 'Tell me.'

For answer, Pascoe shoved Wield's report towards him. He read it quickly.

'Sergeant.'

'Sir!'

'Oh, stop standing there as if you'd crapped yourself,' said Dalziel wearily.

'Think I may have, sir,' said Wield.

This tickled Dalziel's fancy and he grinned and belched. There had obviously been a buffet bar on the train.

'How'd it happen you had a recorder in your car, lad? Not normal issue these days, is it?'

'No, sir,' said Wield. 'It's my nephew's. It'd gone wonky so I'd been having it repaired.'

'That was kind of you,' said Dalziel approvingly. 'At an electrical shop, you mean?'

'Not exactly, sir,' said Wield, uncomfortable again. 'It's Percy Lowe who services the radio equipment in the cars. He's very good with anything like this.'

'Oh aye. In his own time and with his own gear, I suppose,' said Dalziel sarcastically.

'He did a good job on your electric kettle, sir,' said Pascoe brightly.

Dalziel edged nearer the corner of the desk to scratch his paunch on the angle.

'Let's hear what the spirits had to say, then,' he commanded.

He followed Wield's transcript closely as the tape was played again.

'Now that's what I call helpful,' he said when it was done. 'That makes it all worthwhile. Here's us thinking Brenda Sorby was killed after dark when all the time the sun was shining, and that she was chucked into our muddy old canal that's so thick Judas bloody Iscariot could walk on it, and all the time it was some nice crystal-clear trout stream!'

'Sir,' said Pascoe, but the sarcasm wasn't yet finished.

'So all we've got to do now, sergeant, is work out the most likely nesting ground for albatrosses in Yorkshire. Or condors, maybe. Wasn't there a pair seen sitting on a slag heap near Barnsley? That's it! And these dark-skinned buggers'll be Arthur Scargill and his lads just up from t'pit!'

Pascoe laughed, not so much at the 'wit' as in relief that Dalziel was talking himself back into a good mood. He had known the fat man for many years now and familiarity had bred a complex of emotions and attitudes not least among which was a healthy caution.

'All right, Peter,' said Dalziel. 'This crap apart, what's really happened today?'

'Nothing much. House to house goes on, but we're running out of houses.'

'And the lad, what about the lad?'

'Tommy Maggs? I saw him again today while the sergeant was at the Sorbys'. It was just about as useful. He sticks to his story. He's very uptight, but you'd expect that.'

'Why?'

'Well, his girl-friend murdered and the police visiting him twice daily.'

'Oh aye,' said Dalziel doubtfully. He glanced at his watch. 'Well, I'll tell you what we'll do,' he said. 'How's your missus?'

Pascoe's wife, Ellie, was five months gone with their first child.

'Fine, she's fine.'

'Grand,' said Dalziel. 'That's what you need, Peter. A babby around the house. Steady you down a bit.'

He nodded with the tried virtue of a medieval bishop remonstrating with a wild young squire.

'So if she's all right, and my watch is all right, the Black Bull's open and I'll let you buy me a pint.'

'A pleasure, sir,' said Pascoe. 'But just the one.'

'Don't be shy. You can buy me as many as you like,' said Dalziel.

As he passed Wield, he dug a finger into his ribs and said, 'You'd best come too, sergeant, in case we move on to spirits.'

He went chuckling through the door.

Pascoe and Wield shared a moment of silent pain and then followed him.

(HAPTER 2

Brenda Sorby was the third murder victim in less than four weeks.

The first had been Mary Dinwoodie, aged forty, a widow. Disaster had come in the traditional three instalments to Mrs Dinwoodie. Less than a year earlier she and her husband and their seventeen-year-old daughter had been happily and profitably running the Linden Garden Centre in Shafton, a pleasant dormer village a few miles east of town. Then in a macabre accident at the Mid-Yorkshire Agricultural Show, during a parade of old steam traction engines, one of the drivers had suffered a stroke, his machine had turned into the spectators, Dinwoodie had slipped and next thing his crushed and lifeless body was lying on the turf. Five months later, his daughter too was crushed to death in a car accident on an icy Scottish road.

This second tragedy almost destroyed Mrs Dinwoodie. She had left the Garden Centre in the care of her nurseryman and gone off alone. More than three months elapsed before she reappeared. She looked pale and ill but was clearly determined to get back to normality. Ironically it was her first tentative steps in that direction which completed the tragic trilogy.

While the Dinwoodies had made no close personal friends locally, they had not been inactive, their social life being centred on the Shafton Players, the village amateur dramatic group. Mary Dinwoodie had withdrawn completely after her husband's death, but now, pressed by a kindly neighbour, she had agreed to attend the group's annual summer 'night out'. They had had a meal at the Cheshire Cheese, a pub with a small dining-room on the southern outskirts of town. At closing time they had drifted into the car park, calling cheerful goodnights. Mary Dinwoodie had insisted on coming in her own car in case she wanted to get away early. In the event she had stayed to the last and seemed to enjoy herself thoroughly. The other twenty or so revellers had all set off into the night, in groups no smaller than three. And all imagined Mary Dinwoodie was driving home too.

But in the morning her mini was still in the car park.

And a short time afterwards a farm labourer setting out to clear a ditch not fifty yards behind the Cheshire Cheese found her body neatly, almost religiously, laid out amid the dusty nettles.

She had been strangled, or 'choked' as the labourer informed any who would listen to him, a progressively diminishing number over the next few days.

But the alliteration appealed to Sammy Locke, news editor of the local *Evening Post* and 'The Cheshire Cheese Choking' was his lead story till public interest faded, a rapid enough process as the labourer could well avow.

Then ten days later the second killing took place. June McCarthy, nineteen, single, a shift worker at the Eden Park Canning Plant on the Avro Industrial Estate, was dropped early one Sunday morning at the end of Pump Road, a long curving street half way down which she lived with her widowed father. Her friends on the works bus never saw her alive again. A septuagenarian gardener called Dennis Ribble opening the shed on his Pump Street allotment at nine-thirty a.m. found her dead on the floor.

She too had been strangled. There were no signs of sexual interference. The body was neatly laid out, legs together, lolling tongue pushed back into the mouth, arms crossed on her breast and, a macabre touch, in her hands a small posy of mint sprigs whose fragrance filled the shed.

There were no obvious suspects. Her father was discovered still in bed and imagining his daughter was in hers. And her fiancé, a soldier from a local regiment, had returned to Northern Ireland the previous day after a week's leave.

Sammy Locke at the *Evening Post* read the brief accounts in the national dailies on Monday, looked for an angle and finally composed a headline reading CHOKER AGAIN?

He had just done this when the phone rang. A man's voice said without preamble, 'I say, we will have no more marriages.'

Locke was not a literary man, but his secretary, having recently left boring school after one year of a boring 'A' level course, thought she recognized a reference to one of the two boring texts she had struggled through (the other had been *Middlemarch*).

'That's *Hamlet*,' she announced. 'I think.'

And she was right.

Act 3, Scene 1. *I have heard of your paintings too, well enough; God hath given you one face and you make yourselves another; you jig, you amble, and nickname God's creatures, and make your wantonness your ignorance. Go to, I'll no more on't; it hath made me mad. I say we will have no more marriages; those that married already, all but one, shall live; the rest shall keep as they are. To a nunnery, go.*

Sammy Locke did not know his Shakespeare but he knew his news and after a little thought he removed the question mark from his headline and rang up Dalziel with whom he had a drinking acquaintance.

Dalziel received the information blankly and then consulted Pascoe, whose possession of a second-class honours degree in social science had won him the semi-ironical status of cultural consultant to the fat man. Pascoe shrugged and made an entry in the log book.

And then came Brenda Sorby.

She was just turned eighteen, a pretty girl with long blonde hair who worked as a teller in a suburban branch of the Northern Bank. A picture had emerged of a young woman with the kind of simplistic view of life which is productive of both great naïveté and great resolution. She had told her mother that she would not be home for tea that Thursday evening, and she had been right. After work she was having her hair done, and then she planned to take advantage of the new policy of Thursday night late closing by some of the city centre stores to do some shopping before meeting her boy-friend.

This was Thomas Arthur Maggs, Tommy to his friends, aged twenty, a motor mechanic by trade and an amiable but rather feckless youth by nature. He had got into a bit of trouble as a juvenile, but nothing serious and nothing since. Brenda's father disapproved of almost everything about Tommy and his circle of friends, but was restrained from being too violent in his opposition by Mrs Sorby, who opined that it was best to let these things run their course. They did, until the night of Brenda's eighteenth birthday which she celebrated with a party of friends at the town's most pulsating disco. She returned home happy, slightly merry and wearing a rather flashy engagement ring. Jack Sorby exploded—at Brenda for her stupidity, at Tommy for his duplicity, at his wife for her ill-counsel, at himself for taking heed of it. He subsided only when his threats to throw his daughter out were met by the calm response that in that case she would start living with Tommy that very night.

A truce was agreed, a very ill-defined truce but one which Jack Sorby felt had been treacherously and unilaterally shattered when on that Friday morning only four days later he rose to discover his daughter had not come home the previous night. Once again, all Mrs Sorby's powers of restraint were called upon to prevent him setting off for the Maggses' household only a mile away and administering to Tommy the lower-middle-class Yorkshireman's equivalent of a horsewhipping. Curiously, his genuine if rather over-intense concern for his daughter did not admit any explanation of her absence other than the sexual.

Winifred Sorby had a broader view of her daughter, however. As soon as her husband had left for the local rating office where he was head clerk, she had rung the bank. Brenda was usually there by eight-thirty. She had not yet appeared. At nine, she tried again. Then, putting on a raincoat because, despite the promise of a fine summer day, she was beginning to feel a deep internal chill, she went round to Tommy Maggs's house.

There was no reply, no sign of life.

The Maggses all worked, a helpful neighbour told her. And, yes, she had seen them all go off at their usual time, Tommy included.

Mrs Sorby went to the police.

The name of Tommy Maggs immediately roused some interest.

At eleven-fifteen the previous night a Panda car crew had been attracted by the sight of an old rainbow-striped mini with its bonnet up and a young man apparently trying to beat the engine into submission with a spanner.

Investigation revealed that it was indeed his own car which had broken down and, despite all his professional ministrations (for it was Tommy Maggs), refused to start. A strong smell of drink prompted the officers to ask how Tommy had spent the evening. With his girl-friend, he told them. She, irritated by the breakdown and being only half a mile or so from her home which was where they'd been heading, had set off on foot.

Had they been in a pub?

No, assured Tommy. No, they definitely hadn't been in a pub.

But you have been drinking, suggested one of the policemen emerging from the interior of the mini with an almost empty bottle of Scotch in his hand.

A breathalyser test put it beyond all doubt. Tommy was taken to the station for a blood test. His protestations that he had not taken a drink until *after* the breakdown evoked the kindly meant suggestion that he should save it for the judge. The police doctor was occupied elsewhere looking at a night watchman who'd had his head banged in the course of a break-in and it was well after one a.m. before Tommy was released, a delay which was later to stand him in good stead. By this time it was raining heavily and constabulary kindness was once more evidenced by a lift in a patrol car going in the general direction of his home.

When the police approached him the next day at the Wheatsheaf Garage, his place of work, he assumed it was on the same business and his story came out again—perhaps a little more rounded this time. A quiet romantic drive with his fiancée, the breakdown, Brenda's departure on foot, his own frustration and the taking of a quick pull on the bottle to soothe his troubled nerves prior to abandoning the useless bloody car and walking home.

When he realized the true nature of their enquiries, however, his agitation was intense. The police took a statement, then went on to the bank. No one had heard of or seen Brenda since she left the previous evening, but there had been a couple of attempts to get her on the telephone earlier that morning, apart from Mrs Sorby's, that was.

By lunch-time, the police were taking things very seriously. Jack Sorby had created a diversion by going round to the Wheatsheaf Garage and attempting to assault Tommy who by this time was too miserable and demoralized to defend himself. Fortunately, the police arrived almost simultaneously and established peace. Tommy wasn't up to much except repeating his story mechanically but at least they solved the mystery of the other phone calls. He had made them, he admitted. When asked why, he said with a brief flash of his customary liveliness, 'To get her to back up my fucking story about the drink, of course.'

This made sense to Pascoe, who since the two stranglings had been told by Dalziel to keep an eye on all female attacks or disappearances. While it didn't actually confirm Tommy's version of the evening, it helped a lot; or it meant he was ten times more cunning than he looked.

What finally took Tommy off the hook was the last thing anybody wanted—the discovery of the body. It was not pleasant. Right through the heart of the city, a straight line alongside the shallow and meandering river, ran the old canal, a relict of the last century and little used since the war until the holiday companies began to sell the delights of inland cruising in the 'sixties and commercial interests began to react to soaring fuel costs in the 'seventies. It was a barge that quite literally brought Brenda's body to light. Riding low with a cargo of castings, the barge was holding the centre of the channel when a careless cruiser forced it over towards the bank. The bargee swore with proverbial force as the bottom bumped and the propeller stuttered, thinking he'd caught some sizeable bit of rubbish dumped in the murky waters.

Switching off the engine he hurried to the stern and peered over. At first he was just aware that the dark brown water was imbued with a richer stain. Then as he saw what came drifting slowly to the surface, he began to swear again but this time as a kind of pious defence.

The pathologist was able to confirm that all the mutilations on the body were caused by the action of the propeller and had nothing to do with the girl's death. She had been strangled but had not been dead, though possibly moribund, when she entered the water. Asked when death occurred, he refused to be more definite than not less than twelve, not more than twenty hours. Pressed, he became irritable and talked about special circumstances such as the high temperature of the canal water and the opening up of the chest and lungs by the propeller. Pascoe, long used to the imprecisions of science, had looked for other evidence of timing.

Twenty hours took him back to six-thirty p.m. on the Thursday. He was able to move forward to eight p.m. because that was when Brenda and Tommy had met. Their rendezvous had been at the Bay Tree Inn, a half-timbered former coaching inn not far from the city centre which had fallen into the hands of a large brewery group renowned for the acuteness of their commercial instincts and the awfulness of their keg beer. Now the Bay Tree's history attracted the tourist set, its twin restaurants (one expensive, one extortionate) attracted the dining set, and its cellar disco attracted the young set. Thus it was always packed. The meeting had been witnessed by Ron Ludlam, a workmate of Tommy's and one of the friends of whom Mr Sorby so fervently disapproved. He had been drinking with Tommy while he waited for Brenda. Brenda had not wanted to stay at the Bay Tree. Ron Ludlam, who had accompanied the distraught Tommy home after the news of Brenda's death, said she seemed more interested in having a serious talk with her fiancé about marital matters. Alone. They had gone off in the noisy, multicoloured mini.

According to Tommy they had spent the evening just driving around. Without stopping? Of course they had stopped, just parked out in the country to have a fag and a talk. Was that all? They might have played around a bit but nothing serious.

'Nothing serious' was confirmed by the pathologist. Brenda was *virgo intacta*.

The canal was flanked on the one side by warehouses. Access could be obtained to the waterfront, but only by dint of climbing over security gates. In addition, from eleven p.m. on, there had been great police activity in Sunnybank, the canyon-like road which serviced the warehouses, for it was in one of these that the night watchman, whose injuries had kept the doctor from sampling Tommy Maggs's blood, had been attacked.

On the other side of the canal, the side where the body had been found, was a grassy isthmus planted with willows and birches to screen the industrial terrace from the view of those taking the air in the pleasant open spaces of Charter Park. This air on the night in question was filled with music and merriment. The city's fortnight-long High Fair was coming to the end of its first week there. The City Fathers in a fit of almost continental abandon permitted the municipal Boating Station to stay open until midnight during the fair and those who tired of the roundabouts and sideshows could hire rowboats to take them across to the isthmus where the trees were strung with fairy lights and a couple of hot-dog stands provided the wherewithal for a picnic. This area was far too well populated for a body to have been dumped in the canal until eleven-thirty when the clouds which had slowly been building up in the south suddenly came rolling northwards, ate up the moon and the stars, and spat rich, heavy raindrops into the sultry night. Within twenty minutes the isthmus was vacated by laughing holiday-makers and cursing hot-dog men alike, while on the canal the pleasure cruisers had either puttered off to more congenial moorings downstream or battened down for the night.

Now a regiment of corpses could have been deposited without drawing much attention.

But by now, Tommy Maggs was already in deep conversation with the police and was to continue in their company until dropped at his door at one-thirty a.m. His father, watching a late western on the telly, confirmed his arrival. So unless he later stole from the house and, carless, contrived to re-encounter Brenda, lure her to the canal bank some five miles away and there murder her, he was in the clear.

But what had happened to Brenda after she left her boy-friend by his broken-down mini, no one could say. Except one person.

At six o'clock on Friday the news editor of the *Evening Post* picked up his phone.

'I must be cruel, only to be kind,' said a voice. The line went dead.

The news editor yelled for his secretary.

CHAPTER 3

Ellie Pascoe was not enjoying the rich rewarding experience of pregnancy.

At roughly the halfway point she was still suffering the morning sickness which should have died away a month earlier and was already experiencing the backache and heartburn which might decently have waited till a month later.

'For Christ's sake don't make soothing noises,' she said as she returned pale-faced to the breakfast table. 'I'm having a baby, not turning into one.'

Pascoe, warned, returned to his cornflakes and said lightly, 'You shouldn't have bought the ticket if you didn't want the trip.'

'I didn't know it meant the end of civilization as I know it,' she said grimly.

'At least you don't have to go to work,' said Pascoe.

They were well into July and the long vacation had begun at the college where Ellie lectured.

'It's the students who get the holiday, not us,' she retorted. This was an ancient tract of disputed land, full of shell holes. Pascoe made a tactical withdrawal.

'Can I have the butter, please?'

'If by that you mean that if I'd taken your advice and resigned last term I wouldn't need to be thinking about next September's courses then let me remind you that, first, I personally need the work and, secondly, we personally need the money and, thirdly, that women having fought for centuries to get the meagre rights they've got, including the right not to lose their jobs because some careless fellow puts them up the stick, I am not about to renounce those rights just because you're feeling all patriarchal and protective. Excuse me.'

When she came back, Pascoe said, 'Thank God I didn't ask for the marmalade,' but she didn't respond.

'What are you doing today?' he asked as he finished his coffee.

'I'm going to be sick at the Aero Club,' she said.

'Good God,' he said, alarmed. 'You're not taking up gliding, are you?'

'No. Just having lunch there. They do a chicken-in-the-basket. Today they might see it there twice.'

'Come on,' said Pascoe. 'It can't be that bad. Can it? And why the Aero Club? Not your normal stamping ground.'

'I'm meeting Thelma.'

'Lacewing? You surprise me. I shouldn't have thought it was her scene either.'

'And what do you know about Thelma's scene?'

'Me? Nothing. Nothing at all,' said Pascoe uninterestedly.

He had good reason for sounding uninterested in Thelma Lacewing. First she was the leading light of WRAG, the Women's Rights Action Group which put the law a very poor second to its principles; secondly, he had recently helped to put her uncle, a respected local businessman, away on a pornography charge; thirdly, he (in a purely aesthetic sense of course) rather fancied her and sometimes thought she might rather fancy him.

'Anyway, her scene or not, it's her idea,' continued Ellie. 'I promised that when the summer vac came and I had more time, I'd take some of the secretarial work off Lorraine Wildgoose's plate.'

'But you said it was only students who got holidays,' protested Pascoe.

'Oh, go to work!' said Ellie disgustedly. 'See if you can stop that lunatic from killing more than half a dozen women today.'

As he finished his toast, he said crumbily, 'Wildgoose. That rings a little bell. Do I know her?'

'I don't think so,' said Ellie. 'Though she's all the things you admire in a woman. Forty, ferocious, teaches French and is in the middle of a rather unpleasant marital shipwreck.'

Pascoe shuddered and rose from the table.

When he returned with his briefcase ready for departure, Ellie was immersed in the newspaper.

'Hey, there's a little bit here about fat Andy calling in a clairvoyant.'

'Oh God. Let me see.'

He looked at the paper and said in relief. 'It's just a couple of lines and I don't think he gets the *Guardian* anyway.'

'Perhaps not. But just think how large it's likely to be printed in the tabloids! It's a good story. At least, you made it sound like a good story last night.'

'Don't!' he said, kissing her.

'Peter,' she said thoughtfully when he'd finished, 'that transcript of the tape you showed me. Can I borrow it?'

'Why on earth should you want that?'

'Well, it's just come back to me. I woke up in the night and I was lying there thinking and I got this brilliant idea, you know how you do. About that woman in the trance. Well, I know you said it can't have anything to do with what actually happened, but I was remembering, last year the museum organized a dig in Charter Park, do you remember, at the bottom end beyond the War Memorial. Our historians were involved. It was the Roman Level they were interested in, but they took one section of the trench much deeper just to see. It was clear there'd been a settlement thereabouts for as long as men have been settling.'

'Fascinating.' said Pascoe. 'So what?'

'So suppose when you die, time shifts? Well, why not? It certainly *stops*, doesn't it? Briefly for a moment as she dies, she goes back. You know they say your life flashes before you as you drown? So, it's a cliché, but it's what people who've been saved from drowning have said. Suppose it's not just your life but the *whole* of life. And once you're beyond yours, you're beyond the point of being saved.'

'All right, all right,' said Pascoe, disturbed by what for Ellie was an untypical flight of fantasy. 'So…?'

'So for a moment, that girl is out of our time and into, say, the early Mesolithic period. The water runs clear. And because of the time shift, it's still daylight. And those faces, what did she say, "like beasts at their watering," small wary brown-skinned people, Cresswellians perhaps, or some tribe of prehistoric man. And the birds she saw, pterodactyls perhaps.'

'Jesus!' said Pascoe.

'All right. Be dismissive. But it seems to me that this famous open mind you're always yapping about is about as open as a bank on Saturday.'

'I was merely expressing surprise at the depth of your knowledge of prehistory,' he protested speciously.

She looked sheepish.

'I know about as much as you,' she admitted. 'That's why I wanted the transcript. Thelma was in on the dig, it's one of her hobbies. I thought she might be able to put me right.'

'A lady of many parts, that one,' said Pascoe. 'Mainly untouched by human hand, or so she would have us believe.'

'What on earth can you mean?' she said, grinning.

'All right,' he said, opening his briefcase. 'Here it is. We've got a copy at the station, but don't lose it all the same. Though strictly speaking, it's hardly an official document! And in return, promise me you won't let those viragos con you into taking on more than you can cope with. OK?'

'Yes, sir,' she said.

He kissed her again, sternly, and left.

But as he backed out of the drive he suddenly thought *Pterodactyls*! and chuckled so much he almost hit the milkman.

Nevertheless something of what Ellie had said must have tickled his subconscious, for when he found himself crawling in the nine o'clock traffic which seemed likely to stretch all the way to ten, almost without taking a conscious decision he turned down a side street and ten minutes later found himself driving through the gates of Charter Park.

The dry weather had baked the ground so hard that even the odd thunderstorm hadn't softened it and the turf was very little cut up so far. But it was well worn and strewn with litter like the route of a Blind School paper-chase. Pascoe wondered how long the fair would survive. It had changed considerably even in the comparatively few years he had known it.

Up until the First World War it had been one of the great horse-fairs. There were still people who could recall the days when drovers and gypsies came from all over the North and the roadsides for miles on the approaches to the town were lined with caravans, not the sleek, shining motorized caravans of today, but the old wooden ones, gold and green and red and blue. Gradually during the century, its character had changed in the direction of a pure pleasure fair, but horses had still been sold as recently as the early 'sixties. But there had been growing complaints, not least from the regular fairground people who considered themselves several cuts above the Romanys and objected to their presence on all kinds of grounds, notably their hygienic deficiencies, both human and equine. The Showman's Guild added its weight to the protests and when a small herd of gypsy ponies broke loose from the Park and trotted through the centre of town, causing several accidents and much indignation, horses were finally banned from Charter Park. There was still a small gypsy presence at the Fair, but the main gypsy encampment was now on a stretch of the old airfield to the south and most of their business was done door-to-door rather than at the fairground.

So pleasure had won the day, but even the taste for pleasure changes and fairs are limited in the ways they can keep up with these changes. Also, though in the past this had traditionally been the city's holiday fortnight, and many people still stuck to the habit, many more objected to being told when they should or should not go on holiday. Another decade, thought Pascoe, and the High Fair could well be another casualty in the war for individual rights.

But at the moment it still covered a great deal of ground. Quiet now, though there was plenty of movement in the caravan park, his mind peopled it with the milling crowds of a hot summer's night. After ten-thirty when the pubs closed, there would have been a new influx of noisy and not very perceptive pleasure-seekers. Easy for one girl, or one couple, to pass unnoticed here. But how had Brenda Sorby got here in the first place?

Pascoe walked slowly over the fairground, deep in thought. One possibility was that the girl had met someone she knew on the way home last Thursday night and accepted an invitation to go to the fair. But it was after eleven p.m., so he would have needed to be very persuasive. Perhaps she had simply been offered a lift home and it wasn't till the car was moving that the Fair had been mentioned. By the time they got here, the storm would have broken, the crowds be heading for home. But that still left the fair people who would be clearing up, mopping up, counting up for another hour or so. So had she just sat in the car for that time? Perhaps she was already dead or unconscious? Perhaps...

He was walking past a fortune-teller's tent and the sight of it made him think of Sergeant Wield's experience the previous day. He had recounted it jokingly to Ellie when he got home but she had not been amused. *It strikes me you can do with all the help you can get*, she had said. She seemed to be taking these murders very personally. Perhaps an emotional side effect of her condition? He had had more sense than to say so!

He reached the small landing-stage where the hire-boats were moored.

Joe, the boatman, was not there yet for which Pascoe was grateful. He was the kind of surly suspicious Yorkshireman who at birth probably examined his mother's breast closely for several minutes before accepting the offer. But at least he made a definite witness.

No, he didn't recognize the photo of Brenda Sorby. No, there was no boat unaccounted for. No, there was no one who had come back alone.

Forced to admit that the sudden storm had brought the boaters back in a bit of a rush, he grudgingly conceded that a foursome might have come back as a threesome. But no singles, and he'd seen 'em all. Rain or no rain, he checked the gear in each boat before refunding the two pound deposit; and all deposits had been returned.

But the Choker must have used a boat. The nearest bridge giving access to the isthmus was a mile downstream, too far to risk carrying a body. In any case, why come so far to dump it?

The only alternative was that the Choker was one of the barge people, a theory approved by Andy Dalziel who tended to lump all people who lived itinerant lives together as 'dirty gyppos'. Pascoe, however, had done a paper at university on the education of 'travelling children' in England and knew that the attitudes and lifestyles of the different societies varied considerably. Fairground and circus folk, for instance, were generally speaking much concerned about their children's schooling, and where they could afford it, often sent them to private boarding-schools. Gypsies on the other hand were much more suspicious of 'the system,' and much more conscious of their independence from it, a consciousness which made integration of their children into any conventional school much more difficult. The barge people in the same way had once presented an even greater problem, but one which had been in part solved by time and the disappearance of their way of life as canal traffic ceased to be economically viable. There were signs of a resurgence recently and no doubt, thought Pascoe, the problem too would return.

Meanwhile he had ensured that everyone in any kind of craft on the canal that night was traced and interviewed. All had been in company, all reasonably alibied, none had heard anything. In any case the signs were that the girl had been put into the water from the bank, not a boat. There were traces of mud on her dress corresponding to that in a shallow groove in the bank close by the place where the body was found.

Pascoe glanced at his watch. Brooding time over, he decided. There was work to be done. He began to retrace his steps.

The fairground was livelier now. Business wouldn't really get under way till much later in the morning, but meantime there were things to be done, machinery to be checked and oiled, canvas covers removed, brass to be polished. At side-stalls like the rifle-range and the hoopla there were the gimcrack prizes to be set out, gun-sights to check in case they had deviated to accuracy, and hoopla rings in case they had stretched to go over the whisky bottle.

By the fortune-teller's tent a young woman in jeans and a yellow suntop was talking to a man in a tartan shirt and brown cords, gaitered militarily above ex-army boots. He was about forty with the knitted brow and dark craggy good looks of a Heathcliff.

They looked at Pascoe as he passed and the man said something.

A moment later Pascoe stopped and turned as the woman's voice called, 'Excuse me!' She had started after him. The man watched for a moment and then strode away towards the trailer park.

'Aren't you one of the policemen?' said the girl. Anyone under twenty-five now qualified as a girl, Pascoe realized ruefully. This one certainly did; fresh young skin, clear brown eyes, luxuriant auburn hair escaping from the green and white spotted bandanna which she had tied around it.

'That's right,' said Pascoe. 'Does it stand out?'

'I saw you the other day, I think,' said the girl, evading the question. Pascoe nodded. It was likely. He had spent a great deal of time here on Friday afternoon.

'You work here?' he asked.

'Yes,' she said. 'Do you have a moment?'

Without waiting for his answer she set off towards the fortune-teller's tent and lifted the flap.

Pascoe paused before the entrance, partly to establish his independent spirit, partly to read the sign. *Madame Rashid*, it said, *Interpreter of the Stars, Admission 50p*. The lettering was pseudo-Arabic and the words were surrounded by a constellation of varying hues and shapes.

'The price of the future's gone up,' he said.

'You should try having a full horoscope cast,' she said seriously. 'Besides, we're not allowed to tell the future.'

'I know,' he said.

'Oh, of course you would. Won't you come in?'

He passed by her under the flap.

It was a bit of a disappointment, reminding him more of a Boy Scout camp than the Eastern pavilion he had half expected. The smell was of damp canvas and trodden grass and the only furniture was a plain trestle table and two folding chairs.

A suitcase lay on the table and she pointed to this as if sensing his disappointment and said, 'It looks better when I get the props out.'

'I'm sure,' said Pascoe. 'What did you want to see me about Miss—er—Rashid?'

She laughed, very attractively.

'No,' she said. 'I'm Pauline Stanhope.'

She held out her hand. He took it. The name sounded familiar.

'And I'm Detective-Inspector Pascoe,' he said.

'I thought you must be. It's about yesterday, Inspector Pascoe. Won't you sit down?'

He unfolded the chairs and they sat opposite each other at the table, as though for an interrogation. Or a fortune-telling. It depended on your point of view.

'Yesterday?'

'Yes. Aunt Rose was very upset when she read the paper.'

'Was she?' said Pascoe.

Aunt Rose? Of course, Rosetta Stanhope. And this was the niece.

'Rosetta. Rashid,' he murmured as the enlightenment spread.

'That's right. I'm sorry. I thought you'd know all about us. All those questions.'

'Think of all those answers, Miss Stanhope,' he said sadly. 'Someone has to edit.'

Everyone who worked on the fairground had been questioned, naturally. Everyone who admitted visiting it on Thursday night also. Everyone who lived on the same street as the Sorbys. And the next street. And maybe the next. Everyone who worked with her. Everyone who lived on the streets she would have walked through on her way home from the broken-down car. Everyone who had a barge or a cruiser or a craft of any kind which could have been anywhere on that stretch of the canal that night.

The questioning was still going on, was likely to continue till Christmas. Or the next murder.

'My sergeant seemed to have heard of your aunt,' he said cautiously. 'But he didn't mention any connection with the Fair.'

'Mr Wield, you mean. He's awfully nice, isn't he? It's a bit complicated, I suppose. Family history usually is.'

'Perhaps you could give me a digest, if you think it would be helpful, and if you don't have to stray much beyond the Norman Conquest,' said Pascoe.

She grinned.

'I see where Mr Wield gets his cheek from,' she said. 'The thing to understand is that originally Aunt Rose is a Lee on her father's side, a Petulengro on her mother's.'

'You mean the Romany families?'

'You know something about gypsies?'

'I've read my George Borrow,' he said with a smile.

'An expert!' she said. 'That must be very useful when it comes to moving them on.'

Pascoe raised his eyebrows and the girl had the grace to look a little embarrassed before carrying on.

It emerged that years earlier, Rosetta Lee, then nineteen, had met, loved and married ex-sergeant Herbert Stanhope, just demobbed from the Yorkshire Rifles and, after five years spent risking his life to protect the old folk at home, not in any mood to take heed of their melancholy warnings. The couple married and lived happily and childlessly until twelve years later when Stanhope's younger sister turned up pregnant and husbandless and not at all contrite. But she effaced her sin in the best nineteenth-century manner by dying in childbirth, leaving the Stanhopes with Pauline on their hands. Thereafter they lived even more happily for another twelve years till an accident at the railway marshalling yard where Stanhope worked killed him.

'Aunt Rose knew it was going to happen,' said Pauline.

'Why didn't she stop him going to work?' enquired Pascoe, trying not to sound ironic.

'If you know it, then essentially it's already happened so you can't possibly stop it,' said Pauline as if she were talking sense.

'And you? Do you have this—er—gift too?'

'Oh no!' she said, shocked. 'I'm a fully qualified horoscopist and a pretty fair palmist but I've got no real psychic powers. Aunt Rose is different. She's always had the real gift. Her grandmother was a *chovihani*, that's a sort of gypsy witch. She really looked the part, not like Aunt Rose. But Aunt Rose has got the greater gift. She's a true psychic, that's the fascinating thing. It's not just a question of fortune-telling, but she really makes contact. Well, you know that yourself from the other day.'

Pascoe nodded, looking as convinced as he was able.

The girl continued, 'It was strange how it developed in a *gorgio* society. Perhaps all the trappings and superstition of Romany life are a limiting factor, you know, they make a little go a long way but stop a lot from going as far as it might. That was what one of the researchers from the Psychic Research Society said.'

'Your aunt is famous, then?'

'Oh no!' said the girl, 'But she's well known in interested circles. Really all she wants is a quiet life, but she'd always been willing to help friends out.'

'For free?'

'At first. But inflation nibbled away at the pension Uncle Bert left her and she's had to charge fees to make both ends meet. But she's very careful in accepting clients.'

Gullibility being high on her list of criteria? wondered Pascoe.

'Normally she'd have steered clear of a case like Mrs Sorby's, but Mrs Sorby had been coming to her for years, ever since her mother died. Mr Sorby objected but she still kept coming. Naturally when this awful thing happened, Aunt Rose had to help.'

'Naturally. What's your part in all this, Miss Stanhope?'

The girl shrugged.

'I had an office job, but it was pretty deadly. I'd picked up a lot of things from Aunt Rose, she brought me up, you see. Well, I'm not Romany, so I didn't have anything of her gift, but I got quite interested in casting horoscopes. It's pretty scientific that, you only need a very limited degree of sensitivity. Palmistry the same. I got myself properly qualified and gave up the office to work at it full time alongside Aunt Rose. But it's her I want to talk about, Inspector. That awful newspaper story really upset her.'

Pascoe looked surprised. The *Evening Post* had been fairly restrained, he thought.

'It didn't much please my superintendent either,' he said.

'Aunt Rose doesn't mind helping the police, but this makes her sound like a real sensationalist,' said the girl, producing a newspaper.

The mystery was solved. This was not the *Evening Post* but that morning's edition of one of the more lurid national tabloids. Obviously one of the local reporters was a stringer for this rag and knew that provincial standards had very little selling power. Pascoe glanced through the article. Its main source was Mrs Duxbury, the neighbour. She gave a graphic account of what Mrs Stanhope had said before being awoken from her trance. Embellished by Fleet Street licence, the occasion sounded like something out of Dennis Wheatley. Much play was made of the fact that Rosetta Stanhope was also Madame Rashid (Mrs Duxbury again?), fortune-telling in the very fairground where Brenda had been murdered. Not even a *perhaps*, thought Pascoe. He wondered if Dalziel had seen it yet.

'Auntie was really upset this morning,' continued the girl. 'Too upset to work, so I'll be on by myself all day.'

'I'm sorry about that,' said Pascoe conciliatingly.

'Don't be stupid!' she flashed. 'It's not that. It's Auntie's reputation. You may be the police but you've no right to exploit her name like this.'

'Reputation?' said Pascoe, beginning to feel a little irritated. 'Surely you're rating all this stuff a little bit high, aren't you, Miss Stanhope? I mean, that sign outside! Isn't this just the bottom end of the entertainment business?'

He didn't want to sound sneering and the effort must have shown for the girl was equally and as obviously restrained in her reply.

'Aunt Rose is Romany. She's never turned her back on that all these years she's lived among *gorgios*. This used to be mainly a Romany Fair, Inspector. Now what with one thing and another, the only gypsy presence you get here is a couple of tatty stalls and a bit of cheap labour round the fringes. Dave Lee, for instance, his grandfather...'

'Who's Dave Lee?' interrupted Pascoe.

'I was just talking to him,' said the girl. 'I suppose he's a kind of cousin of Aunt Rose's. His grandfather might have brought two, three dozen horses here, being a big man. Now he helps around the dodgems while his wife sells pegs and bits of lace. He's not allowed to bring the ponies he still runs anywhere near the park! This tent is the last real link between the fair today and what it used to be for centuries. There was a fortune-teller's tent on this pitch before there was a police force, Inspector. Not even the big show-people with their roundabouts dare interfere with that. And for nearly fifty years it was run by Aunt Rose's grandmother. When she died four years ago, that looked like the end. Oh, there were fakes enough who might have taken over, but the Lees have more pride than that. So Aunt Rose stepped in. For a couple of weeks a year she's back in the family tradition, in the old world.'

'And which world are you in, Miss Stanhope?' asked Pascoe.

'I help as I can,' she said. 'Collect the money, look after the props, do a bit of palm-reading when Auntie needs a rest. Yes, I did say *props*. It wasn't a slip, so don't look so smug. Of course most people come into a fortune-teller's tent at a fairground for the entertainment. But *we* take it seriously, that's the important thing.'

She spoke defiantly. Pascoe answered seriously, 'I hope so, Miss Stanhope. You spoke of protecting your aunt from exploitation just now. I too am employed to stop people being exploited.'

She flushed angrily and said, 'Auntie was just concerned to bring any comfort she could to that poor woman. We shut up shop here for the afternoon, which lost us money, and Aunt Rose wouldn't accept any fee from Mrs Sorby. So we're the only losers, wouldn't you say, Inspector?'

'There are all kinds of gain, Miss Stanhope,' said Pascoe provocatively. 'I mean in the entertainment world, there's no such thing as bad publicity, is there?'

Now she was really angry.

'Tell me, Inspector,' she said in a hard, clear voice, 'I'd say you were a bit younger than Sergeant Wield, right?'

'A bit,' he admitted.

'And yet he is so much pleasanter than you. It looks to me as if the nastier you are in the police force, the higher you're likely to get. Right? I bet I'm right. Goodbye, *Inspector*!'

Wait till you meet my boss, thought Pascoe as he left. You don't know how right you are!

As he drove away he saw in his rear-view mirror the man Dave heading back towards the tent.

Keen for a report on the conversation? he wondered. But wasn't everybody fascinated by a connection with a murder case?

He put it out of his mind and hurried towards the station, eager to tell Sergeant Wield he'd got an admirer.

CHAPTER 4

Alistair Mulgan sipped his tomato juice carefully. He would have preferred a large gin partly because he wasn't paying and partly because his metabolism seemed to be very sympathetically inclined towards large gins these days. But the Northern Bank did not care to have its staff breathing alcohol over its customers and since becoming acting manager of the Greenhill branch after the manager fell under a bus (nothing to do with alcohol of course) three weeks earlier, Mulgan had determined to set a perfect example. Now nearly forty, he had come a long way from his humble beginnings in rural Derbyshire, but for the past few years had felt that his career was bogged down. Each full week as acting manager had given him hope that the appointment would be made permanent, hope reinforced when clients started inviting him out to lunch. Though even here fate, as usual, had distributed its gifts with grudging hand and instead of the looked-for filet mignon at the White Rose Grill, he had just been offered the choice between chicken-in-the-basket and scampi-in-the-basket at the Aero Club bar.

'First time here, Mulgan?' said his host. 'How d'you like it?'

Mulgan looked round. A group of young men were drinking pints and noisily exchanging gliding experiences. Three women were sitting in a corner beneath a fluorescent notice announcing that Friday and Saturday were disco nights. On the blue emulsioned walls a formation of china Spitfires banked through photographs of smiling young men in flying kit towards an old school clock whose face was ringed in RAF colours. The hands, propeller-shaped, stood at twelve-fifteen.

'It's very nice,' said Mulgan politely.

'Yes, I thought we'd meet here. It's handy for us both and I hate them stuck-up places with their fancy prices. Besides, I'm going up a bit later on, so I'd have to be here anyway. You ever tried it, Mulgan?'

His host was Bernard Middlefield who with his brother John was co-owner and dictator of a small electrical assembly plant on the Avro Industrial Estate. *Middlefield Electric* was feeling the pinch of the latest credit squeeze and Mulgan guessed that these new friendly overtures in his direction were just so much bread scattered on the waters. He was not offended. Middlefield under his abrupt, loud-mouthed manner was a sharp enough operator. Chicken-in-the-basket today meant that he had been spotted as being possibly worth filet mignon tomorrow. That was one thing about these Yorkshiremen. You knew precisely where you were with most of them.

'No, I haven't,' said Mulgan. 'What kind of plane do you fly?'

'Plane? Not a *plane*, Mulgan. Do you never look up from that desk of yours? It's gliders we fly here. Though planes have been known to land, isn't that right, Austin? Alistair Mulgan. This is Austin Greenall, our CFI, that's Chief Flying Instructor, secretary, and master of all trades.'

'As you see,' said the man who had taken the place of the middle-aged woman who had been behind the bar to start with. 'Except cooking. We're short-handed today. Summer flu, would you believe! Jenny has to keep an eye on the kitchen too, so if there's anything else you require from the bar, I'm your man.'

'No, thanks. These'll do us. I'm flying and Mr Mulgan's got to keep his head clear else he'll get his sums wrong at the bank.'

'I thought I recognized you,' said Greenall. 'The Club account's there.'

'Watch him,' said Middlefield to Mulgan. 'He'll be wanting to screw some money out of you for another couple of planes if he can.'

'The Club does own some planes already, then?' said Mulgan.

'A plane. We've got a Cub we use for towing but it's long past its best. And there's a Cherokee owned by a consortium of local businessmen, Mr Middlefield included. No, it's the gliding that keeps us going. Just.'

'But not if you have your way, eh, Austin? He's only been here five minutes and he's got ambitions to turn us into Heathrow.'

'Hardly. I just think there's a lot that can be done to improve facilities and attract members.'

'As long as you keep in mind it's not like Surrey up here. We know what we like and we like value for money. How's our grub coming on? Take a look, there's a good chap.'

Greenall smiled amiably and left the bar.

❈ ❈ ❈

In the corner Ellie Pascoe said to Thelma Lacewing, 'Why doesn't your secretary hit him with a bottle?'

'Middlefield's on the committee, also a JP,' said Thelma. 'But mainly he's a reactionary shit. For instance, trying to get the weekend discos stopped on the grounds that they breed immorality. I keep a very close eye on that sod, I tell you.'

The two women made a striking contrast. Ellie was long-limbed, mobile, though the taut line of her athletic figure was now slackened by the contours of pregnancy; black haired, grey eyed, and with a face that after thirty-odd years was handsome rather than pretty, and her chin gave promises of determination her character kept. Thelma's face had the frank wide-eyed pensive beauty that goes with folded wings and flowing white robes and that a monk might dream of without sin. She was a dental hygienist.

'Let's get down to business,' she said. 'Ellie, are you going to sink cow-like into the placid, man-pleasing, expectant-mother role, or are you going to cut your brain off from your belly and start doing some real work for WRAG?'

'Depends what you mean by real work,' said Ellie.

The third woman spoke. This was Lorraine Wildgoose, teacher of French at a local comprehensive school. She had a striking face, with high cheekbones and intense eyes. Her hair was at fag end of an old freak-out cut and her figure had the kind of thinness that derives from nerves rather than diets.

'Vacancies in all areas,' she said. 'Typing, telephoning, tea-making.'

'Propagandizing, preaching, protesting,' murmured Thelma.

'Not to mention subverting, suborning, and sabotaging,' added Lorraine.

'I rather fancied assailing, assaulting, and assassinating,' said Ellie, not to be outdone. 'But seriously, look, I want to help, but also I want some time to write. I'm into another novel. I've finally got over my feelings of failure with the first. I mean twenty-two publishers can't be wrong! And I really want to get this new one sorted out before *this*.'

She patted her stomach disgustedly.

'We've all got calls on our time,' flashed Lorraine. 'Two kids, a pending divorce and an unbalanced husband takes a bit more of your time than a couple of neatly turned paragraphs.'

This unexpected outburst brought a hiatus in the conversation which was filled by the timely arrival of Greenall with their baskets of food. At the bar the discussion seemed to be getting a little heated too.

'Well, you know your own employees best, I dare say,' Middlefield was saying. 'But give me leave to know something too. When you've been on the bench a bit, you get to read between the lines. I mean, just look at the facts. A field behind a pub! A shed on an allotment! The canal bank! Not the kind of places you'd look to meet the vicar's wife, are they?'

'I can assure you, Brenda Sorby was as nice and decent a young woman as you could hope to meet,' protested Mulgan, his rather fleshy face pinking with indignation or embarrassment.

'That's how they all *seem*,' scoffed Middlefield. 'You see a bit more of the world in my line than yours, I dare say.'

'You're not saying those poor women deserved what happened to them?'

'Don't be daft! But them as take chances can't complain overmuch when things go wrong.'

'Those women certainly can't complain, can they?' said Thelma in a clear, carrying voice.

'I beg your pardon?' said Middlefield turning on his stool to view her. 'Oh, it's you, Miss Lacewing.'

'I'll just fetch the tartare sauce,' murmured Greenall. He retreated to the kitchen.

'I suppose you might say that unaccompanied women coming to places like this take the chance of overhearing primitive sexist prejudices being expressed by loud, ill-informed men,' continued Thelma.

'I expect I know as much about it as you, young woman,' said Middlefield grimly.

'Really? Perhaps we ought to put the police in touch with you, then. Fortunately one of my friends is married to one of the officers on the case. Ellie, perhaps you'll pass the word to your husband that Mr Middlefield knows more than he has yet been willing to volunteer.'

Ellie smiled warily. There weren't many people left in the world who could embarrass her, but Thelma was certainly one of them. Which was probably why, as Peter had theorized, she allowed her the moral ascendancy.

Greenall had emerged from the kitchen with two more baskets which he placed before the two men at the bar, saying blithely, 'Here you are. Piping hot.'

Thelma turned back to her friends, completely unruffled. That's what I envy too, thought Ellie. I get all pink and abusive.

'Is your husband really on the case?' asked Lorraine Wildgoose.

Ellie nodded.

'Are they getting anywhere?' pursued the woman rather intensely.

'I'm not sure. I expect so,' said Ellie cautiously.

Lorraine Wildgoose looked as if she might be going to say something more and Ellie's heart sank at the prospect of having to listen to an attack on the police, no matter which of the many possible forms it took. But Thelma, as if spotting the danger, said lightly, 'What about all this clairvoyant help?'

'You read about that?' said Ellie, relieved. 'Listen, I've got a theory. I pinched a transcript of what this woman actually said from Peter. It might interest you in your archaeological hat.'

She produced the transcript and was holding forth when Greenall returned with the tartare sauce.

'Sorry to interrupt,' he said, putting the sauce on the sheet of paper in front of Thelma.

'Don't do that, Austin!' she said. 'You may offend the spirits.'

'You're doing a bit of table rapping, are you?' he said. 'Be careful. It's Mr Middlefield you don't want to offend!'

'It's OK. This is police business,' said Thelma. 'My friend is a Mrs Detective-Inspector. These are official documents.'

Greenall picked up the transcript and pretended to rub it with his sleeve, murmuring at the same time, 'By the by,

Middlefield's threatening to drop in at the disco on Friday on a fact-finding tour.'

'Is he? I may join him. Thanks, Austin. Join us for a drink later?'

'I'd love to, but another time. I've got things to do and his lordship's got to be launched after lunch. *Per ardua ad astra*, as they say.'

He left and Ellie fluttered her eyebrows at Thelma.

'Now he seems nice, Thelma.'

'He's bearable,' she said noncommittally. 'When he came six months ago I thought *Christ, another ex-RAF wizard-show chauvinist pig*. But he was a nice surprise. I think he's got genuine sympathy with the feminist position.'

'I bet,' grinned Ellie.

'That, if I may say so, is the kind of crack that comes from too close an association with the racist, sexist constabulary.'

'Is that so? And perhaps you'll now explain how you come to be rolling around with evident pleasure in this male chauvinist sty,' said Ellie.

'Why, to overcome my fear of flying, of course,' said Thelma, wide eyes wider with surprise. 'Now let's eat. Ellie, you've nearly finished your drink. Would you like something else? A quart of warm milk, perhaps.'

Ellie giggled girlishly.

'You'll think I'm silly,' she said coyly. 'But being like this and all, I get these funny urges, you know how we mothers-to-be are, and whenever I eat scampi and get put down at the same time, I've just *got* to have a couple of glasses of Dom Perignon. It brings up the wind so nicely!'

CHAPTER 5

Andy Dalziel, according to much of his acquaintance, had a very simplistic approach to life. He saw everything as either black or dark blue. In this they were mistaken. Life was richly coloured for the fat man; full of villainy and vice, it was true, but with shifting shades and burning pigments, like Hogarthian scenes painted by Renoir.

Pascoe understood this. 'He detects with his balls,' he had once told Ellie gloomily.

To Pascoe's rational mind, there was still some doubt whether Brenda Sorby's murder was truly in sequence with the other two strangulations.

'She wasn't laid out like the other two,' he said. 'In fact the body was hidden, whereas with the others, the killer obviously wanted it to be found. Also, to let herself be picked up at that time of night (and there had to be a car—she wasn't going to *walk* five miles to the canal!), it had to be someone she knew.'

Dalziel wasn't much interested. He *knew* it was part of the sequence. But he didn't mind exploding a younger colleague.

'Mebbe she just scrambled away and fell in. He wouldn't be about to jump in after her, would he? Or mebbe he left her for dead, all neatly laid out, and she recovered enough to roll over. Splash! Or mebbe he was disturbed and just slipped her over the edge, not wanting her to be found while he was still so close in the vicinity. And as for the car, mebbe he pulled her into it, threatened her with a knife, even knocked her out. Or mebbe it was someone she'd trust without knowing him, a copper, say. What were *you* doing that night, Peter?'

Laughter (Dalziel's). End of discussion.

Curiously, the one thing which seemed to confirm the superintendent's judgement that Brenda's death was linked with the others, he had treated most dismissively.

'Anyone can make a phone call,' he said. 'And everyone's got a Complete Shakespeare. *I've* got a Complete Shakespeare!'

Pascoe sat in his office and studied the pathologist's reports which he knew almost off by heart. All three women had been strangled by someone using both hands. The bruising on their necks indicated this and the cartilage in the area of the voice boxes was fractured to a degree which demonstrated the violence and strength of the attack. But the pathologist was adamant that Brenda Sorby had not been quite dead when she went into the water...*all over me, choking, the water, all boiling at first, and roaring, and seething...* Pascoe shook the medium's taped words out of his mind and went on with his reading.

There was a degree of lividity down the left side which was unusual for a corpse taken from the water, but it could be explained by the fact that the body seemed to have been wedged in the debris by the canal bank rather than rolling free in the current. Also (another difference from the previous cases) there was some bruising around and underneath the breasts, possibly indicating a sexual assault, though the lacerations caused by the barge propeller had made examination difficult in this area. Elsewhere there was no indication of sexual interference.

Pascoe sighed. The bloody pathologist thought *he* was having things difficult!

Sergeant Wield came in.

'I just had CRO run some of those fairground people through the computer,' he announced.

'Including Miss Stanhope?' said Pascoe with a grin.

Wield's creased and pitted face had shown no response to Pascoe's twitting about Pauline Stanhope's interest earlier that day. Now he managed something not unlike a grimace.

'There was a statement from her and her aunt,' he said. 'Like all the rest. Nothing. This was interesting, though.'

David Lee had been in the hands of the police several times. Disorderly conduct had cost him half a dozen fines. In 1974 he had been put on probation for assault on his common law wife. Assaulting a council officer in charge of an operation to move on a gypsy encampment got him three months in 1976, and this had been doubled in 1978 when he punched a police officer who was attempting to stop him from beating another common law wife.

There was also a charge of rape in 1979, dismissed by a majority verdict.

'What made you pick on this one?' wondered Pascoe. 'Not because I saw him chatting up Miss Pauline, I hope?'

'There's half a dozen others,' grunted Wield. 'If you'd care to have a look.'

Pascoe thought for a moment.

'Tell you what,' he said. 'If Mrs Sorby's such an enthusiast for peering over the Great Divide, perhaps Brenda got roped in too.'

'And might have known about the Madame Rashid connection,' said Wield.

'And met Dave Lee through it?'

Pascoe shook his head even as he spoke.

'It's stretching things a bit,' he said. 'Still, it's worth checking. Fancy a trip to the fairground to have your fortune told?'

Wield shrugged.

'I go where I'm sent,' he said indifferently.

'All right,' said Pascoe. 'It's twelve now. Have your lunch, then with your vigour fully restored go and cross the lady's palm with silver. Either lady, depending whether you prefer mutton or lamb.'

I must stop this nudge-nudge, wink-wink bit, he thought as Wield left. I'm getting more like Dalziel every day!

A few moments later the phone rang. It was the desk sergeant.

'There's a lady here wants a word with someone in CID, sir,' he said. 'It's a Mrs Rosetta Stanhope.'

'What? Oh, look, Sergeant Wield probably wants to speak with her anyway, so let him sort it out, will you? He should be on his way out any moment now.'

'He just went past, sir. I don't think he noticed the lady. He seemed in a bit of a hurry.'

'The bastard!' swore Pascoe. 'He's opted for lamb. All right. Wheel her in.'

Rosetta Stanhope had adapted well to her chosen environment. In her late fifties, her hair tightly permed with just the suggestion of a blue rinse, dressed in a stylishly cut grey suit with toning shoes and handbag, she could have chaired a WI meeting or opened a flower show without remark. Only a certain rather exotic stateliness of bearing and darkness of skin which even a carefully layered mask of make-up could not disguise hinted at her origins.

Her voice was quiet, a little hoarse, perhaps; the result of twisting her vocal cords to produce her spirit voices? wondered Pascoe.

'I met your niece this morning,' said Pascoe. 'You haven't seen her?'

The woman considered, then smiled.

'You're quite right, Mr Pascoe. I wouldn't do Madame Rashid dressed like this. And I wouldn't go home specially to change just to impress a policeman.'

Pascoe was impressed. She'd cut right to the source of his question. Not that you needed to be a mind-reader, but it was a good policeman's trick.

'So you've left your niece in charge of the future?'

Lucky old Wield.

'I didn't feel able today,' she said. 'I don't put on a show. It's got to be right.'

'What about Pauline?'

Mrs Stanhope made an entirely un-English *moue* of dismissal.

'Palmistry,' she said. 'It's a craft. You learn it.'

Pascoe decided to do a bit of short-cutting himself.

'I'm afraid you're not going to be able to get an apology out of us, Mrs Stanhope. It wasn't our doing. A denial perhaps, but I tried that yesterday and you saw the report. I'm sorry it upset you.'

'I'm not upset, Inspector,' she said. 'Don't heed our Pauline. She probably told you I'm not very practical? Well, I'm practical enough to let her think so. She needs to be looking after folks, that one. It probably comes of never knowing her mother.'

'You brought her up from birth, I believe,' said Pascoe. 'I'm surprised she doesn't regard you as her mother.'

'She did when she was young, poor mite. But she had to be told. I remember she was twelve and casting her own horoscope. It wouldn't come right. Well, it wouldn't, would it? Bert and me had always decided to tell her. It was a relief in a way.'

'Why so?'

'She knew about me and my background. I'm proud of it, why not? And Bert always used to joke that he'd stolen me from the gypsies. Pauline and me, we got very close, but I could see it was a bit difficult for a young lass thinking she'd got a gypsy mother but not feeling of the blood, if you follow. It were odd, but when we told her, it seemed to bring us even closer together.'

'And finally she joined that side of the family business?'

'She could hardly become an engine-driver, could she, even in this age,' said Rosetta Stanhope lightly.

'I believe it's possible,' said Pascoe, suddenly picturing Thelma Lacewing wiping her brow with an oily rag on the foot-plate of the 'Flying Scotsman'. 'But tell me, Mrs Stanhope, if you're not here to complain, threaten, or cast a gypsy's curse, why have you come?'

She leaned forward and tapped his desk significantly. Or perhaps she was knocking on wood?

'I was upset last night, Inspector. Not by the paper, though that irritated me. I was upset by the contact I'd made with that poor girl. I hardly slept. I just kept on getting impressions; no, not visions or words, nothing definite like that; but, like colours and feelings. I let Pauline think it was just the newspaper report that had upset me. I wanted to think things out for myself.'

'So what *do* you want, Mrs Stanhope?'

She opened her youthfully clear brown eyes in big surprise.

'I want to do what that *Evening Post* said I was doing already,' she said. 'I've come to help you with your enquiries.'

CHAPTER 6

When Sergeant Wield reached Charter Park the fairground was doing good business. It was a fine sunny day with just enough breeze to cool a fevered brow and send little puffs of cloud, picturesque to the point of artificiality, drifting across the deep blue cyclorama above. The green of the grass and trees, the sparkling band of the river, the bright brash music of the steam organ, all these combined to produce a pleasantly euphoric sensation in the sergeant's breast which he allowed to surface in the form of a light almost soundless whistle through gently pursed lips.

His reaction when he reached the fortune-teller's tent and found the flap closed and a folding chair pushed against it to which was pinned a card saying BACK SOON was disappointment, but it was a purely professional emotion. Pascoe's winks and nods about Pauline Stanhope's fancy for him were seeds on the stoniest of ground. Wield's self-containment and reticence were not linked, as the amateur psychologist might have guessed, to his fearsome appearance. They derived from his early recognition that the best way to conceal one thing was to conceal all things, to have so many secrets that the only important one would not be suspected. And this was that he was wholly and uncompromisingly homosexual. In the police, the usual circular syndrome applied. Homosexuals were disapproved of because they were blackmail risks because they were secretive because they were disapproved of...

Ten years earlier Wield had found himself growing increasingly fond of a man called Maurice Eaton, a Post Office executive who was even more anxious than Wield about the damage an open liaison might do to his career. But they had reached the stage of discussing setting up house together in Yorkshire when Eaton was offered a promotion in the North-East. To Wield, the move had seemed tragic at the time, but soon a routine of weekends in Newcastle and holidays abroad had been established which, while it was not without its tensions and dangers, had proved viable for a decade. But though having the centre of his emotional life a hundred miles away had made him 'safe', it also made him a bit of a cypher. Institutions do not like what they do not understand and now he was stuck at sergeant with younger men like Pascoe leapfrogging over his head.

Eventually something would give, he felt it in his bones. Meanwhile, on with the job.

The stall closest to the fortune-telling tent was an old fashioned 'penny-roll' at which coins were rolled down grooved ramps to land on a numbered chequer board, winning the amount stated if the coin fell plumb in the middle of a square. The man in charge shrugged indifferently, but his sharp-featured helpmeet believed she had seen Pauline leave about twenty minutes earlier. So BACK SOON could mean an hour or so yet.

He ought to get back to the station. He felt a little guilty at the way he had turned a blind eye to Rosetta Stanhope as he left, but it had seemed amusing to reinforce Pascoe's impression that he was more concerned with the good-looking niece than the old aunt. But it was very pleasant being out in the sunshine and he found himself asking the penny-roll woman if she knew where he might find Dave Lee.

She gave him a sharp, inquisitive look, then said, 'He could be on the dodgems, or the waltzer. He helps around when they're busy.'

'He doesn't have anything of his own then? A stall, I mean?'

The woman answered sneeringly, 'He's pure *didicoi*, not real fair people, don't like regular work, them. There is a stall, a lot of gypsy tat if you ask me. Over there, by the river. You're a copper, aren't you?'

'No, I'm his rich uncle from Australia,' said Wield gravely.

The dodgems and the waltzer producing no sign of Lee, he made his way to the stall which did nothing to make him feel the penny-roll woman had been unjust. Even in this temple of tawdriness, this looked extra tawdry and the dark-skinned woman with high, aristocratic cheekbones, one of which was livid with a wide bruise, seemed to be making little effort to entice customers.

'I'm looking for Dave Lee,' said Wield.

'What for? Are you going to arrest the bastard?' she answered.

'Just talk.'

'Pity. Why not put him in jail for a while?'

She seemed sincere.

'Why? What's he done?'

'Him? What hasn't he?'

Suddenly she seemed to tire of the conversation as if even resentment and hatred could not stimulate her interest for long.

'He's not here,' she said flatly.

'Where might he be?'

She shrugged. Wield consulted his notebook.

'You don't have a trailer here, do you? Could he have gone back to the encampment?'

Another shrug. Wield's patience began to go.

'All right. Come on.'

'Come on where?'

'To the station.'

'Me? What have I done?'

The interest had been restimulated.

'You? What haven't you?' mimicked Wield.

She swore. He didn't understand Romany, but he had no doubt what she was calling him.

'He went in the van,' she said, gesticulating at the nearby trailer park. 'Half an hour. To the camp, perhaps. Does he tell me where he goes? If you see him tell him he can...'

'What?' asked Wield.

The woman's face went sullen, flat, once more. Only the bruise gleamed.

'Nothing,' she said.

Wield strolled down to the river's edge. Boats were in large demand and the isthmus was full of people. For two days as a couple of dozen coppers crawled on their hands and knees from one end to the other, it had been closed to the public. The only result had been the most efficient litter-clearing operation in the city's history. Now the picnickers were back, their appetites doubtless whetted by the thought that on this very spot perhaps a girl had been done to death. And if they got bored with that, they could stroll a hundred yards or so down the canal bank and peer greedily across at the blank wall of Spinks's Electrical Depository where earlier the same night a watchman had had his skull fractured for the sake of a few cheap transistor radios made in Hong Kong.

Though typically he kept them to himself, Wield had his own carefully worked out ideas about crime and punishment. They included doling out in exactly measured and scientifically monitored doses the kind of pain to the attacker which he had inflicted on the attacked. Nothing to do with barbarities like chopping off hands or cutting off ears. Just the pain.

Though how to measure the pain of terror which these murdered women must have felt, he did not know. But something was needed, something better than we had.

He went back to Madame Rashid's tent. The notice was still there. He glanced at his watch. One-thirty. The station? Or could he justify going after Dave Lee? It was just a fifteen-minute drive at the most.

'Sod it,' he said and headed for his car.

He drove rapidly and efficiently, roughly following the course of the river out of town till he reached the old airfield which lay to the south-east. There had been a time in the affluent days of Super-Mac at the end of the 'fifties when it had teetered on the edge of development into a full-scale airport. But the moment had passed and now it was two-thirds disused, the remaining one-third being in the hands of the local Aero Club. Occasionally small private planes landed, particularly when there was a big race meeting at the city track, but generally speaking only the breathless *swoosh* of the gliders disturbed the air. There were a couple up now. Wield watched them, admired their soaring freedom but felt no desire to share it. He was a motor-bike man himself. Black leather and 100 mph up the motorway. Something else he kept quiet about at the station.

The disused section of the airport, where the urgent weeds and grasses had turned the runway into crazy paving and a couple of derelict buildings gaped like dead mouths at the unremembering sky, was now the site of an unofficial/official gypsy encampment.

It was 'unofficial' because the local council had been arguing for years about the need to provide an official site in the area; it was 'official' because during the hard months of the winter and during the two weeks of the High Fair the council and the police operated a 'no-hassle' policy. But come the spring and come the end of fair fortnight, the stand-pipes were turned off and the travelling folk invited to travel. There was a strong lobby in the gliding club which wanted them cleared off permanently, claiming that apart from polluting the nearby river with their sewage, their ponies (the same which had been banned from Charter Park) were a menace to gliders and small aircraft landing only a quarter-mile away. The council had erected a picket fence to prevent the ponies from straying but this was not proving one hundred per cent effective, as Wield realized when he got out of his car close to the gaudily painted caravans.

Normally the arrival of a stranger would have been viewed with close suspicious interest, but at this moment all attention was focused on a noisy and potentially violent confrontation taking place in the middle of the caravan circle.

On the one side was a group of gypsies with Dave Lee at their head. On the other were two men, one slight, blond, wirily built, in slacks and a sports shirt, the other much bulkier and sweating in a thick windcheater and flying helmet. All around them at a discreet distance stood a circle of interested women and kids.

The heavier man was wagging a finger that wouldn't take much bending to make a fist in Lee's face.

'Listen, you,' he grated in a harsh Yorkshire accent, 'I see one more bloody pony on the Aero Club's ground and I'll shoot it, you hear? And then I'll come and shoot the bugger who owns it.'

Dave Lee bared brown-stained teeth in a sneer and answered in an unpunctuated and rather high-pitched gabble. 'Listen mister what's up here you come here fucking threatening and talking about some pony which pony show us the fucking pony and what do you think anyway that ponies have no fucking sense to get out of the way of those machines more fucking sense than some fucking idiots who go up in them!'

The wagging finger folded. Wield had recognized the face beneath the flying helmet. It was Bernard Middlefield, JP. Not a man he cared for, but not a bad magistrate from a police point of view. At least he jumped hard on first offenders, believed police evidence like Holy Writ, and started from the useful premise that ninety per cent of what most social workers said was crap.

It would be interesting but not diplomatic to witness him thumping the gypsy. The blond man seemed bent on acting as a peacemaker but there was no guarantee of his success.

Wield advanced, warrant card at the ready, and addressed himself to Lee.

'Mr Lee?' he said. 'Can I have a word?'

The big gypsy laughed scornfully and said in the direction of Middlefield, 'No wonder he wants to fight when already he's called the cops!'

'Are you the police?' said Middlefield. 'Just in the nick!'

Wield didn't want to get involved but he had to hear the tale. The blond man was Austin Greenall, Chief Flying Instructor of the Aero Club. He had been manning the launching winch to get Middlefield's glider airborne when a pony had come wandering across the path of the accelerating aircraft and nearly caused an accident. Middlefield had come straight to the gypsy encampment closely attended by the secretary.

'Ultimately it's the council that are responsible, sir,' said Wield. 'They own all this land. You lease from them, I believe? So keeping fences in repair is their job.'

'Thanks for nothing,' said Middlefield. 'If I'd got killed, you might have taken heed, is that it? Well, I'll tell you something, these buggers need sorting out, and I'm the man to do it. They're anti-social, dirty and dishonest. I've got my works on the estate not a quarter-mile from here. When this site's occupied, I double my security staff. *Double* it. And that costs brass!'

'I'm sorry, sir,' said Wield. 'Unless there's been a breach of the law...'

Middlefield snorted indignantly, turned on his heel and marched away. Greenall gave an apologetic shrug to Wield, said, 'For God's sake, Mr Lee, watch those animals of yours,' and went after him.

'Yorkshiremen!' said Lee. 'Tough buggers, they think. Always wanting to fight.'

'Not me,' said Wield. 'I want to talk.'

They went to sit in the sergeant's car. Gypsies don't invite strangers, especially policemen, readily into their caravans and though the day was balmy, Wield knew that if he talked with Lee out of doors, he would quickly inherit the circle of curious kids.

Away from the excitement of confrontation, the gypsy's torrential speaking style declined to a reluctant dribble.

'It's about last Thursday night,' said Wield.

'I've told all that.'

'I read what you said,' said Wield.

'Well then.'

'You said you were at the Fair from eight till eleven, mainly on the dodgems.'

'Yes.'

'And you didn't see anyone resembling the dead girl during that time.'

'That's right.'

'You don't sleep at Charter Park, do you?'

'No. They stopped the ponies a few years back. Said they were dangerous. Like that short-arse fool.'

'So you came back here to your caravan at night. How?'

'I've a van. That's it there. Licensed and insured.'

'I never suggested it wasn't,' said Wield. 'But I'll check. I've done a lot of checking on you already, Mr Lee.'

'So?'

'So I know all about you. You've a nasty temper.'

The man shrugged.

'Against women too. I saw a woman today at your stall. She'd had a nasty crack.'

'She's a clumsy bitch.'

'Yes. Rape too. You've not stopped short of that, have you?'

This at last restarted the torrent of words, but not English. Wield said finally, 'Shut up or I'll pull your balls off.'

The man subsided, then burst out again. 'There wasn't no rape! No conviction! Rape that slut? Stick feathers on a chicken!'

'All right, all right,' said Wield impatiently. 'Where was your van parked?'

'Behind the stall,' he answered sullenly.

'And you just drove back here? Straight back? At eleven?'

'Eleven, half past. I don't know. It started raining. We packed the stuff from the stall into the van like every night.'

'We?'

'My wife and me. You met her you said. Then back here.'

'And no doubt she'll confirm this? And that you then went to bed and slept peacefully all night?'

The man didn't bother to answer.

'All right,' said Wield. 'Now tell me about Madame Rashid.'

He had a sense at that moment of the gypsy's receptivity being turned up a notch, though there was no outer physical sign.

'You know her?'

'Yes.'

'In fact she's a relation of yours, isn't that so?'

'She married a *gorgio*,' he said. 'Many years ago.'

'And her niece. You know her too?'

'I see her at the park.'

Wield paused. He'd no idea why he'd introduced this line of questioning. It wasn't going anywhere.

He decided on the heavily significant abrupt conclusion.

'All right,' he said. 'That's it.'

'What?'

'Out.'

The big gypsy got out of the car and shut the door with a force that shook Wield. An older grey-haired man with a ruddy open face who had been hanging around close by approached Lee and exchanged words with him in rapid Romany. Wield leaned out of his window and beckoned to the newcomer.

'Who're you?' he demanded.

'Me, pal? I'm Silvester. Silvester Herne's my name, pal.'

'Are you the boss of this lot? The king or whatever you call it?'

'Me, pal?' he said again, looking amazed. 'Just an old gypsy, just old Silvester.'

'Well, old Silvester, see if you can get it into your friend's thick skull. I'm not happy about him. I'll be back. Meanwhile, get that fence mended, stop them ponies straying. Or you'll all be in trouble. Right?'

'Right, pal,' said Herne, beaming co-operation. 'Straightaway!'

That was telling them! thought Wield as he drove away, but years of experience had taught him that telling gypsies anything was like talking to the trees. Not that he objected to gypsies as such, though the untidiness of their life made him shudder. If anything, he felt a sneaking sympathy with them as outcasts and envy of them as defiant outcasts. And perhaps there was some atavistic fear in his attitude also. He had certainly been more affected by Rosetta Stanhope's trance yesterday than he cared to reveal.

He should have gone back to the station but instead he found himself driving to his own flat, where he made himself a cup of tea. It was a gloomy place, he thought dejectedly. Even on the brightest of days the small north-facing windows let little light in. And it was drab and impersonal. Not many people visited him here apart from his married sister and the young nephew whose cassette recorder he had used at the seance. But the secretive element in his make-up drew him to the anonymous and noncommittal in all but the most private areas of life.

Reacting against the thought, he picked up his phone and dialled Maurice's business number in Newcastle. But when the phone was answered he replaced it without speaking. They had an agreement. All contact to be private except in extreme emergency. This was no emergency though somehow it felt as if there might be an emergency in the offing, like an area of low pressure over the Atlantic on the telly weather chart.

When he finally drank his tea it was quite cold and he saw with dismay that he had been sitting totally abstracted for more than an hour. It was after three-thirty.

He left the flat hurriedly. Pascoe was going to want to know *how* he'd spent his time. He would not be pleased. As for Dalziel...

At least he ought to be able to say he'd spoken to Pauline Stanhope.

He drove back to Charter Park, but swore under his breath when he saw the chair with the BACK SOON sign still outside Madame Rashid's tent. What the hell did SOON mean to a fortune-teller?

It ought to mean something.

Suddenly uneasy, he pushed the chair aside and opened the flap.

It was dark inside, dark and musty. The triangle of light from the opening fell across a plain trestle table.

'Oh Jesus,' said Wield.

He took two steps forward. Looked down. Retreated. As he pulled the flap down and replaced the chair with the sign a pair of young girls approached. One said boldly while the other giggled, 'Are you the fortune-teller, mister?'

'No,' said Wield. 'She's gone.'

'When will she be back?'

He gestured at the sign, then hurried away towards his car to radio for assistance.

BACK SOON. But from where?

Across the trestle table, her legs dangling off one end but her arms neatly crossed over her breast, lay the body of Pauline Stanhope.

She had been strangled.

CHAPTER 7

'Not a good advert, this,' said Dalziel. 'Like a butcher getting food poison.'

'Yes, sir,' said Pascoe, though his more exact mind found the analogy imprecise and therefore dissatisfying. He didn't say so, but wondered what the newspapers might make of a murder in a fortune-teller's tent.

The press were imminent, of course. The discovery of a crime by an experienced officer gives the police a head start in getting their investigation under way free from public or professional interference. But once they start, the news speeds like a run on the pound even from sites much more sequestered than a busy fairground. A rope barrier had been erected around the tent to keep the public back. The police doctor had examined the body briefly, pronounced the girl dead, probable cause strangulation, probable time two to four hours earlier. Next, at Pascoe's suggestion, because of the smallness of the internal area, a single detective had been sent in on hands and knees, armed with a high-powered torch and a plastic bag, to pick over every inch of the floor space before the photographer and fingerprint men further trampled the already well crushed grass. Another couple of men were put to examining the turf in the environs of the tent, but the passage of so many feet there made it a token gesture.

Next, photographs were taken from all angles, sketches made, distances measured. Then the fingerprint boys, who had been dusting the chair and notice outside, moved in and did the chair and table inside with the body still *in situ*. Finally, after Dalziel had stood and looked phlegmatically at the corpse for a few minutes, he gave the order for it to be slid into its plastic bag and taken to the mortuary where the clothes would be carefully removed and despatched to the lab for examination.

Now the print men did the rest of the table before it and the chairs were also packaged and despatched to the lab.

While all this was going on, a police caravan had been towed into the car park and here already statements were being taken for the second time in a week from the fairground people, with particular attention paid to those whose stalls or entertainments were within sighting distance of the tent.

Of these, the sharp-faced woman on the penny-roll stall was the most positive. Her name was Ena Cooper.

'Just before twelve she went. I told the ugly fellow. No, I didn't speak, well, she weren't all that close, like, and we was busy. Things don't really pick up while afternoon, but you get a lot of kids round late morning and the roll stalls are always popular with the kids. No, I didn't see her come back, I went across to our Ethel's, she's got a hot-dog stand by the Wheel, for a bite to eat later on, so she could have come back then. About two o'clock, just after the ugly fellow was here the first time. I was away mebbe forty-five minutes. No, it's no use asking *him*. He's so short-sighted he can hardly see the pennies. Kids cheat him rotten when I'm not here!'

Cooper, her husband, nodded melancholy agreement. He'd seen nowt, heard nowt.

Loudspeaker appeals were made to the crowd requesting anyone who had visited Madame Rashid's tent earlier that day to come forward, but so far without success.

Notable by his absence was Dave Lee. After Wield had described his encounter that afternoon, he was sent to pick the gypsy up and bring him in for questioning. At the same time, Dalziel sent a man round to the Wheatsheaf Garage to check the movements of Tommy Maggs.

Pascoe nodded approvingly. Investigation is ninety per cent elimination. In his mind, Maggs was almost completely in the clear as far as Brenda Sorby's death was concerned, and he didn't see the young man as a psychopathic mass murderer. But the obvious has got to be seen to be done.

When he was bold enough to utter these thoughts to Dalziel, the fat man grunted, 'Oh aye?'

A policewoman had been sent to tell Rosetta Stanhope the tragic news. Pascoe had steered her out of the office earlier that afternoon, with assurances that they would certainly consider her kind offer of psychic assistance.

Later he had been summoned to Dalziel's office where the fat man was conferring with Detective Chief Inspector George Headingley who was in charge of the Spinks's warehouse case. This was now murder. The watchman had died in hospital that morning, and Headingley was in search of more manpower. They had gone over the staff dispositions together and seen how tautly stretched they were. Then Pascoe had mentioned Rosetta Stanhope's offer of help and frivolously wondered if they might not take it up.

'Aye,' said Dalziel. 'She can try to make contact with the ACC for a start. That bugger's been dead from the neck up for years!'

They had all laughed. And not long afterwards Wield had phoned with his news.

Now Pascoe awaited uneasily the arrival of the dead girl's aunt. She would have to be taken to the mortuary for a formal identification of the body. It was always an unpleasant business, and though Rosetta Stanhope had impressed him as a strong-willed albeit rather eccentric character, experience had taught him there was no way of forecasting reactions.

He felt almost relieved when the policewoman called in with the news that Mrs Stanhope was not at home so she had stationed herself outside her flat to await her return.

Shortly afterwards Wield returned to say that Dave Lee had gone off in his van right after the sergeant's visit. No one knew, or at least was telling, his destination.

Finally the DC sent to check on Tommy Maggs arrived, also unaccompanied. Maggs had not returned to work after the dinner break and there was no reply to repeated knockings at the door of his home.

'Check with the neighbours,' ordered Dalziel. 'See if he's contacted his parents at work. Find out who his doctor is. Sergeant Wield, you've got Lee's van number? Right. Put out a call. Peter, you go and deal with the press, will you? You're better at shooting shit than anyone else.'

'Thanks,' said Pascoe. 'What do I tell them?'

'What you know, which, unless you're holding some thing back, is bugger all.'

'They'll be keen to know if it's the Choker again,' said Pascoe.

'Won't know that till the PM. And then we'll only know it's *a* Choker!'

'It looks a pretty clear case,' protested Pascoe. 'I mean, compared with the Sorby girl...'

'You think so? We'll have to see,' said Dalziel.

The old bastard thinks he's on to something, thought Pascoe. Or perhaps he just likes being contrary.

The journalists who had gathered at the fairground were not just local. Word had spread, and there were even a couple from London already, though it emerged that they had travelled up attracted by the clairvoyance story, and Pauline Stanhope's murder was just a bonus. In the car park, a television crew were unshipping their cameras. They would get some good atmospheric footage if nothing more, thought Pascoe. The fairground amusements, after a brief hiatus, were back to full steam, whirling, glittering, blaring. Did the laughter, the music, the excited shrieking hold perhaps a more than usually strident note of hysteria? wondered Pascoe. It was almost indecent, but at the same time it was inevitable. Death, the biggest barker of them all, had gathered together a huge crowd and the fair people could hardly be expected to ignore this opportunity. It wasn't even as if Pauline Stanhope was one of their own. Nor Rosetta, for that matter. Once a year they joined the show while the rest of them formed a shifting but constant community.

He stonewalled the questions for ten minutes. As he'd anticipated, they were most eager for confirmation that this was a Choker killing.

'What about the *Hamlet* calls, Inspector?' asked one of the reporters. 'Has there been one yet?'

'I don't know.' Pascoe smiled. 'You'd better ask your colleague from the *Evening Post*. His boss gets them first.'

One of the TV men caught his sleeve as he turned away and asked if they could do a filmed interview in about five minutes.

'I'll have to check,' said Pascoe.

'Well, it's not with you, actually. It's Superintendent Dalziel we'd like.'

Piqued, Pascoe returned to the caravan where he found Dalziel on the phone which the Post Office had just connected.

'The telly men request the pleasure of your company, sir,' he said when the fat man had finished.

'What's up with you, lad? Not photogenic?'

'Perhaps I don't fill a twenty-six-inch screen,' said Pascoe acidly.

'What? Put you out, has it, lad?' chortled Dalziel. 'Here's something to put you back in. I've just been talking to Sammy Locke at the *Post*.'

'There's been a call?' said Pascoe eagerly.

'I knew that'd please you, Peter. You reckon you'll get the bugger through these calls, don't you? Well, best of luck. There's two of the sods at it now!'

He was wrong.

By the time Pascoe got home that night there'd been four *Hamlet* calls.

The first, at four-forty-two, said, *Now get you to my lady's chamber, and tell her, let her paint an inch thick, to this favour she must come.*

The second, at five-twenty-three, said, *One may smile, and smile, and be a villain.*

The third, at six-fifteen, said, *To be, or not to be, that is the question.*

The fourth, at seven-nine, said, *The time is out of joint:—O cursed spite, that ever I was born to set it right.*

Ellie, for a change, was in bright good spirits and Pascoe was so pleased to see this that he restricted himself to no more than a forty degree roll of the eyeballs when she announced that she was now the membership secretary of WRAG. In any case, she seemed much more keen to talk about the Choker.

'These phone calls. Are they really going to be any use?'

'We don't have much else,' said Pascoe, tucking into his re-heated beef and mushroom pie. 'But they can't all be the Choker. Sammy Locke's memory of the first voice is a bit vague. He reckons that two, possibly three, of this lot are not so very different from it.'

'You've got all today's calls on tape, you say,' said Ellie. 'What you want is a language expert to listen to them.'

'Good thinking,' said Pascoe, who'd already made the suggestion to Dalziel but wasn't about to be a cleversticks. 'Anyone in mind?'

'Well, there's Dicky Gladmann and Drew Urquhart at the College. They impress their students by working out regional and social backgrounds by voice analysis.'

'And are they right?'

'One hundred per cent usually, I gather. But I think they probably check the records first. Still, they're certainly incomprehensible enough to be good linguists.'

Pascoe finished his pie, drew breath and started in on the apple crumble, also warmed up.

She wants *me* to get fat too! he suddenly thought.

'I'll give them a try. Though they're probably enjoying their little vacation in Acapulco,' he said. 'By the way, you never said, how did la Lacewing respond to your theory about the medium message?'

'Thought it was a load of crap,' said Ellie moodily.

'Did she now? Well well. Let me have the transcript back, won't you?'

'Yes. And she got pretty close to embarrassing me by talking about you being in charge of the case.'

'That embarrasses you?'

'Of course not. No, I mean she was trying to put down some loud-mouthed fellow called Middlefield, he's a JP or something, thinks all murdered women are *ipso facto* whores. I tell you what was interesting, though. I gathered the fellow *he* was talking to was the manager of the bank where that other girl worked. The one on the tape. Or not.'

'Brenda Sorby. Now that is interesting,' said Pascoe. Later as they lay in bed, Ellie said drowsily, 'This poor woman at the fairground. You say she was Rosetta Stanhope's niece?'

'That's right.'

'Then maybe she'll get in touch with her. I mean, they must have been close.'

'Maybe,' said Pascoe. 'We'll call you in if it happens.'

She dug her elbow in his ribs and soon her breath steadied into the regularity of sleep.

Pascoe found sleep difficult, however, and when it did come, it came in fits and starts and flowed shallowly over a rocky bed. Ellie was partly responsible by putting the thought of Pauline Stanhope into his mind, but she would have been there anyway. He always slept badly the night before attending a post-mortem and tomorrow he was due at the City Mortuary at nine a.m. to attend the last forensic rites on the body of Pauline Stanhope.

CHAPTER 8

The police pathologist was a swift, economical worker who never took refuge in the kind of ghoulish heartiness with which some of his colleagues sought to make their jobs tolerable. Pascoe was glad of this. He liked to enter an almost trance-like state of professional objectivity on these occasions and had already offended the Mortuary Superintendent and the nervous new Coroner's Officer by his brusque response to their efforts at socialization.

The pathologist examined the neck first before asking the Superintendent to remove the clothes which were then separately packaged and sent on their way to the laboratory. After a further careful examination of the naked body, turning it over on the slab so that nothing was missed, the pathologist was ready to make the median incision. As the scalpel slipped through the white skin, the Coroner's Officer swayed slightly. This was his first time, Pascoe had gathered from the man's nervy conversation with the Mortuary Superintendent. He reached into his pocket, pulled out a notebook, and tapped the man on the shoulder.

'Borrow your pen a moment?' he asked brusquely.

'Yes, of course,' said the man.

Pascoe scribbled a few notes, then returned the implement.

'Thanks,' he said. 'You'd better have it back. Your need's greater than mine. Your boss is a stickler for detail in all these forms, isn't he?'

The man managed a pale grin, then began writing at a furious rate.

After a while Pascoe took his own pen from his pocket and followed suit.

There was another disturbance, more obvious this time, about thirty minutes later.

Voices were heard distantly upraised. After a while the door opened and a porter came in and spoke quietly to the Mortuary Superintendent who relayed the information to Pascoe.

'There's a woman outside with a man. She says she's the girl's aunt and she's making a fuss about seeing the body.'

Pascoe looked at the cadaver on the examination table. The sternum and frontal ribs had been removed and the omentum cut away so that heart, lungs and intestine were visible.

The pathologist continued with his work, undisturbed by the interruption.

'I'll sort it,' said Pascoe.

He went out of the examination room, through the storage room, into a small reception area, where a clerk was holding Rosetta Stanhope at bay.

With her, to Pascoe's surprise, was Dave Lee.

'Mr Pascoe,' she said, 'they say my niece is here. I've a right to see her, haven't I? I'm entitled. I want to see her.'

Emotion was giving her voice rhythms and resonances from her childhood, forcing them up through the heavy overlay of conventional urban Yorkshire.

'You can't stop her, mister,' said the man. 'It's her niece.'

'I'm sorry, Mrs Stanhope,' said Pascoe quietly. 'There's an examination going on just now. When it's all over we'll make arrangements, I promise you.'

'You've no right to stop her,' said the man belligerently. 'Like she says, she's entitled.'

'I don't think you'd want to see her now, Mrs Stanhope,' said Pascoe. 'Please. Later. It's for the best.'

'You mean, they're cutting her up?' asked the woman.

'There has to be a post-mortem,' said Pascoe gently.

She nodded and Pascoe took her arm and led her through the door of the Superintendent's office. The clerk looked uncertain at this procedure but Pascoe who knew all about social dynamics said to him, 'Get us a cup of tea, will you?' and he went away quite happily feeling his function reinforced.

'We tried to get hold of you last night,' said Pascoe after Rosetta Stanhope had sat down. There were only two chairs in the room and Pascoe took the other, leaving Dave Lee to stand awkwardly and with ill grace by the window.

'I went away,' she said.

'You didn't say anything about going away when we talked yesterday lunch-time,' said Pascoe. 'Unexpected, was it?'

'Yes. Unexpected. I left a note in the flat for Pauline.'

Her voice choked as she spoke the girl's name. Pascoe looked at her carefully. She was wearing the same grey suit as on the previous day, only it wasn't quite so smart now, a little crumpled, a little awry and straggly.

'How did you hear about your niece, Mrs Stanhope?' he asked.

She shot a glance at the man.

'I heard...this morning,' she said. 'In the papers.'

'Yes, I see.'

Pascoe reminded himself to check the papers. Most of them were very co-operative in not revealing a victim's name till next-of-kin had been informed. On the other hand the background and setting were unusual enough to make identification easy for anyone in the know.

'So, where did you spend last night?' he gently insisted.

'She was with me,' interposed the man harshly. 'We drove up north. Spent the night with some friends.'

'Rather a sudden decision, wasn't it? For both of you, I mean.'

They exchanged a rapid jabber which Pascoe's academic acquaintance with Anglo-Romany did not help him to understand.

'*Qu'est-ce-que vous voulez cacher de moi?*' he demanded loudly. He wasn't sure of the preposition but he could see from their blank stares it didn't matter.

'French,' he said in a normal tone. 'You don't understand it? Then you must find it exasperating, or offensive, or stupid, or even suspicious that I use it.'

The man continued to look blank, but Mrs Stanhope gave him a thin apologetic smile.

'It's just habit, Mr Pascoe,' she said. 'Dave said you were being a bit bloody nosey, that was all.'

'And you replied?'

'That all I wanted to do was see my niece,' she said wearily. 'Yes, it was sudden. I went home after I saw you. Dave called round a bit later. Pauline had told him I wasn't too well that morning and he was a bit worried. He suggested a little drive out, see some friends from the old days, might do me good. So on the spur of the moment, I agreed.'

This picture of a concerned Dave going out of his way to soothe his old cousin's troubles by a little drive in the country was too petit-bourgeois to be true, thought Pascoe.

'What happened yesterday, Mr Pascoe? Can you at least tell us that?' she continued.

'The post-mortem will help us to be sure, but it seems probable that someone went into your tent at the fairground in the early afternoon, strangled your niece, then left, putting up the back soon notice,' said Pascoe carefully.

'Early afternoon, you say?' said the woman in a puzzled voice. 'And no one saw anything? Or heard anything?'

'Well, of course there's a lot of noise on a fairground,' said Pascoe. 'But no, we haven't been able to find anyone yet who saw anything odd. But we're still taking statements. We'd like one from you, of course, Mr Lee.'

'Me? Why?' demanded the man.

'Because you work at the Fair. Because you spoke with Miss Stanhope yesterday morning. I saw you myself.'

'I was away from the park,' retorted Lee angrily. 'I was back at the camp. Your mate, the funny-looking bugger, he saw me.'

'So I understand. That would be about one-forty-five, I reckon. What time did you leave the fairground?'

'I don't know. Dinner-time, summat like that.'

'You went back to the encampment for your dinner, then?'

'That's right.'

'But your wife was still at Charter Park. You prepared your own dinner, did you?'

'I'm not helpless,' said the man.

'Did you?' insisted Pascoe. 'And did you eat alone? Who else saw you at the encampment?'

'I had a beer and a pie in a pub on the way back if you must know,' snarled the man. 'So I was seen all right, pal.'

'Good,' said Pascoe. 'And the pub?'

'What?' The man was suddenly hesitant, unsure.

'What was the name of the pub?' Pascoe enunciated clearly, watching Lee with interest.

'The Cheese,' said Lee surlily.

'The Cheshire Cheese?' said Pascoe. 'Well, well.'

Even Rosetta Stanhope looked at Lee curiously.

'A little out of your way,' said Pascoe provocatively.

'It's dead handy!' retorted Lee, defiant again. 'I often have a drink there.'

'Do you now?' said Pascoe. This was interesting. Probably a red herring, but extremely sniffable. But not at this time and place.

The door opened and the clerk came in with a cup of tea. He looked uncertain whom he should offer it to. Pascoe nodded towards Rosetta Stanhope and glanced at his watch.

'If you'll excuse me, I'll go back in. I'm sure it will be all right if you wait here, though it may take some little time, you realize.'

The clerk didn't look at all sure, and Dave Lee did not seem all that happy either. But Mrs Stanhope nodded emphatically.

'Right, then,' said Pascoe. He stepped into the outer office, closing the door firmly behind him, picked up the phone on the clerk's desk and dialled HQ. When he got through he asked for Dalziel. The fat man wasn't available, however, so he got on to Sergeant Wield and told him succinctly what had happened and suggested he got down to the mortuary with a policewoman as quickly as possible.

Then, with reluctant steps, he returned to the examination room.

❀ ❀ ❀

Ellie Pascoe was stretched out on the broad springy sofa which she and Peter had chosen with overt sensuality aimed at embarrassing the too enthusiastic salesman. They had failed. But the sofa had certainly succeeded, she thought, turning a page of the romantic thriller she was currently using to postpone work on her own great novel.

The doorbell rang.

In best suburban fashion, she peeked through the living-room window before answering it. There was a blue Marina parked at the gateway. In it she could see a man and a couple of children, early teens. She recognized neither car nor inmates.

The bell rang again.

She went to the door.

'Hello,' said Lorraine Wildgoose.

She was dressed in jeans and a loose shirt. From behind Ellie guessed her slim figure would probably pass for that of a teenager, but they'd get her under the Trades Description Act when they saw the face. It was not unattractive, but fortyish beyond the disguise of eye make-up and blusher.

She was carrying three thick and rather tatty cardboard files.

'I said I'd drop this stuff in,' she explained. 'I was passing, so here it is.'

'Great,' said Ellie with as much enthusiasm as she could manage. 'Come on in.'

She led the way to the living-room and had to stop herself from straightening the cushions on the sofa and at the same time pushing her romantic thriller under them.

'They look a mess, but they're all in sequence,' said Lorraine. 'I think we covered everything yesterday, but any problems, just give a ring.'

'Thanks,' said Ellie. 'Would you like a coffee or something?'

To her surprise, her visitor said, 'Yes, why not?'

Well, mainly because you seem to have left a car full of people broiling in the hot sun, thought Ellie, but she didn't know the woman well enough to say it.

'So this is what a policeman's house looks like,' said Lorraine, following her into the kitchen. 'Nice.'

'The bribes help,' said Ellie.

'Your husband's working on this Choker thing, you said yesterday. Full-time job by the sound of it.'

'He does other things,' said Ellie.

Ellie was quite capable of waking Pascoe up in the middle of the night to tell him that he and his colleagues were stupid, brutal and fascist, but she was very wary of invitations to bring her special relationship to the liberal bar in public debate. But Lorraine went no further, contenting herself with peering into a couple of cupboards Ellie would rather have kept closed.

'What about your...friends?' she said as she spooned the instant coffee into mugs.

'Who? Oh, *them*. They're not friends, they're family,' she said with a tight smile which might have been meant to indicate a joke. 'My kids. And my husband.'

'You're separated, aren't you?' said Ellie.

'So far as you can be when you work in the same school,' she said. 'Still, the hols are here now, so we can get some real separation in. I go off next week for three weeks in Italy, Mark's off the week after for practically the whole of the vacation, and the kids are going up to the Dales with some friends who've got a cottage there.'

'Then you won't be seeing much of each other for a while,' said Ellie, pouring the boiling water.

'No, thank Christ. This is a kind of last rite. We're off for a picnic lunch by the sea. We'd all rather be doing something else, but even the kids don't like to say it.'

'Well brought up,' suggested Ellie.

They went back into the living-room. She managed a glance through the window. The man had got out of the car and was leaning against it. He was wearing shorts and a T-shirt with something printed across the chest.

'The usual thing is to say there were faults on both sides,' said Lorraine Wildgoose abruptly. 'Well, there weren't, not this time. You know, I used to enjoy being domesticated. It was nice. I was into the WRAG thing too, but I never pushed it at home. Then it changed.'

'Another woman?' said Ellie conventionally.

'Maybe, I don't know. The bastard just started hating me. I suddenly realized that, whatever the cause, he actually hated me! So I got out. You don't have to take that kind of risk, do you? Not if you're not a prostitute.'

Ellie cast a longing eye at her romantic novel.

'Where are you living now?' she asked to fill a small silence.

'Oh, I'm back in the house and *he's* out now. I went straight to Thelma and she got things sorted very quickly. She's marvellous, isn't she? Not that Mark raised much objection, to give him his due. Suburbia probably cramped his style, anyway. Too open. Too many eyes behind too many lace curtains.'

She sipped her coffee, then added abruptly, 'This fellow your husband's after. There was another one yesterday. I read it in the paper.'

'They're not certain yet it was the Choker,' said Ellie, cautious again.

'Whoever, he must hate us pretty much too,' said Lorraine, frowning into her coffee. The doorbell rang.

'That'll be him,' said Lorraine. 'He won't wait. We've a right to protect ourselves, haven't we? A duty.'

'I suppose so.'

Ellie stood up.

'Don't bring him in. I'm finished,' said the woman, draining her mug. 'You'll get a shock when you see him. I hope it doesn't affect the baby. He's gone weird. You know what he's doing this vac? He's going to Saudi Arabia with a mini-bus camping party. I think he lied about his age, told them he was thirty. The kids get embarrassed. Shit! *I* get embarrassed!'

Ellie opened the front door.

Mark Wildgoose was leaning against the jamb and didn't bother to straighten up. He had a thin dark mobile face which might just about pass for a dissolute thirty. The legend on his T-shirt said *The Greatest!* It looked as if it could do with a wash and he smelt sweaty.

'The kids are pissed off,' he said over Ellie's shoulder. 'Me too. Are you going to be all bloody day?'

'See what I mean?' said Lorraine. 'Despite his language, they let him teach English and Drama at the Bishop Crump Comprehensive School. He used to be my husband. He might even know your husband.'

'Hello,' said Ellie, pretending this was an introduction. 'I'm Ellie Pascoe.'

'Hello,' said Wildgoose. 'Look, I'm sorry, I didn't mean to be rude, but she said a minute and the children *are* very hot. Your husband...Pascoe? Works in the education office, does he?'

'He's a policeman,' interjected his wife. 'He may have interviewed you. When that woman was killed, remember?'

'Of course I remember, but I don't remember the policeman's name. Look, are you coming now or not?'

He was plainly exasperated but Ellie could not really see anything amounting to hatred in his expression, though he did look as if he might have pushed half a grapefruit in his wife's face if he'd happened to have half a grapefruit.

'Yes, I'm coming,' said Lorraine Wildgoose wearily. 'Thanks for the coffee, Ellie.'

'Coffee!' Wildgoose cried with an expressive movement of the shoulders as he headed back for the car.

His wife lingered still.

She wants me to press her, thought Ellie.

'Which woman?' she said.

'I forget her name. The one they found in the allotment shed. They talked to everyone who had an allotment.'

'And your husband...?' Ellie was surprised.

'Yes,' said Lorraine wearily. 'Last year he was into self-sufficiency. Grow your own veg. I wouldn't let him dig up the lawn so he applied for an allotment. I knew it wouldn't last. He hardly goes at all now.'

'Why are you telling me this, Lorraine?' asked Ellie.

'Telling you what? I'm just talking. My life's in such a turmoil, I don't know what I'm doing half the time,' said Lorraine. 'That's why I'm so glad you can take over this job. You'll let me know if there's anything you don't understand.'

'That's very likely,' said Ellie. 'OK.'

Outside a horn blew. One short, two long blasts.

'*Qu'il est triste, le son du cor, au fond du bois,*' said Lorraine. 'That girl Brenda Sorby. She went to the Crump Comprehensive, you know.'

Now the car had started up, the engine revving noisily. '*Ciao,*' said Lorraine. 'Don't forget, ring if there's anything I can do.'

'I will,' promised Ellie. 'I will.'

When she returned to the sofa, for a long while she found her romantic thriller unpickupable.

CHAPTER 9

Sergeant Wield had had another unsatisfactory session with Dave Lee. The gypsy stuck to his story that he had driven Rosetta Stanhope up north on a visit to friends 'to take her out of herself'.

When pressed for detail he said vaguely, 'Teesdale, somewhere near Barnard Castle,' adding that as they were on the move, he couldn't say where they'd be now. Thereafter all that he would add to his story was a mounting degree of exasperated profanity.

He was equally vague and equally profane when the topic changed to his movements earlier in the day. He couldn't remember when last he'd seen Pauline. *Early. Nine o'clock perhaps.* Nor what they'd talked about. *The other cop, the good-looking one, had just gone, so mebbe it was about him.* Nor when precisely he'd left the fairground. *Dinner-time, somewhere about then.*

But he was certain about his pint in the Cheshire Cheese and that he'd been back at the aerodrome no later than one-fifteen which all present would confirm.

Wield didn't doubt it, but turned to the landlord of the Cheshire Cheese for less partisan confirmation of Lee's timetable. Wally Furniss was a round, rubicund man who, had he been an actor, would have made a large fortune playing jovial English landlords in costume dramas. Instead, he made a small fortune playing the same role in real life. Death seemed to be his friend. Recently widowed, he had emerged from the ordeal redder and jollier than ever. And the awful fate of Mary Dinwoodie behind his pub had crowded his bars and broadened his smile in the weeks since.

Wield, used to landlords who were surlily resentful or distastefully sycophantic, found himself greeted with what felt like genuine pleasure and a large vodka and tonic.

'You remembered,' he said. It sounded a foolish thing to say but Furniss grinned delightedly, tapped his brow, and said, 'Trick of the trade.'

His memory was equally good when it came to Lee.

'The gyppo? About twenty-five past twelve. A pint of mild and a pastie. Said it was stale, and I asked him how *he'd* know! He ate it up, though. Yes, we have one or two of his lot in when they're camping on the 'drome. It's just the other side of the by-pass. No, I don't mind 'em, as long as they stick to the taproom, which they mostly do.'

'The night Mrs Dinwoodie was killed, were there any of them in then?'

Furniss pursed his lips. 'Not that I can say definite, else I would've done, wouldn't I?'

Wield had to agree.

'Mind you, they were about,' added Furniss. 'I remember saying, just a bit before, that some of 'em were back early this year. It's usually just the week before the Fair that they start congregating. Poor sods probably got turfed out of their last spot a bit unexpected.'

'That's interesting,' said Wield. 'Dave Lee, now, the fellow I was asking about, was he one of them?'

'Couldn't say for sure,' said Furniss regretfully. 'Are they mixed up in this Choker business, you reckon?'

'Just enquiries, Mr Furniss,' said Wield heavily. 'And I'd appreciate it if they stayed between you and me.'

'My lips is sealed,' said Furniss with a contradictory breadth of smile.

'And you're sure they were around before Mrs Dinwoodie's death?'

'Oh yes. Ask at the Aero Club if you want to find out just when. They keep a close eye on them down there. Lots of valuable stuff around that place, not to mention the bar! If I catch any of them hanging around outside here, I send them packing pretty quick. Paying customers are one thing, light fingers another! Same again, Sergeant?'

Wield shook his head and put his glass down.

'Work to do,' he said. 'Thanks all the same.'

'Any time you're passing. Watch how you go now.'

Furniss accompanied him to the door and saw him out into the eye-blinding sunshine. Returning to the cool shades of his taproom he said to his barmaid who was checking the bottled beer, 'Bloody cops. Drink you out of business if you let 'em! And, Elsie, keep an eye open for those gyppos who sometimes get in here. The coppers reckon they had summat to do with that Dinwoodie tart's death.'

Wield meanwhile was taking a circuitous route back to the centre of town. The old aerodrome was barely a half-mile away across the by-pass. Roughly rectangular, it was flanked by the river and open country on one side, the by-pass itself on another, and by the Avro Industrial Estate and the suburb of Millhill on the other two. During the war when Wellingtons and Lancasters took off from here nightly, the 'drome had been well outside the city limits, though too close for the comfort of those who unpatriotically wanted to keep the war as far away from themselves as possible. Now the city had caught up with it, industry and suburbia had nibbled into it, and increasingly there were voices raised in council meetings pointing out what a valuable piece of real estate it was. The Aero Club's lease ran out in three years and Wield guessed that with the squeeze on local authority finances getting even tighter, the speculators would be invited in to do their worst.

Wield felt as indifferent to this possibility as he had done during the recent battle between the motorway planners and the city's premier golf club. His ideas of recreation were oriental in every sense. Judo, kung-fu, karate—his fondness for these martial arts had the official seal of approval. Every good policeman should be able to take care of himself.

And every good policeman should be able to make connections too. He thought of the coincidence of Lee's use of the Cheshire Cheese. Could it be significant?

He pulled the car to a halt by the side of the road. From here he could see the open expanse of the old airfield. A bright orange windsock hung flaccid from its pole.

Wield took out his map of the city and its environs and studied it for a while. Then he carefully drew circles round the Cheshire Cheese, Charter Park and the Pump Street allotment. Next he put a cross against the northeast corner of the airfield where the gypsies had their encampment.

Apart from its comparative proximity to the Cheshire Cheese, it had no apparent significance. Now he put squares round the murdered women's homes. Again nothing. They were widely scattered. Only June McCarthy had been killed near her home.

Wield frowned. Much more of this and he'd run out of shapes. He began to set triangles round the victims' places of employment.

That was better. That was what had been niggling away.

Two of the triangles, McCarthy's factory and Sorby's bank, were situated not too far from the airfield, in the Avro Industrial

Estate and the adjacent Millhill residential suburb respectively. Mrs Dinwoodie's Garden Centre was several miles out of town and, for the purpose of the enquiry, Pauline Stanhope's place of work would have to go down as Charter Park. But a fifty per cent statistic might be significant.

Though, he thought gloomily, gypsies were hardly famed for using banks or indeed seeking employment in the factories.

He started his engine again. As he did so, his radio crackled into life with his call sign. He replied and was told to contact Inspector Pascoe as soon as possible. There was a call-box only a hundred yards ahead.

'Sergeant, where are you?'

Wield explained and also gave a brief run-down of his talk with Furniss and his subsequent geographical musings.

Pascoe said doubtfully, 'It might mean something. I'll toss it around. Meanwhile, on your way in, call at the Wheatsheaf Garage. You probably heard Tommy Maggs is still missing. He didn't arrive home yesterday and he's not at work this morning. See if anybody can give us a line, particularly that lad, Ludlam. Watch him. If he's covering up for Tommy, he can be slippery. You know about Ludlam, don't you.'

'Oh yes,' said Wield gravely. 'I know.'

Ludlam, like Maggs, had had some juvenile problems with the police, but a little more serious—shop-lifting, robbing a phone-box, taking and driving a car without permission. Since his mother died when he was seventeen, he had lived with his married sister, Janey, who had been glad of his company two years ago when her husband, Frankie Pickersgill, had been jailed for his part in an off-licence robbery. Frankie was a careful, clever and previously unconvicted criminal. The police had been delighted to get him at last, disappointed that his clean sheet got him off so lightly as a 'first offender'.

What few people knew, especially not Frankie and his wife, was that a few days before his arrest, Ron Ludlam had been picked up trying to flog some cheap Scotch round the pubs and after a couple of hours alone with Dalziel he had been ready to co-operate fully in return for a guarantee of anonymity.

Dalziel's guarantees usually made the South Sea Bubble look firm and substantial, but this time enough evidence materialized to convict without Ron's appearance in the box.

'On the other hand, if he knows anything about Tommy, a bit of pressure and he'll give. We know that,' continued Pascoe. 'Now, to kill two birds with one stone. We've got so many of the lads tied up on the Choker case that Mr Headingley's finding himself a bit thin on the ground. He's going down a list of possibles for the Spinks's warehouse break-in. Frankie Pickersgill's on it, of course. He's been out three months now, might be feeling the pinch though it doesn't sound like his style. Anyway he says he was home that night watching telly with his wife and brother-in-law.'

'We know Ron was at the Bay Tree at half eight,' interposed Wield.

'Yes, I know. This is after ten we're talking about,' said Pascoe. 'Well, Janey and Ron, it's not the best of alibis. And while Mr Headingley doesn't really reckon Frankie, it might be worth pressuring Ron ever so lightly at the same time as you ask about Tommy.'

'Right,' said Wield.

When he got to the Wheatsheaf Garage, he wandered around for a while chatting to all and sundry and got confirmation of the story as told before. Tommy had worked normally in the morning. He was not his old chipper self, but that was only to be expected in the circumstances. At midday he had cleaned himself up and driven away.

Wield found Ludlam half in, half out of an Austin Princess, working under the dashboard. He climbed into the passenger seat and said, 'Very nice.'

'You reckon? Me, I like something with a bit more zip.'

Ludlam was a fresh-faced youth of about twenty with shoulder-length blond hair that obviously got nothing but the best treatment, wide-set blue eyes and good teeth. There was a smudge of oil on his cheek. Wield, looking down on him with an undetectable pleasure, was tempted to erase the smudge, but resisted easily.

'You still living at your sister's place, Ron?' he asked.

'That's right.'

'Frankie's out now, isn't he?'

'Yeah. He's working as a driver. He only did sixteen months with the remission.'

'Only sixteen months? I expect it seemed long enough to him. You're good mates, are you?'

Ludlam wriggled out of the car then climbed back into the driver's seat.

'Yeah. Fine. Why not?'

'I can think of a reason, Ron,' said Wield gravely. 'Frankie never suspected though? That's good. But you must feel you owe him a favour, like. I mean even though it was *only* sixteen months, you must feel you owe him a favour. And your sister too. You owe Janey a lot, I should think.'

'What do you mean?'

'The night Brenda disappeared. What were you doing, Ron?'

'Nothing. I went home early. Sat and watched a bit of telly with Janey and Frankie.'

'You left the Bay Tree, didn't go into the disco, didn't pull yourself a bird, just went home for a quiet night? Not your style.'

'I just felt like it,' insisted Ludlam. He sounded agitated.

'Tell you what, Ron. We're going to be asking questions down at the Bay Tree. We get one sniff that you were having your usual knee-tremble in the back lane at the time you say you were home, you'll be in real trouble, son. You knew Brenda pretty well?'

The change of direction disconcerted Ludlam.

'Yeah.'

'She'd been round to your place?'

'Yeah, but with Tommy, I mean. And Janey was there!'

'But you fancied her? I mean, you wouldn't have said no.'

'What do you mean? She was Tommy's bird. We were friends!'

'*Friends*. So if you'd been driving along and you saw her walking, you'd stop and give her a lift?'

'Yes. I mean no. I mean, I told you, how could I, I was home that night and anyway I haven't got any wheels!'

Wield gave what Pascoe had once described as his Ozymandias sneer and made a gesture which took in the car-packed garage.

'We're worried about Tommy,' he said abruptly. 'It's not like him, his mam says, just going off like this.'

'I'm worried too,' said Ludlam. He sounded as if he meant it, though whether he was referring simply to Tommy's disappearance was another matter.

'If you know anything, better tell us,' said Wield. 'He seemed really cut up about Brenda. He's in no fit state to be off by himself.'

'He wouldn't do anything like that.'

'Like what?'

'Like hurting himself.'

'I'm glad to hear it. You should know. You're his mate. How'd he seem yesterday morning?'

'Quiet, like. He'd just come back to work. The boss said he could have longer off, but he seemed to want to be occupied. When he didn't turn up after dinner, we just thought he'd taken the boss up on his offer.'

'Don't you usually have your eats with him?'

'Yeah. We usually have a pie in the Wheatsheaf across the road. But it got to midday and he just took off.'

Wield got out of the car and walked round to the driver's side.

'You hear anything, you tell us now, Ron. You remember anything, you tell us. All right?'

'Sure, yeah. I will.'

He couldn't keep the look of relief off his young fresh open face. It seemed a pity to do anything to spoil that beauty but Wield knew his job was not to bear comfort but a sword.

'Be sure you do, Ron,' he said, his face close to the boy's. 'We helped you once. We reckon you still owe us. And we like to keep the books balanced. One way or another.'

Worry put five years on Ludlam's face at a stroke. At least, thought Wield as he walked away, features like his own could take the hobnailed march of time and trouble with scarcely a trace.

He felt troubled now, without knowing why. Pascoe would have approved the obliquity of his interrogation, Dalziel the threat, but he did not feel satisfied. He glanced at his watch and wondered if he'd get away early enough that evening to drive up to Newcastle. It was his friend's birthday and he'd promised. But he knew that in the police the strongest oaths were often straw to the fires of duty. He glanced at his notebook. One more call to make, on Mrs Sorby, and then he should be done. He crossed his fingers.

❀ ❀ ❀

As it turned out, everyone got away early that evening. Nothing was happening, the investigation was in the doldrums, and Dalziel, who had no qualms about dragging his men on holiday out of their hotel beds at midnight if a case required it, said, 'That's it. Everyone sod off, get a bit of rest while you can.'

Wield headed up the A1 at seventy mph, Dalziel opened a bottle of Glen Grant and grimly settled down to read all those reports and statements which he had hitherto ignored, while Pascoe went home to a quiet nonconstabulary evening and found his wife much concerned with murder.

'She was practically telling me she thought he'd done it!' she said excitedly. 'Honestly, Peter, she came as close as damn it to saying, "You want the Choker? He's outside in the car with the kids!"'

'Wildgoose,' mused Pascoe. 'I knew I'd seen the name. Sergeant Brady did the interviews with the allotment holders. Just a formality to check if they'd noticed anyone hanging around in the past few days.'

'He's a teacher. English and Drama!' said Ellie triumphantly.

'So?'

'So, *Hamlet*!'

'Well, yes. But it *is* the most famous play in the language. Even Andy Dalziel had heard of it.'

'And he's gone odd.'

'Who? Dalziel?'

'No, you twit. Mark Wildgoose. Lorraine says she thinks he hates her. She's frightened of him.'

'She sounds a bit odd to me,' grunted Pascoe, looking at the *Radio Times*. 'Hey, *The Man Who Shot Liberty Valance* is on tonight. Didn't we go to see that in our distant student days?'

'Did we?' said Ellie. 'I sometimes forget we were once young together.'

'What are we now?'

'*You* are showing many of the symptoms of senility. Such as deafness. Mark Wildgoose I'm telling you about. He's going to Saudi Arabia in a mini-bus. He wears a T-shirt saying *I'm the Greatest*, and God knows when he last had a bath.'

'For Christ's sake, love,' said Pascoe. 'What's that you've got in your belly? Tory twins?'

'What's that mean?'

'Well, suddenly you're sounding like a large Conservative majority.'

'Ha ha. Well, how about this? Do you know which school Brenda Sorby went to?'

'The pterodactyl girl? Sorry! No, I don't.'

'The Bishop Crump Comprehensive!' said Ellie triumphantly. 'Which is where Wildgoose teaches.'

'And did he teach her?' enquired Pascoe.

'I don't know. I don't see why not.'

'There are upwards of two thousand kids at that school,' said Pascoe. 'These places are so big that some kids never even find out who the headmaster is.'

'Teacher,' said Ellie.

'What?'

'Head-teacher. Not headmaster.'

'All right. Head-teacher. I'm sorry. I'll go round to see Thelma in the morning and get her to drill all my teeth without anaesthetic as a penance.'

'Oh, don't be so bloody patronizing!' yelled Ellie.

The explosion took Pascoe by surprise. There was a moment of quietness.

'I'm sorry,' he said. 'I thought I was just being sarcastic.'

'And I thought I was just being helpful,' said Ellie.

'You are. And I'll look into it, I promise. It's just that I was trying not to track my work into the house too much, particularly this case.'

'A woman-killer? This is one case I want to see you solve,' said Ellie grimly.

'Yes. You and everyone. Hey, talking of help, I took your advice and got in touch with those linguists, Urquhart and Gladmann. They're coming in tomorrow.'

'Both of them? You'll enjoy that. They make a point of not agreeing with each other.'

'That is no barrier to true love,' said Pascoe sententiously. 'As we should prove.'

'Yes,' said Ellie. 'That's one way of looking at it.'

CHAPTER 10

One of Dalziel's maxims was that briefing sessions should be brief. Nevertheless, after the announcement of new developments and the disposition of forces, he allowed a general airing of ideas while he scratched whatever area of his large frame attracted his roving fingers that morning. End of scratch, end of talk.

The main news of Friday was that Tommy Maggs's Harlequin mini had been found with its big-end gone in the southbound car park of the Watford Gap service area on the M1.

Dalziel said, 'He probably hitched a lift in a lorry. He'll be in the Smoke by now. The locals are checking for sightings at Watford Gap. We'll need to check with Maggs's family for likely contacts in London. Relations, friends, the usual.'

Pascoe made a note. It was his task to make a note of everything. This was Dalziel's idea of not wasting his university education.

The briefing continued. Dalziel was sarcastic about the linguists.

'We've got four calls on tape. We don't know if any one of them is really the Choker, so it'll likely not help us much to know which street in Heckmondwike these four come from.' Pause for syco-phantic laughter. 'But we'd be daft not to use any expert help we can get. I've asked Dr Pottle of the Central Hospital Psychiatric Unit to give us an opinion too. He's been given all the details we have. Mr Pascoe, perhaps you'd see he gets copies of the tapes as well.'

Pascoe made another note, concealing his surprise. He had encountered Pottle on another case, a small, chain-smoking, rather irritable man with a ragged Einstein-type moustache. Dalziel reck-oned nothing to psychology and had the large man's distrust of little men. 'Has to be something missing,' he opined. So there must have been pressure here.

The PM on Pauline Stanhope had confirmed the time of death as between eleven-thirty a.m. and one-thirty p.m. The heat in the enclosed tent had complicated things a little. The cause of death was two-handed strangulation. Bruising to the stomach was probably caused by a violent blow aimed at pre-empting struggle or noise. There were no signs of sexual interference. And wherever else she was going when Mrs Ena Cooper, the penny-roll woman, glimpsed her leaving the tent before midday, it wasn't to lunch. Traces of a light breakfast were all that were found in her stomach.

Co-ordinating the collection of statements from stallholders and visitors to the Fair was Sergeant Bob Brady, a gum-chewing taciturn man who always looked more knowing than Pascoe suspected he ever was. But he had a reputation for being method-ical and had also co-ordinated the statements from the allotment holders after the McCarthy killing.

As far as the Stanhope murder went, Brady's method so far had produced only the following: that no one had noticed anything or anyone about the tent during the significant time, and that after Mrs Cooper's sighting, no one had seen Pauline Stanhope till she was found dead.

'Just like the Sorby girl,' said someone.

'She could have come back with someone. Or someone got into the tent while she was gone and was waiting for her on her return,' said Brady, lengthily for him.

'Meaning *he* got in without being seen, *she* came back without being seen, *he* got out without being seen,' said Dalziel.

'Why was she killed anyway?' wondered Wield.

'Why were any of them?'

'I know that, sir. But there's a connection here for the first time.'

'The girl's aunt, you mean?' said Dalziel. 'You checked they never met, though, didn't you?'

'Yes, sir. I contacted Mrs Sorby. She says that she always visited Rosetta Stanhope, never the other way round because of her husband. Not until that last session, that is, and then Mrs Stanhope insisted because of the atmosphere.'

'And Brenda never went with her mother.'

'No. Brenda wasn't interested in that kind of thing. Practical, down-to-earth, sporting type of girl. More like her father.'

When it was clear that no more was going to come from this particular discussion, Pascoe said, 'Sergeant Brady, could we go back a bit to the June McCarthy case? You interviewed an allotment holder called Wildgoose, Mark Wildgoose.'

'I remember.'

'Anything special about him.'

'It'll be in my report.'

'It's just like the others,' said Pascoe adding, in case that sounded critical, 'Just what you'd expect, of course. Though in fact it's even slighter than the others. He only went down to work on his allotment once or twice a week, if that. He didn't know June McCarthy and had never observed anyone suspicious around the place.'

'Same as most of the rest,' agreed Brady. 'A few carrots stolen, that's about all the excitement previous.'

'A couple did recall June McCarthy from when she was on the day shift,' said Pascoe. 'Including Dennis Ribble whose shed she was found in.'

'Aye. But Ribble and t'other fellow are in their eighties. Couldn't choke a dead pigeon between 'em,' said Brady to laughter.

'What's your interest in Wildgoose?' demanded Dalziel. 'You've heard summat?'

'That he is odd. Potentially violent. And he teaches English and Drama at Bishop Crump Comprehensive which is, incidentally, Brenda Sorby's old school.'

'Oh aye,' said Dalziel. 'Was any of that on your report, Sergeant Brady?'

Brady shook his head.

'None,' he said with the laconic assurance of one who is not at fault.

'What's your source, Peter?'

'Information,' said Pascoe uncomfortably. He didn't mind telling Dalziel privately but saw no reason to label Ellie as a snout before all this lot.

'Malicious?'

'Possibly. But also authoritative.'

'Aye. Sergeant Brady?'

'Sir?'

'Come on, lad. You're the only one here that's met the bugger. Don't be coy.'

Brady lit a cigarette from the one he was smoking. 'Lives on Wordsworth Drive on the Belle Vue estate about half a mile from Pump Road. Detached house, just.'

'Garden?' asked Dalziel.

'Grass, roses, flower-beds. No veg. It's not a vegetable estate.'

'And you interviewed him at the house?' said Pascoe.

'Yes.'

Dalziel looked at Pascoe interrogatively.

'I heard he was separated from his wife,' said Pascoe. Living apart.'

'Well, she was there that evening. Mind you, she did shuffle the kids out pretty sharpish when I said what I was.'

'And her personal reaction?'

Brady looked puzzled.

'Was she shocked, worried, indignant, inquisitive? What?' demanded Pascoe.

'Nothing much. She just showed me into a room where he was sitting with these two kids, said, "Police, for you. Come on children," and that was that. I didn't see her again.'

Pascoe and Dalziel exchanged glances.

'Probably just visiting,' said Pascoe. 'And Wildgoose himself?'

'Ordinary fellow. Just answered the questions. Nothing special.'

Dalziel said to Pascoe, 'Any ideas?'

'It might be as well to check when June McCarthy was last on the day shift and ask around if anyone ever saw Wildgoose talking to her as she passed the allotments.'

'Would he need to talk to her in advance?'

'He'd need to find out somehow that she'd be passing that way in the early morning.'

'Right. At the same time check him out on the times of the other killings.'

Pascoe made a note, saying, 'It'd better be fast. He's off to Saudi Arabia any moment.'

'Jesus!'

The briefing proceeded.

Wield reported on his visit to the Cheshire Cheese and diffidently wondered if there might be any significance in the closeness of the gypsy camp to three locations linked with the murders.

Dalziel said, 'One scene of killing, two work-places. Not much, is it?'

Wield muttered something about the widow's mite.

Dalziel said, 'Let's keep religion out of this. All right. Check on sinister gypsies lurking round the bank or the factory. Anyone else got any straws for us to grab hold of? No? Right, then here's what I think. There's things not being noticed on this case. I say *case*, not *cases*, because that's what it is, and that's what the trouble is. Too many of you are acting as if there's four individual investigations going on. Well, there's not, there's *one*, and when you're asking questions, taking statements, I want you to remember that. *Detectives*, that's what you're called. From what I've seen and heard, some of you couldn't detect piss in a urinal! So get your fingers out. Let's get back to the beginning. Everything new that happens changes everything that's past. So I want you all looking at what you've done already in that light. We're going to go over all the old ground again, but this time we'll shift around a bit, see what a new eye can do. I want all of you to know all of this case inside out. There's some people reckon getting into the CID means you're licensed to sit on your arse supping pints all hours that God sends. They'd better get disenchanted. Let's get some sodding work done!'

His right hand which had been scrabbling beneath his shirt like a ferret in a sack suddenly emerged into the light and slapped ferociously on the table top before him. The meeting broke up.

'Sergeant Wield!' called Dalziel.

'Sir.'

'You reckon Ludlam knows something?'

'That's what I think, sir. But whether it's about Tommy or whether it's about his brother-in-law, I don't know.'

'I've been talking with Mr Headingley,' said Dalziel. 'He's about as far on as we are. So if you think that Ludlam really is holding back, let's keep up the pressure. Call in at Pickersgill's house, stir things up a bit. You're interested in Tommy Maggs, right. But anything you can get on Frankie Pickersgill will be fine.'

'Poor sod,' said Wield.

'Why?'

'Well, I'm trying to get Ron to grass on Frankie again by threatening to tell Frankie that Ron grassed on him last time!'

This tickled Dalziel and he bellowed with laughter.

'There's no chance that the two of 'em could have been on the Spinks's warehouse job together?' he wondered when he had laughed his fill.

'I doubt it. Frankie puts up with Ron for Janey's sake. He really thinks he's a bit of a halfwit and Frankie doesn't suffer fools gladly.'

'No. That's what Mr Headingley reckons too. Well, see what you can do, but don't spend more time on it than necessary. The other thing, you didn't have much to do with Brenda Sorby's bank, did you?'

'I was around, but Mr Pascoe did most of the talking.'

'Right, Sergeant. I want you to go over all that stuff again. Get pictures of everyone concerned in the case, see if any of 'em mean anything to any of the girl's workmates. Peter, don't look so hurt. I meant what I said just now. New eyes. I want you to check through Mrs Dinwoodie's background again, all right? And *I* did that in the first place.'

'Sir,' said Wield.

'You still here, Sergeant? You want a rest perhaps? Come to think of it, you look a bit knackered. You ought to try getting to bed at a decent time.'

'I was just wondering, sir. How far do I go with this business of putting the pressure on Ron Ludlam?'

Dalziel looked surprised.

'Bluffs for con-men and card-sharps,' he said. 'My rule is, never threaten owt you won't perform.'

After Wield had left, he turned to Pascoe and said, 'What's the background on this Wildgoose stuff, Peter?'

Pascoe told him and he nodded sombrely.

'His wife, eh? Well, women can get pretty bitter when there's a break-up. They don't see straight.'

He sighed deeply. His own wife had left him many years ago and her reasons for doing so had long since fossilized in his mind in the form of hysterical female delusions.

'All the same, the bugger needs checking out. Better go and see him.'

'Wouldn't Brady be better? After hearing me mentioned yesterday, it's going to alert him, me turning up so soon.'

'If he's our man, the bugger'll be alert enough already,' said Dalziel. 'Which is more than I can say for Brady. No, you go, Peter. Don't worry about alerting him, as long as you bloody well terrify him into the bargain!'

'Is that such a good idea? Perhaps we should wait till Dr Pottle produces his profile first,' probed Pascoe.

'That quack! Christ, I'd as lief sit through one of Rosetta Stanhope's seances,' said Dalziel disgustedly. 'It's the sodding ACC's idea, wouldn't you know it? I think that twerp's one of Pottle's best patients.'

A phone rang on the table.

Dalziel picked it up and bellowed 'Yes?' as though he wanted to make it obsolete. He listened a moment.

'Talk of the devil,' he said. 'The sod's here.'

'Pottle?'

'Yes. And a pair of linguists. Peter, get them sorted, will you, or at least out of sight. We can't have the public coming into a respectable police station and finding it looking like a senior fucking common room!'

'Sir, where will you be?' called Pascoe as Dalziel headed for the door.

The fat man grinned, brown teeth bared like a moon-touched churchyard.

'Out of touch,' he said. 'I'll practise what I preach. There was a break-in at the Aero Club bar last night. Just a couple of bottles missing, but there's any number of suspects. That gang of gyppos just across the fence! Me, I don't know any of these buggers yet, but they seem intent on getting in on the act. This gives me a nice excuse to go visiting.'

CHAPTER 11

Sergeant Wield was no intellectual. The only books he owned were the complete works of H. Rider Haggard which he read and re-read avidly. But he knew a prick-teaser when he saw one.

Janey Pickersgill crossed and recrossed her long legs with maximum slither and maximum exposure. Her skirt had the fashionable side slit and Wield observed that stockings had made a comeback after a decade of tights. She noticed him noticing and stretched sensuously in her armchair, arching her back to obtrude her tiny bust.

Wield yawned. It wasn't altogether an affectation. There had been a lot of talk, not much sleep, the previous night. Maurice, his friend in Newcastle, had been ill at ease, not wholly welcoming. Their talk had not got to the heart of things but Wield suspected the worst.

As he did now.

'Janey, if you're trying to take my mind off my job, forget it,' he said pleasantly. 'I've seen better tits on a Turkish wrestler. Tell me again about that Thursday night.'

'You can't talk to me like that. I'll tell Frankie,' she threatened. But she arranged her skirt into more decorous folds and lit a cigarette, holding it and puffing it like a beginner. There was something of the tyro about everything she did. Still in her mid-twenties, she had not yet developed the patina of hardness, or worse, of dreary resignation which is worn by those whose contact with authority is invariably defensive or on visiting days. But it would come, thought Wield. Meanwhile, though there was no chance of his being seduced by her charms, he must be careful not to be charmed by her naïveté.

She had married Frankie Pickersgill knowing what he was and had lied constantly and vehemently while he was being investigated for the off-licence job.

'Didn't they tell you at the depot Frankie's driving a load across to Manchester? He won't be back till late this afternoon.'

'Yes, I know,' said Wield, settling comfortably in his chair. 'What I don't know is what you're trying to take my mind off with all this leg-waving, Janey. I mean, all I'm interested in is Tommy Maggs. Now the three of you were here the night it happened. Right?'

'The night what happened?' she said warily.

'Why, the night young Tommy Maggs's girl-friend got killed,' said Wield innocently. 'Did anything else happen that night?'

'Yes, all right, we were all here, watching the telly. We've told your lot already. What are you bothering us again for?'

'You see, Janey, Tommy's disappeared,' said Wield earnestly. 'We're worried about him. He's naturally very upset. A young lad like that, wandering around in a distressed state, anything could happen. You can see that, can't you?'

'I can't see what it's got to do with me,' complained the woman, nervously pecking at her cigarette.

'No? Well, it's Ron, really. You know what these youngsters are like. False sense of loyalty, not really knowing their friends' best interests, that sort of thing. There's a chance he may know more than he's letting on. I wondered if you could help.'

'No. I don't know anything. He's said nothing to me.'

'Are you sure? Throw your mind right back. Back to that night when the three of you were sitting here watching telly together.'

'Well, he wouldn't be likely to say much then, would he, as nothing had happened yet,' said Janey with the pride of one stumbling on an oasis of logic in a wasteland of feminine intuition.

'Of course, he wouldn't. You're right,' said Wield. 'Unless he said something about Tommy's state of mind when he left him in the Bay Tree.'

The woman looked at him in alarm.

'You don't think Tommy's got anything to do with killing that lass, do you? It was the Choker, everyone knows that.'

'But who's the Choker, Janey? Who knows that? You've met Tommy?'

'Couple of times. Ron brought him round to the house.'

'Nice lad.'

'He seemed very nice. Very decent,' she said emphatically. A scrap of tobacco had got stuck to her tongue. She picked at it with a scarlet fingernail. The effect was much sexier now that she wasn't trying.

'And Brenda, did you meet her?'

'Just the once. She was in the car when Tommy called, so I made him bring her in. Nice girl too. Well spoken.'

'Bit posh for Tommy, you thought?'

'No. Just well spoken.'

'Frankie, did he meet her?'

'Yes. He said hello.'

'And what did he think of her?'

Now alarms were ringing in her mind.

'What's that mean? He didn't think anything of her. Just for a minute they spoke. What the hell are you driving at?'

Wield looked at her with a blankness not altogether affected. He had stumbled on this line of questioning by chance just as he was about ready to give up and go. There was no way that Frankie was going to let hints about his brief acquaintance with Brenda Sorby scare him into admitting the Spinks's warehouse job. But Janey might let something slip out of sheer indignation.

'We're interested in anyone who knew Brenda,' he said, suddenly very stiff, very official. 'There's a strong possibility that she was picked up by a car after she left Tommy that night. And for her to get willingly into a car at that time of night, she would almost certainly need to know the driver.'

She was on her feet leaning over him, so close and so angry that he felt little specks of spittle hit his face as she spoke.

'Are you pigs so hard up you want to pin this one on any poor sod who's handy? Well, you've come to the wrong shop if it's my Frankie you're after. He was here with me all that night, and I mean all that night, from when he got home till next morning when he went to work. And nothing's going to make me say different, not even if they send a whole battalion looking like you do!'

'What time did you go to bed?' asked Wield calmly.

'What?'

'Bed. You did go to bed? What time.'

'I don't know. Half eleven, midnight.'

She was confused as people often are by a lack of reaction to an emotional outburst.

'What about Ron?'

'*What* about Ron?'

'Did he go first? Or was he still up when you and Frankie went to bed?'

'I don't know. First I think.'

'So there was a period when you and Frankie were downstairs by yourselves between eleven and midnight.'

'I don't know! What's it matter? Mebbe we went first.'

'Leaving Ron by himself?'

'No! I mean, most likely we all went up together.'

'I didn't know you were that close a family,' said Wield.

She slapped at his face, a full round-arm blow. Wield parried unhurriedly, the chopping edge of his left hand held palm forward at head height like a gesture of peace.

'Jesus!' she swore as she nursed her wrist.

'Pick someone your own size,' said Wield.

He rose, put his hands on her shoulders and pushed her down on to the chair he had just vacated.

There was something here, he was sure. But it was probably something for Chief Inspector Headingley, and he had already spent too much Choker time on it.

Casting bread on waters was a good exit ploy for a policeman. Leave them worrying. It was often very effective. It was also often very unpleasant but, as any Rider Haggard fan knew, duty must be done.

'Janey,' he said sternly. 'If your Frankie's relying on Ron for an alibi, he shouldn't sleep too well at nights.'

'What the hell do you mean?' she said sullenly, still rubbing her wrist.

'Come on, Janey! Don't be naïve. You must know your brother well enough by now. When Frankie got done for the whisky, did you never wonder how we got on to him?'

She was with him so quickly he knew he must have touched some deep hidden suspicion.

'You're lying,' she said. 'Prove it.'

'Oh Janey,' he said sadly. 'That's the one thing people like you and people like me have in common. We know when each other's lying or telling the truth. It's only juries that need proof.'

He made for the door. There was nothing else for him here just now. Later, perhaps...

Wield knew he'd taken a risk. It was one thing to threaten Ludlam, quite another to blow the gaff to Janey. But Wield had his intuitions too. It crossed his mind that the last time he had followed one was when he sat in on the seance with a cassette recorder in his pocket.

He shuddered at the memory and drove to Brenda Sorby's bank.

❈ ❈ ❈

Millhill was a typically 'mixed' suburb, middle-class, owner-occupied on the side nearest the river moderating to council house and commercial towards the neighbouring industrial estate. The Northern Bank was in a smallish shopping precinct at about the midway point. The previous weekend after the discovery of Brenda Sorby's body, Pascoe had interviewed the bank staff while Wield had checked round the shops. Only the hairdressing salon a quarter of a mile along the road had provided any witness. Brenda had kept her appointment, been bright and chatty and left just after six-fifteen. Indeed, as they knew that she had met Tommy in the Bay Tree at eight, anything the bank staff or shopkeepers could tell them hardly seemed likely to be significant, but Dalziel wanted the ground turned over again, and Dalziel was Ayesha.

Wield checked his notebook. A couple of the smaller shops had been closed for the annual holidays. It was surprising how many people still stuck to the old tradition of taking their vacation during the High Fair.

The first one he tried, *M. Conrad, Jeweller and Watch-Repairer*, was locked. The second, *Durdons Confectioners*, was open. Mr and Mrs Durdon had just got back from a week in Spain that very morning, and were clearly bent on recouping their expenses as rapidly as possible.

Yes, they had read about the killing, they always bought the English papers on holiday. Yes, they had been here that Thursday, they didn't go till early Friday morning. Yes, they remembered the lass vaguely.

But no, they didn't recall seeing her that day, and no, there was nothing they could tell Wield though he got a distinct impression they had lorded it at their Costa Brava hotel on the strength of their intimate connection with the case.

In the bank he was greeted with less enthusiasm. Mulgan, the acting manager, had (according to Pascoe's notes) been genuinely distressed at Brenda's death, but also perhaps a little too concerned that somehow it would reflect on him.

Now, a week later, this personal concern seemed to dominate. About five nine, with brown hair, thick, luxuriant and anointed, he was a good-looking man in a fleshy kind of way. His full cheeks were razored to a roseate glow and gave off strong emanations of one of the more macho aftershaves. Wield's memory was stirred. Maurice had given him a bottle last Christmas, but he had never used it.

He took Wield into his office, an act, so the sergeant felt, more of concealment than courtesy.

'This is very nice, sir,' said Wield, looking appreciatively round the well-proportioned office. 'It's a pretty large establishment. I mean, for a suburban bank.'

'Yes. It was built as the Avro Industrial Estate developed,' said Mulgan. 'Head Office anticipated a lot of business.'

'But didn't get it?'

'Pardon?'

'I meant, you sounded as if things didn't quite work out.'

'Oh no,' said Mulgan with loyal indignation. 'It's very flourishing. Very flourishing.'

Then, relaxing a little, he said, 'Mind you, they're a very conservative lot, your Yorkshire businessmen. You'd be surprised how many of them insist on maintaining their accounts at the main office in the town centre. Not that they couldn't have been persuaded with a little more dynamism perhaps. Well, perhaps it's not too late.'

Wield glanced at his notebook. Mulgan was the acting manager, he saw. They were clearly touching the world of his ambitious dreams.

'So you don't carry many local business accounts?' he said, probing a little further, though for no particular reason.

'Oh yes,' said Mulgan, bridling again. 'Nearly all the local shops.'

'But from the estate?'

'One or two.'

Suddenly seeing a glimmer of a connection, Wield asked, 'Would those include the Eden Park Canning Plant?'

But he was disappointed.

Mulgan shook his head and fiddled impatiently with the blotter on his desk.

'How can I help you, Sergeant?' he asked.

'We're just going over the ground again, sir,' said Wield. 'Routine. Often things come to mind after a few days that get forgotten when everyone's shocked and upset to start with.'

There was a knock at the door and a young girl's head appeared.

'I'm sorry to interrupt,' she said. 'But Mrs Mulgan's here and would like a word.'

'What?' said Mulgan irritably. 'Oh very well, I'll come out. Excuse me.'

'No,' said Wield, getting up. 'You see your wife in here, it's all right. I'll just have a quick chat with any of your staff that aren't too busy.'

Outside the door he saw the girl talking to a thin-faced, rather defeated-looking woman who appeared a good ten years older than Mulgan.

'Thank you, dear,' she said in a fairly broad rural Derbyshire accent. 'You take care of yourself, won't you? I'll go in now, shall I?'

'Excuse me, Miss,' said Wield to the girl before she could move away. He introduced himself and discovered she was Mary Brighouse. She was not bad-looking with a good figure and big brown eyes which moistened as he began to talk about Brenda.

'You were good friends,' said Wield sympathetically.

'We didn't see much of each other outside,' said Mary. 'But I liked her a lot. I was so upset when we heard what had happened, I had to go home. I didn't come back in till Wednesday.'

Wield glanced at his notes from Pascoe's report. The girl had been no help at all and had broken down very early on during questioning. From the look of it, he doubted if he was going to get any further this time. He took her arm and gently led her as far to the back of the bank as they could go.

'That was Mrs Mulgan, was it?' he said lightly. 'Bit of a surprise after meeting your boss.'

'She's very nice,' said the girl defensively.

'Yes, I'm sure she is,' said Wield. 'I only meant...'

'Yes. I know,' she helped him out. 'They were born in the same village.'

'But he's moved on while in a manner of speaking she hasn't, you mean?' said Wield. 'It's always sad, that.'

He was very good at gossip. A right old woman, Dalziel had called him once. Wield had smiled bleakly.

'Yes, and it's not just the job either,' Mary replied, eyes clear again, voice confidentially lowered.

'It never stops there,' agreed Wield without much idea what he was agreeing to.

'No. There're some men think a bit of power gives them all sorts of rights. And he's only acting, after all.'

'I know,' said Wield, suddenly with her. 'It can be very embarrassing, that kind of thing. I mean, what's a bit of a giggle at the office party can cause a lot of unpleasantness when it's out of place. Has it bothered you a lot?'

'Not really,' she said. 'Well, it wasn't really me, just some-times he'd say something. It was more...'

Her eyes filled again.

The door of Mulgan's office opened and Wield had no time for sympathy now.

'You mean, it was more Brenda?'

'Oh yes,' she said with fast-fading coherence. 'I think he asked her out a couple of times and he was always calling her into the office or standing behind her, really close, like. She said that now she had an engagement ring, perhaps it would...' The memory was too much for her.

'Sergeant Wield!' called Mulgan.

'Blow your nose, love,' said Wield. 'Then go and wash your face. You're a good girl.'

He patted her on the arm and returned to the manager's office where he studied his digest of Pascoe's interview notes once more. He felt disappointed. The Inspector hadn't got on to Mulgan's lech for Brenda, but his customary thoroughness had led him to check the acting manager's whereabouts between ten and midnight that night. He had been at home. Confirmed by his wife. Wield frowned.

'I hope you haven't been upsetting Miss Brighouse again,' said Mulgan. 'We've had to do without her for half the week already.'

'She seems a very sensitive sort of girl,' said Wield.

'Yes. Now what else can I do for you, Sergeant? We are extremely busy.'

'I'm sorry. I should have called outside banking hours,' said Wield.

'We do work then also,' said Mulgan acidly.

'I'm sure you do.'

Wield closed his notebook with a snap.

'I'll tell you what you can do for us, sir,' he said. 'Is it possible to check back and see what business Brenda dealt with that day, when she was at the counter, I mean?'

'It's possible. But why on earth should you want that?' wondered Mulgan.

Wield looked mysterious. It wasn't difficult. It was a mystery to him. But he wanted a bit of time to think things over.

Mulgan gave him more.

'I'd need to get authority from Head Office,' he said. 'It would mean revealing banking information, you see.'

'That's all right, sir. No rush. I'll call back later, if I may. Or if I don't get back in working hours, stick it in your brief-case and someone can pick it up from your home.'

He rose and took his leave before the man could raise an objection.

Outside in the car he tried to consider possible burgeonings of the seeds he had sown that morning, but all he could think of was the bittersweet tang of Mulgan's aftershave.

CHAPTER 12

Dr Pottle and the two linguists sat and listened to the tapes of the four telephone messages which had followed Pauline Stanhope's murder.

Pascoe had provided them with a typed transcript with the *Hamlet* references for good measure.

(A) *Now get you to my lady's chamber,*
    and tell her, let her paint an inch thick,
    to this favour she must come.
    (Act 5, Scene 1)

(B) *One may smile, and smile, and be a villain.*
    (Act 1, Scene 3)

(C) *To be, or not to be, that is the question.*
    (Act 3, Scene 1)

(D) *The time is out of joint:—O cursed spite,*
    That ever I was born to set it right.
    (Act 1, Scene 3)

This was the order in which they had been received. Sammy Locke, the *Evening Post* news editor, felt that (A) and (D) came nearest to his memory of the voice which he had heard on the first two occasions. But which of the two (if there *were* two, they sounded very alike to Pascoe) it was, he couldn't say. Pascoe had not felt it necessary to pass this information on to the linguistic experts.

After the tape had been played for the fifth time, there was a long silence. Pottle lit another cigarette and scribbled some notes. Pascoe looked interrogatively at the linguists who were looking interrogatively at each other.

They were an ill-assorted pair. Dicky Gladmann was a small dapper man, fortyish, with bright blue eyes and demi-mutton-chop whiskers, dressed in an old tweed jacket with a red bandanna trailing from his breast pocket and a spoor of gravy running down his old something-or-other tie. The other, Drew Urquhart, was much younger. A small, round, rosy-cheeked face showed fitfully through a dark tangle of beard like a robin in a holly bush. Dressed in jeans and a T-shirt, he seemed to have little liking for his surroundings.

'Well, we'll see what we can do, shall we?' said Gladmann in a self-parodyingly fruity upper-class voice.

'I suppose so,' said Urquhart, broad Scots, not Glasgow but somewhere close.

They rose. Gladmann took the cassette from the player and slipped it into his pocket.

'Aren't you going to work here?' said Pascoe, taken aback.

'My dear chap, you must be joking!' said Gladmann. 'Not that it isn't nice. You can hardly see the blood on the walls, can you, Drew, my son? But your equipment's hardly space-age, is it? No, the language lab at the college is the place. And if it seems worthwhile we can even drive across to the university and run it through their sonograph.'

'Well, all right,' said Pascoe. There were, after all, several copies of the tape.

Urquhart said, 'Inspector, I'd like to be sure what you intend. How do you propose to use whatever we tell you?'

'Sceptically, I dare say,' replied Pascoe.

Gladmann hooted, but Urquhart did not smile behind his tangle.

'So long as it's clear I'm not interested in helping the polis find a scapegoat,' he continued.

Pascoe sighed. His own background made him a lot more sympathetic with academic liberalism than most of his colleagues, but he could understand the feeling behind Dalziel's complaint on another occasion, 'If these are the clever buggers, no wonder crime pays!'

'Believe me,' he said, 'a scapegoat's no good. The man we're after is an unbalanced killer. He's not going to stop murdering women just because someone else has been arrested.'

Urquhart did not look wholly convinced but he left without further comment. Gladmann followed, saying, 'My love to the delectable Ellie. We'll be in touch.'

Pascoe closed the door after them and turned his interrogative gaze on Pottle not with a great deal of hope.

The psychiatrist's opening comment confirmed his pessimism.

'Not a great deal to go on yet,' he said.

'Four murders!' expostulated Pascoe. 'Not a bad start, surely?'

'Come now,' said Pottle, amused. 'What's your best chance of catching this fellow?'

Pascoe considered.

'Another murder,' he admitted unwillingly. 'Or at least an attempt. Get him in the act.'

'Quite so. Similarly, though in rather a different way, the more I have, the better results I can hope for. Now, to start with, I am making two assumptions which may turn out to be false. One is that these four deaths have been caused by the same man. The other is that basically in each case the motive has been the same, or at the least an aspect of a single consistent motive. As I say, these assumptions may be false. Indeed, there is much in the evidence as you have laid it before me which suggests that they are false.'

'Such as?' interposed Pascoe.

'The eccentricities of pattern,' replied Pottle. 'They are all young unmarried women—except for Mrs Dinwoodie who is a middle-aged widow. They are found neatly laid out with arms crossed on the chest—except Brenda Sorby who has been dumped in the canal. The murders all take place in circumstances made remote by time of day or location, except for Pauline Stanhope's which occurs in the middle of the day in the middle of a fair-ground. But it's only by making these two assumptions that I can even begin to pretend I have something to work at. That's where another murder would come in so useful. Better still, two. Then we would begin to have enough trees to make a wood!'

Only the suspicion that this ghoulishness was being used to provoke him in some way kept Pascoe from voicing another protest.

'You'll be the second or third person to know, Doctor,' he said. 'Carry on.'

'Right you are. I summarize, of course. What it would seem to me we have here is an older rather than a younger man, that is, heading away from thirty five rather than towards it. He is of course unbalanced, but not in the usual pattern of the psycho-pathic woman-killer, whose murderous impulses tend, as it happens, to become more controllable as he gets older. You must catch your psychopath young, Inspector, if you are to catch him at all. No, this man's motivation does not seem to be based so much on hate as on, I can find no better term, compassion.'

'Compassion? You mean, he kills women because he's sorry for them?' asked Pascoe with interest.

'In a way, yes. There's good case-law here. The impulse to euthanasia is a strong one in all advanced civilizations.'

'But you can't be saying these murders are just a form of euthanasia?'

'Only in the same way that you could say Jack the Ripper's killings were a form of moral protest. In a way, it's strange that there aren't more Choker-type killings than Ripper-type. Euthanasia is, after all, half accepted and by definition involves killing, while punishment for sexual immorality eventually disappears from advanced societies and only ever involved death in primitive ones.'

'The Church used to roast you for buggery,' objected Pascoe.

'Precisely,' said Pottle drily. 'Look, I must go, Inspector. I have work to do. You'll have a written report eventually!'

'Hang on just a minute. The phone messages, the tapes. What about them?'

'Of the taped messages, either (A) or (D) would fit my man, with my money being on the former. The voice seems to me to have that genuinely regretful intonation which fits my ideas. (B) and (C) sound far too delighted with it all. But it's the first of the messages received that really needs looking at.'

'You mean *I say, we will have no more marriages?*'

'That's it. You know how it goes on? *Those that are married already, all but one, shall live; the rest shall keep as they are.*'

'Yes, I know. So far we've had one widow, three spinsters. We're still waiting for Mrs Right to come along.'

Pascoe had a nice line in ghoulishness himself.

'Perhaps that's the way to look at it, Inspector. Odd thing, marriage and engagements. Often kept very secret. I assume you've checked very carefully indeed to see if Pauline Stanhope was engaged? The other two girls were, and very recently too.'

'You think that...'

'No, I offer no conclusions, Inspector. But a woman widowed can still be regarded from a certain point of view as a married woman. After all, she retains the title. I should be very interested, if I were you, to know why poor Mrs Dinwoodie should of all the married ladies in the world be the one singled out (if you'll excuse the expression) to be killed. Now I must go.'

After he had left, Pascoe sat for a while and wondered whether it were really possible for a man to go around killing people out of compassion. One, yes. That he could understand. Someone near and dear who was suffering greatly. But strangers? And compassion for what? He should have asked that.

But he couldn't sit here all day, thinking. It was leg work that solved cases, not metaphysical speculation.

❀ ❀ ❀

He headed first for the suburban estate where the Wildgoose family lived. He knew Mark Wildgoose would probably not be there but he had no other address for the man and, though he might have been able to track him down via the school authorities, this gave him an excuse to talk to the woman.

Lorraine Wildgoose was in the front garden passing a small electric rotary mower over the lawn. She switched it off at his approach and nodded when he introduced himself.

'Yes, I know,' she said.

'Oh? We haven't met, have we?'

'No. I saw your photo when I called on Ellie yesterday. Come into the house.'

He followed her. She wore a thin cotton skirt and a brief halter whose shifts as she stooped to disconnect the mower lead gave no hint of a limit to her deep sun tan. The observation was quite objective. Pascoe felt no sensual tingle at these mammary glimpses. There was an intensity of expression on her thin, slightly pock-marked face which precluded any suspicion of prick-teasing and suggested that any man showing an interest in her had better lead with his head, in a manner of speaking.

'Mrs Wildgoose, I'd like to have a word with your husband. I understand he's not living with you any more.'

'Would you like a drink?' she said. 'Coffee or something harder? A couple of years ago, you wouldn't have got either. We were into organic eating in a big way. That's when he got interested in the allotment. That's what you'll want to talk to him about.'

'You do your own gardening now?' said Pascoe whose response to obliquities was always oblique. 'It's quite a job.'

He was looking out of a french window which opened on to the back garden. A small patio led on to a rectangle of lawn some fifty feet deep bordered by roses and ornamental shrubs.

'I always did. He showed no interest till he decided he wanted to dig it up to plant beans and ginseng. That's when I put my foot down, so he got the allotment. I feel responsible for that girl's death.'

This was too fast for Pascoe.

'That drink,' he said. 'It's early but I'm quite thirsty. Perhaps a small beer.'

She went out into the kitchen and returned with a pint can and two tumblers.

'I drink anything now,' she said. 'If it poisons the system, then I suppose my system's done for.'

Pascoe took the can from her thin nervous fingers, opened it, poured the beer and chose his words carefully.

'Mrs Wildgoose, from what you said to Ellie yesterday and what you've just said to me, would I be right in saying you think your husband may know something about these so-called Choker killings?'

'Yes,' she said in a low voice, followed almost immediately by a *No!* in a semi-scream that startled Pascoe into spilling some drops of beer.

'How could I say that?' she demanded. 'I don't know. He just seems so odd, so fearful. In every sense. So frightening and so full of fear. Do you follow me?'

'I think so,' said Pascoe, more in response to her compellingly intense gaze than the dictates of reason. He could recall a junior schoolteacher whose urgent questioning had similarly seemed to preclude a negative response. He could also remember her wrath when, inevitably, he had had to admit his real ignorance.

It was time to take the initiative.

The door burst open before he could speak and a girl of about thirteen rushed in, closely followed by a slightly younger boy. They stopped dead as they saw Pascoe.

'Oops, sorry,' said the girl.

'This is my daughter, Sue. My son, Alan. This is Inspector Pascoe, dears. We won't be long. If you're finding time's hanging a bit heavy, you might like to finish off the front lawn for me.'

The girl made an unenthusiastic face and withdrew. Neither she nor her brother looked much like their mother in their features, though they shared her dark colouring. At least they were obedient, thought Pascoe when almost instantly the whine of the electric mower was heard. A desirable quality in children, one which he and Ellie would look for in their own family. He hoped.

'Mrs Wildgoose, your husband's mental state may be relevant, but it's not primary, not yet. Think carefully. Is there anything at all, anything *concrete*, which links your husband to June McCarthy—or any of the other girls for that matter?'

Her eyes opened even wider in amazement at his denseness. Doesn't she ever blink? wondered Pascoe.

'The allotment,' she said.

'We know about the allotment,' said Pascoe patiently. 'Did he ever mention June McCarthy? Or any girl he'd met or seen when he was in Pump Street?'

'Why should he?' she demanded. 'He'd want to keep something like that pretty quiet, wouldn't he?'

'Like an affair, you mean?' said Pascoe doubtfully. 'You're suggesting he could have been having an affair with this girl?'

'It wouldn't have been the first,' she retorted bitterly. 'He's got a little greenhouse down there. Very handy.'

'A greenhouse is not the most discreet of places to have an affair in,' observed Pascoe pedantically.

'The wall panes are whitewashed,' she said triumphantly. 'So you can't see in. And the children went down there once and he wouldn't let them in.'

Pascoe had a quick mental vision of Wildgoose fornicating among the tomato plants. Green thoughts in a green house.

'And that's all?' he said.

'What else do you want? Photographs?' she flashed.

'Did he ever drink in the Cheshire Cheese, do you know?' asked Pascoe.

'We have done,' she said. 'Of course that was before we went off alcohol.'

'Was your husband back on alcohol before you broke up?'

'Yes, he was,' she said. 'I remember he came home one evening and I smelt it on his breath. It was round about then that I felt things were beginning to go desperately wrong.'

'In what way?'

'This hate I told you about. This resentment. It seemed to flare up then.'

'*Then* being?'

'Earlier in the summer. I don't know. End of May, I think.'

Pascoe took out a diary and thumbed through it. 'And you actually left him when?'

'June 14th,' she said promptly. 'I remember that. It was Alan's birthday. Mark was late. I complained. There was a great row. Mark flew out of the house. He didn't come back till after midnight, in a worse mood than when he'd left and stinking of drink. I slept in the spare room that night with the bed pushed against the door. First thing next morning I got out with the children and went round to Thelma Lacewing's flat. You'll know her, I expect.'

'Oh yes.'

'She's marvellous, isn't she?'

'Uh-huh. And your husband...?'

'Still sleeping, of course. The drink did that for me at least. That at least. Yes, the fourteenth. Just a month. Christ.'

Pascoe regarded her keenly and waited.

For a woman so eager to suggest her husband might be the Choker she was missing a golden opportunity.

Or perhaps she was clever enough to know that some things don't need underlining. Perhaps she felt she could rely on even the most bumbling of bobbies to recall that it was on the night of June 14th that Mary Dinwoodie had been choked to death behind the Cheshire Cheese.

He asked one last question as he rose with Mark Wildgoose's new address in his notebook.

'Despite your suspicions of your husband you still see him. Why's that?'

'He's entitled to access to the children. In any case, I certainly don't want him to think I suspect,' she said defiantly.

It didn't ring true.

'How was your trip yesterday?' he enquired idly as she escorted him to the open front door.

The girl was in the garden propelling the electric mower. She seemed to have made very little progress, observed Pascoe.

'Fine,' said Lorraine Wildgoose. 'It was OK. The children enjoyed it. Oh, excuse me.'

Behind her a telephone was ringing. She retreated, closing the door firmly.

Pascoe walked down the path. The girl was standing still watching him. The mower blades had a different note when it wasn't in motion.

Pascoe paused and smiled at the girl.

'Your mother's upset,' he said. 'Don't take notice of everything she says. It's a bad time for her.'

The girl didn't return his smile but she made no effort to deny her eavesdropping.

'Are you going to arrest Daddy?' she said.

'No. Why should I? But I'm going to talk with him.'

'It's not always his fault,' she said. 'She spoilt it yesterday.'

'Yesterday?'

'Yes. She went into some woman's house first of all and didn't come out for ages. We were roasting in the car. Then when we got to the seaside she nagged all the time. Daddy wanted us all to have tea together later and not come home till the evening, but she started to row with him and we were back home by tea-time.'

'So it wasn't a very good day for you?' said Pascoe thoughtfully.

'It could have been,' she retorted.

Pascoe dug into his pocket and came up with a 50p piece. In the distance he could hear the carillon of an ice-cream van.

'It's a funny old world,' he said. 'But the grass keeps on growing. Why don't you find your brother and share a cornet or whatever else you can buy with this nowadays?'

The silver coin spun through the air. She caught it two-handed, smiled with great charm, said 'Thank you!' and ran off out of the garden gate.

Pascoe watched her go and suddenly felt sick that he might be close to solving this case.

CHAPTER 13

Though Dalziel rarely showed he was impressed by anything his subordinates suggested, nothing went unnoticed. Pascoe he was always very attentive to. Wield also. He hadn't yet quite fathomed the sergeant, but he seemed to have his feet planted on the ground, the seance aside, that was.

So he drove slowly round the locations and wondered whether indeed there might be a significance in the relative closeness of Brenda Sorby's and June McCarthy's places of work.

Wield's car was parked outside the bank (Dalziel had spent an hour at his desk before setting off on his travels) so the superintendent did not pause. But he sat outside the entrance to the Eden Park Cannery for long enough to attract the gateman's attention.

'Can I help you?' enquired the man in a belligerent tone.

'What do you think I'm doing, casing the joint?' said Dalziel. He held out his warrant card. The gateman was not particularly impressed but when Dalziel heaved his bulk out of the car, he became a little more respectful.

'You knew June McCarthy?' enquired Dalziel.

'Sure,' said the man. He was rising sixty, grey-haired, with a cynical mouth and a knowing eye.

'How well?'

'Not well enough to choke her,' said the man.

'How well's that?'

'With some women, just one look at 'em's well enough,' laughed the man. 'But she seemed a nice enough lass.'

'Liked the boys, did she?'

'Not really. She went steady with that soldier lad. He was a big burly chap, knew how to handle himself. So I reckon the others kept clear even when he was away.'

Dalziel knew all this from the records.

'Are you going inside?' asked the gateman.

The fat man stood there undecided. A blue Mercedes drew up alongside the kerb and the electrically operated window slid silently down.

'Andy!'

Dalziel went across to the car.

'Hello,' he said.

It was Bernard Middlefield JP, not a man he cared for all that much, but a friend to the police who needed all the friends they could get these hard days.

'Thought it was you,' said Middlefield.

'Well, you wouldn't think it was Fred Astaire,' said the fat man.

'What brings you round these parts? That poor girl, is it?'

'Sort of. What about you Bernard?'

'Me? That's my works next door,' said Middlefield in a pained voice.

'So it is,' said Dalziel, looking towards the long single-storied brick and glass building. 'You didn't know her, by any chance, did you, Bernard?'

'The dead lass? No. But I see enough of them. What a

sample you get in this place! It's like the flight out of Gomorrah when the hooter goes.'

'Oh aye. Aren't yours the same?'

'No. I employ skilled labour! Electrical assembly's a lot different from canning peas. Why don't you come in, have a cuppa and a look round?'

'Too busy, Bernard, thanks all the same. How's Jack? Business OK?'

'Fine, both fine. Will I see you at the Mansion House tomorrow?'

The High Fair holiday fortnight traditionally ended with a civic luncheon on the last Saturday, a custom some ratepayers thought might be more honoured in the breach.

Dalziel shook his head.

'Pity. It's usually a good do. By the way, I hope your lot are going to clamp down on those tinkers a bit more promptly this year.'

'Tinkers?'

'The gypsies. It's always the same. Give some people an inch. Because they've been coming for centuries, we put up with them for a couple of weeks while the Fair's on. But is that enough? Oh no. It was nigh on September when they got shifted last year, and then half of them were back before Christmas. There's no shortage of wet wonders in this town, either, that'd like them to be let stay here permanent. What I say is, they call themselves travellers, well, let them travel. You got the message?'

'Did I? What was that?' asked Dalziel.

'The other day. One of their ponies got loose by the Aero Club, nearly killed me as I was taking off. It's not the first time either. I told one of your men to let you know. A funny-looking bugger. Wouldn't have been out of place in a caravan himself!'

'Aye. I think I did hear something,' said Dalziel.

He glanced at his watch. He was going round to the encampment anyway, but Middlefield didn't know that. There was no harm in making a virtue out of it. There'd come a time when he might want to trade off favours with Middlefield.

'I've got a moment now,' he said. 'I'll look into it myself.'

'Will you? Good man. I knew I could rely on you, Andy. I often say, if men like you and me had the running of this country, we'd soon set it right!'

The Mercedes purred away.

Dalziel raised a hand and smiled after it. Running this country from a kraut car! It took a lot to make him feel liberal, but Middlefield could manage it.

'Get fucked,' said Dalziel.

'Pardon?' said the gateman at his shoulder.

'Not you,' grunted the fat man, climbing into his car.

'Though on second thoughts,' he added as he closed the door, 'why not?'

❀ ❀ ❀

The Aero Club seemed deserted but as Dalziel was peering through the club house window a voice behind him asked him civilly what he wanted.

Dalziel didn't like to be crept up on and was ready to reply most uncivilly till he turned and saw the man was wearing a tracksuit and gymshoes which explained the quietness of his approach.

'Police,' he said, showing his warrant card.

'About the break-in? I'm Greenall, CFI.'

'Eh?'

'Chief Flying Instructor. To tell the truth,' added the man, smiling slightly, 'the only Flying Instructor. I've got an assistant, Roger Minstrel. But he's away on a course. So I do everything. Including tending bar when our girl doesn't turn up or she's rushed. Will you have something for the heat?'

He had opened the club house and led Dalziel into the bar

as he spoke. The fat man's estimate, lowered by the track suit for he despised joggers, rose sharply.

'Nice place,' he said, looking round after he'd reduced the level of his malt by an inch.

'You haven't been here before?'

'There's few places that serve drink round here that I've not been to,' said Dalziel. 'But it's many a year since I was in here. It's been tarted up since then.'

'I dare say. It's the social side that makes money in clubs,' said Greenall. 'Any club. You need to be packed at night to be viable.'

'That doesn't sound as if it makes you happy.'

'I'm a flier,' said Greenall. 'I came out of the RAF and wanted to stay in the flying business. Running discos for teen-agers isn't my idea of the flying business.'

'I thought all you lot ended up flying Jumbos, earning millions, and putting the smile on those air-hostesses you see in the ads.'

'I failed my last air-crew medical, that's why I came out,' said Greenall, sipping the grapefruit juice he'd poured for himself. 'They're just as strict at the commercial end. Light planes and gliders is all I'm good for.'

'You look fit enough to me,' said Dalziel, glancing from the fruit juice to the track suit.

'I live in hopes. A bit of jogging, bit of squash. With a bit of luck, I might get back to the real stuff one of these days.'

'You don't like gliders, then?'

'Oh, the gliders are all right. That's something quite different. But the small planes are like getting into a rubber dinghy after you've been captaining a battleship.'

'Still, at least they must go slow enough so that you can see things as you pass.'

'They do that,' agreed Greenall. 'Useful for some kinds of police work, I dare say. Though choppers are better. Still, if you ever fancy a trip, just say the word.'

Dalziel smiled at the unlikelihood of this and finished his drink.

'Let's have a look at the damage?' he said.

Entry to the store-room had been through a forced window, not much more than eighteen inches square.

'Kids, your constable reckoned. They only took a few bottles, about as much as a couple of youngsters could carry. He went along to the gypsy encampment and had a look round, but naturally he didn't get anywhere.'

'Naturally?'

'Well, they're fairly expert in hiding things, I should imagine.'

'You've had some other bother with them, I gather. Or with their livestock.'

Greenall grinned and ran his fingers through his blond hair, looking younger than his forty years.

'You heard about Mr Middlefield? He was very upset. Not that he wasn't right. It could have been very dangerous. It's happened a couple of times, horse straying I mean. But this was the first time there'd nearly been an accident.'

They went outside together and looked towards the distant encampment.

'I'll have a word with them myself,' said Dalziel. 'Can I get through that fence without rupturing myself?'

'There isn't a gate, if that's what you mean. But kids and ponies don't seem to have any difficulty.'

Dalziel looked down at his ample girth.

'It's not the eye of a needle, is it?' he said.

'No. And it's not much like the kingdom of heaven over there either,' said Greenall.

But the scene as the two men strolled together across the grass had something idyllic about it. There were a couple of tradi-tional wooden caravans, brightly coloured. But even the modern trailers were not unattractive as their polished surfaces gave back the morning sun. There was scarcely any movement. A fillet of smoke hung almost straight in the still air. Half-a-dozen dogs lay in the shade under the wheels. Ponies grazed. A trio of children wrestled in the grass. Distantly the sound of other children at play drifted from somewhere out of sight.

Only when they reached the picket fence did the scrap and the litter which surrounded the caravans become truly apparent.

'Here we are,' said Greenall, pulling back the fence where it had been detached from one of the main stake-posts.

'Thanks,' said Dalziel. 'You not coming along?'

'I don't think so. I mean, if you find anything, then of course I'll co-operate. But I don't want to be always appearing on the side of the complainers. They're a nuisance, I know, but they've got a right to exist, haven't they? And at least they try to stay free, you've got to admire them for that.'

'Free?' said Dalziel. 'I've seen better-looking gaols!'

He strode away, pleased to feel his political equilibrium, upset by Middlefield's extremism, had been restored by Greenall's liberalism.

As he approached the caravans, the dogs and children watched him warily, but he could see no sign of adult life. He made no particular effort at stealth, but he could move extremely lightly for a man of his bulk, and as he slipped between two caravans, it amused him to think of a fat, urban policeman being able to steal up on these sons of nature unobserved.

Then he was seized from behind, his arms pinioned at his side, and he was thrust so forcefully against the side of a caravan that the vehicle shook.

'Fucking snoop around, would you? What's your game, fatty?' said a rough voice close to his left ear.

Too close.

Dalziel jerked his great cannon-ball of a head to the left. There was a sickening clash of bone and flesh. The grip on his arms slackened. He shrugged it off and turned to the thickset, dark-skinned man at his side.

'I'm a police officer,' he warned. 'Who are you?'

The man rushed at him.

Well, he'd been warned, thought Dalziel, and hit him in the stomach. Once was really enough, but it was as well to be sure, so he hit him again in the same spot.

Then he stood back and waited for the man to show signs of being ready for communication.

'I'll ask you once more,' he said finally. 'Who are you?'

'You've bust my gut,' gasped the man.

'*Name!*' snarled Dalziel.

'Lee. Dave Lee.'

'I might have guessed. It's a hobby of yours, assaulting policemen.'

'I didn't know you was police. I thought you was another of them council snoopers.'

'And it's OK to thump council officers, is it?' queried Dalziel. 'Well, you may be right. This your caravan? Let's have a look.'

He went up the steps, thrust open the door and entered. A woman in an inadequate shift was standing in the narrow living area. Dalziel ignored her and looked around. The place smelt of sweat, tobacco and sex, but it looked clean and tidy enough. There was a richly coloured carpet on the floor and a sense of extra space was given by two large, ornate, cut-glass mirrors. One wall was almost covered by a mahogany display cabinet which held a strange variety of traditionally patterned china, crystal bowls and vases and some goblets and smaller objects in what looked like silver.

'Who the hell's this?' demanded the woman.

'Mrs Lee?' said Dalziel, turning his attention to her as if he hadn't noticed her till now. He let his eyes move slowly up from the rather flaccid breasts clearly visible through her shift to her face, the left side of which was stained with a fading bruise.

'That's nice,' he said. 'You'll make a matching pair.'

Behind him Lee spoke sharply in what he took to be Anglo-

Romany and the woman retreated to the sleeping area and began to pull some clothes on.

Dalziel moved around the trailer opening drawers and cupboards, looking under cushions and behind curtains.

'What's your game, mister?' demanded Lee.

'Thought you were never going to ask, Dave,' said Dalziel cheerfully. 'I'm looking for stolen property. I haven't got a warrant, so why don't you shoot off and call your lawyer?'

'What stolen property?' demanded Lee.

'Break-in at the Aero Club last night. Bottles of booze,' answered Dalziel.

Lee laughed harshly. And with relief? wondered Dalziel.

'No stolen booze here, mister. Look all you like.'

Dalziel returned to the living area and stood in front of the display cabinet.

'I believe you, Dave,' he said. 'Your gut's too big for the window. You ought to watch that. I nearly lost my fist in there just now. This is nice stuff. The gypsy bank, they call it, don't they? Worth a pretty penny, I'll be bound. Good investment, no bother with the tax man.'

He opened the cabinet and took down a plate. 'What rank did you say you was, mister?' demanded Lee with sudden suspicion in his voice.

'Detective Superintendent,' answered Dalziel.

'And you says you're looking for a couple of bottles of booze?' said Lee incredulously. 'Here, watch that stuff!'

A cup had nearly slipped from Dalziel's hand.

'Sorry,' he said. 'That's sharp of you, Dave, spotting that. You've got to be sharp in your line of work, no doubt. Whatever it is. Me too. Spot what's not quite right. Now, I'd say this is not quite right, but I'm no expert.'

He had taken down from the extreme end of the topmost shelf a plain stone jar.

'Here, copper, you've got no right!' protested Lee. 'You said you'd no warrant. Right, you can just fuck off and get one before you touches another thing here!'

Dalziel opened the jar.

'Flour,' he said. 'Looks the real stuff. Not this modern muck with all the goodness bleached out of it.'

He took out a handful and sniffed at it.

'Oh yes,' he said to the woman who was dressed now and standing watching him with a look of complete indifference.

He held it out to her. She looked away. He opened his hand, spread his fingers, let the flour filter through on to the rich red carpet.

'The real stuff,' he repeated taking another handful. 'But it can't be all *that* valuable, can it, Dave? I mean, it's in with the family antiques here, though.'

The second handful followed the first.

He dipped in again.

'Hello,' he said. 'I think it's getting lumpy.'

He withdrew his hand. In it was a gent's gold-plated digital watch with an expanding bracelet. Carefully he blew the flour off it.

'Still going,' he said. 'It's like a telly ad, isn't it?'

In went the hand again. And out.

This time his find was a tight roll of five-pound notes.

He put them down beside the watch.

In again.

'I think that's it,' he said. 'No, hang about. Nearly missed that.'

That was a gent's gold signet ring. He tried it on his stubby little finger and looked at it admiringly.

'There it is,' he said. 'I was CPO once, Dave. Crime Prevention Officer. Persuading people not to leave their valuables in silly places was one of the jobs. Oh, these *are* your valuables, aren't they?'

The man and woman exchanged glances.

'Never seen 'em in my life,' she said.

'And you, Dave?'

Lee swore foully and said nothing more but looked around with a kind of wild contemplation.

'Aye, lad,' said Dalziel cheerfully. 'I'm on my own, so you could try thumping me, but I thought we'd settled all that already. Or you could run, in which case either I catch you and break a leg so you can't run no more, or else I send for some of my lads who'll break *both* your legs when *they* catch you. Best thing is to have a quiet stroll with me back to the Aero Club and on the way you can tell me all about the ponies of yours that keep on straying.'

'I've done nothing,' said the gypsy.

'No one's done nothing,' said Dalziel mildly, wrapping up his treasure trove in the small khaki blanket which he used for a handkerchief. 'Off we go. You too, love.'

Outside, the children paused in their play to observe the passing trio.

Dalziel grinned at them, pulled a handful of coppers from his pocket and tossed them into the air. They fell upon them, and each other, yelling wildly. A large lad, a stone or so heavier than his playmates, got the bulk of it.

'That's always the way of it,' said Dalziel philosophically.

❀ ❀ ❀

Greenall looked with some surprise at Dalziel's companions when they reached the Aero Club.

'These two broke into the bar?' he asked.

'Mebbe,' said Dalziel.

'Are you sure? He couldn't possibly have got through that window, and it'd be a tight squeeze for her.'

'They'll have done something,' said Dalziel indifferently. 'All gyppos are guilty of something. Can I use your phone?'

He told the Lees to sit down in the bar and left them there while he went into the office.

When he emerged he found the secretary looking distinctly unhappy.

'What's up?' he said.

'Are you going to be long?' asked Greenall.

'Not long. Why?'

'It's just that it's nearly twelve and there will be members arriving shortly.'

'So? Oh, I see. The gyppos. I thought you didn't mind them, Mr Greenall. Something about free spirits, wasn't it?'

'Hardly free when they're in custody, Superintendent,' said Greenall acidly.

'That's a point,' said Dalziel. 'But don't worry. They'll be picked up just now.'

'Picked up? You're not taking them yourself?'

'No way,' said Dalziel. 'I've got better things to do than chauffeur a pair of tinkers around. No, they'll be safely locked away and I'll get round to them by and by.'

'But you can't do that, can you?' protested Greenall.

'Can and will,' said Dalziel. 'They're not going to go squawking off to a lawyer, that's for sure. And a couple of hours locked in a cell's often worth a day's questioning with a gypsy.'

Greenall regarded him with distaste and went away.

Dalziel joined the Lees in the bar.

'You're not very jolly,' he said to them.

'He says you've hurt his belly,' said the woman.

'More likely it's eating all them hedgehogs,' said Dalziel. But he went behind the bar and poured a large brandy which he handed to Dave Lee.

The police cars arrived at the same time as Bernard Middlefield whose indignation when he discovered the two gypsies in the bar was assuaged only slightly when he realized they were under arrest.

'Not before time,' he said. 'The police cells are the one part of this town that lot are welcome to.'

Mrs Lee said something rapidly to her husband.

'What was that?' enquired Dalziel.

Lee answered, 'She says this loudmouth hangs about the river bank where the kids swim and tries to give them money to feel him.'

Middlefield went such an interesting colour that Dalziel couldn't resist saying, 'You stay like that, Bernard, and you'll have to resign from the golf club.'

A more dangerous encounter occurred as he was giving his instructions to the constables from the cars. To one of them he handed a plastic bag borrowed from Greenall's kitchen into which he had transferred his floury finds.

'To the lab,' he said. 'I want to know all there is to know. And I want it yesterday.'

As the other escorted the Lees to the police car, a pale blue Lancia drew up and Thelma Lacewing and Ellie Pascoe got out.

Thelma was wearing a thin cotton suit in cream with a grey leaf pattern which ought not to have suited her colouring but somehow did. She frowned slightly at the sight of the police cars and went right past Dalziel without a glance.

Ellie who looked hot and uncomfortable in a smock which was stretched as far as it seemed likely to go said, 'Hello, Andy. Checking on pilots' licences, are you?'

'Hello, Ellie,' said Dalziel, beaming widely. 'You're looking grand. There are some flowers that look best in pod. Another business lunch, is it?'

'Another?'

'Aye. Peter told me about your last. You did right to mention Mrs Wildgoose to us. We'll make a snout of you yet.'

Ellie looked around uneasily but Thelma was out of ear-shot talking earnestly to Greenall.

'No, not business this time. Thelma just called unexpectedly. She's off this afternoon, thought she might try a flight.'

'Oh aye?'

Dalziel shot her a questioning glance.

'You're never thinking of going up yourself, lass?'

'I may do,' said Ellie. 'What about it?'

'In your state? Does Peter know about this?'

'Look, Andy,' said Ellie with growing indignation. 'What I do is my business. I make my own decisions. I'm a big girl.'

'That's what I mean,' said Dalziel.

But further discussion was prevented by the return of Thelma Lacewing.

'Those people you have just despatched, Superintendent, have they been charged?' she said in her quiet, rather over-precise voice.

Dalziel scratched his neck, winked at Ellie who turned away from this attempt at conspiratorial familiarity, and said, 'No, Ms Lacewing. They have not.'

'Are they going to be charged?'

'They're helping with enquiries. At this time I am not in a position to forecast the possible outcome of these enquiries,' said Dalziel, deliberately self-parodying.

'Not till they've been questioned, you mean?'

'Right.'

'By you?'

'Right again.'

'Starting when?'

Dalziel looked reproachfully towards the club house but Greenall was no longer in view.

'After lunch,' he said. 'What's the food like here?'

'Let's stick to the point, Superintendent. Just what are you questioning these people about?'

'There was a break-in here last night, did your friend not tell you that?'

'Yes. A couple of bottles. Hardly work for one of your eminence, I shouldn't have thought.'

'I look into crimes. You look into gobs. Neither of us can be selective,' beamed Dalziel. 'What's your interest anyway? The Lees are just a pair of gyppos. You don't strike me as a candidate for a bit of rough.'

Ellie shuddered. Peter wouldn't believe this. On second thoughts, alas, yes he would.

'I dislike abuse of power, especially against women,' said Thelma. 'What you're doing here is on the face of it fascist, racist and sexist.'

'Not sexist,' said Dalziel cunningly. 'I'm treating both of 'em the same.'

'I have a friend who is a solicitor. Adrienne Pritchard, you may know her? I shall instruct her to visit your station as soon as may be this afternoon to ascertain the position regarding the illegal holding of Mr and Mrs Lee and to act on their behalf if they so desire.'

'Well, that's settled then,' said Dalziel. 'Grand! I think I will stay here for a spot of lunch. It's not a bad little place, is it? Ladies, will you join me in a drink?'

Thelma Lacewing said coldly, 'As a policeman, you should be aware that non-members are not allowed to purchase drinks on club premises.'

'Is that right?' said Dalziel, placing one huge hand against each of the women's backs and urging them forward. 'In that case, it looks like your shout, lass. Mine's a pint.'

CHAPTER 14

Mark Wildgoose's flat was in a district of old Victorian terraces where you were more likely to find nests of students than solitary teachers.

Not that he was solitary when Pascoe arrived. Directed up the stairs by a bearded youth with a beatific smile, he arrived on the first floor landing just as a door opened and a girl emerged. She didn't look to be out of her teens. There was a man behind her and she turned to give him a parting kiss. It was an uninhibited affair on her part, almost exhibitionistic, but his eyes remained open and fixed on Pascoe who after a cursory glance at the other two doors had worked out this must be the one.

The girl finished, slipped past Pascoe and flew down the stairs with the lightness of youth and joy.

The man began to close the door.

'Mr Wildgoose?' said Pascoe.

He nodded.

'I'm Pascoe. Detective-Inspector Pascoe. My warrant card. Could we talk?'

Wildgoose studied the card carefully, then ushered him into what must once have been a morning room. Like good bone structure, its dignified proportions had been able to absorb the ravages of age, neglect and even student taste. It contained an unmade bed, a scarred mahogany wardrobe, a couple of dilapidated armchairs, a table with the remnants of breakfast on it, three folding chairs, a washbasin and an electric hotplate. Some makeshift bookshelves, planks on stacks of bricks, were packed to danger point, and an overspill pyramided in one corner.

Bad to heat in winter, thought Pascoe looking up at the leafily corniced ceiling. But at the moment it was warm enough, too warm in fact, stuffy with a rich mingling of smells. He sniffed. Coffee, perspiration, tobacco...

'There is a bit of a fug,' said Wildgoose, flinging open windows. The girl must have looked up as she left the house for he leaned out and blew a kiss. Pascoe could see his face in the pane of glass.

'It's about your allotment, Mr Wildgoose,' he said, and watched the tension come into the averted face.

But when the man turned, there was nothing but alert frankness there.

Small, dark, sharp, mobile, it was a good face for a French singer of disillusioned but not despairing ballads. The children got more of their looks here than from their mother.

'Wasn't that your wife I met yesterday?' said Wildgoose.

'I believe so.'

'Coincidence?' His eyebrows added their own double questionmark.

'Coincidence?' echoed Pascoe. 'A funny thing, coincidences. On the other hand, less funny because less rare than many people believe. It's noticing them that's rare.'

'I don't follow.'

'And you an English teacher,' smiled Pascoe. 'That was a coincidence, wasn't it? I mean you actually taught Brenda Sorby, didn't you?'

'Brenda...?'

'Sorby. Choker victim number three. The girl on your allot-ment was number two.'

'Not *my* allotment, Inspector. And no, I can't remember teaching a Brenda Sorby, though I'm willing to accept I did, if you tell me so. Is that it? For coincidences, I mean?'

'Not quite. You drink at the Cheshire Cheese, don't you?'

The man sat down in an armchair and lit a cigarette. His face was thoughtful now. He used the smoke as a mask.

'I have done,' he said.

'What about the fairground, Mr Wildgoose? Have you been to the Fair this year?'

'Yes. I always go. I like fairs.'

'When were you there?'

'Last week. Thursday night if you like.'

He smiled and Pascoe felt irritated. But it had been his own idea to start playing this game. He couldn't blame the other for joining in.

'What about lunch-time two days ago? Wednesday, that is?'

'I think I was out walking,' said Wildgoose after some thought.

'By yourself?'

'I believe so.'

'And where did you walk?'

'Oh, here and there. I expect I strolled along the river bank. It's so pretty down there, don't you think?'

'Along the bank, and through Charter Park, you mean.'

'That's where the river flows, Inspector,' said Wildgoose. 'Now, how are we doing for coincidences?'

He doesn't give a bugger! thought Pascoe. He's mocking me.

Yet there had been something there when we started. Where had they started?

'If you don't mind, I'd like to take a look at your allotment, Mr Wildgoose,' he said abruptly.

That was better. The tension had flickered back momentarily.

'It's a stretch of wasteland, Inspector,' he said lightly. 'I haven't bothered much with it this year. In fact, I'm not sure it's even still mine, officially. The rent could be overdue.'

'All the same, I think I'll have a look,' said Pascoe. 'Would you care to join me?'

Wildgoose stood up. His muscles were aggressively tensed.

'Where'd you get my address from, Pascoe?' he asked. 'Have you been talking to my ex-wife?'

'Your wife, surely? There's no divorce yet, is there?'

'Hardly. But there will be, whatever she thinks. Even the law's delay doesn't last for ever these days.'

Pascoe said, 'The law's delay. That's *Hamlet*, isn't it?'

'I suppose so. So what?'

'Coincidence, that's all.'

Wildgoose laughed and relaxed and pulled on a cotton jacket over his T-shirt which was not the one described by Ellie, unless he was wearing it inside out.

'Half the clichés in the language are Shakespeare and most of the rest Pope,' he said. 'Not a very valuable coincidence, is it?'

'That's what I've been saying about coincidences all along,' said Pascoe. 'Isn't it?'

As they drove along the road which was the quickest route to Pump Street, Pascoe said, 'Why aren't you coming all over indignant, Mr Wildgoose?'

'Why should I?'

'Well, for a start, you've obviously worked out I've been chatting to your family about you. That would annoy a lot of men. And there'd be very few men indeed who wouldn't get extremely indignant when they realized the police were trying to tie them in with the Choker killings.'

'Including the Choker?'

'Perhaps especially the Choker,' said Pascoe.

'Then perhaps I'm busy establishing my innocence, Inspector,' said Wildgoose calmly. 'If you turn down here, you'll cut off the traffic lights.'

Pump Street consisted mainly of two long rows of terraces opening on to the pavement. One side had been built for railway workers in the mid-nineteenth century, the other, still known as the New Side although identical in style, had been put up speculatively about ten years later as the demand for low-cost housing exploded in this area. What gave Pump Street some individual character and even beauty was the ground contour which had made it easier to build on a curve, and chance had produced an arc fit for a Nash crescent. The allotments were situated in a break in the New Side where a Dornier with its full load had come down one still-remembered night in '41 and reduced a hundred yards of terracing to rubble, and thirty-nine men, women and children to corpses. There was no time for rebuilding then, but gradually the site had been cleared, and eventually planted on, by the gardenless locals eager to plug some of the gaps in their diet. Eventually, after complaints of piracy and land-grabbing, the council stepped in and regularized matters, and so things continued for more than thirty years till the June morning when the death toll rose to forty.

There were two or three old men working on their allotments and they watched with open curiosity as Pascoe and Wildgoose picked their way across to the latter's strip. It was indeed sadly neglected though no more so than half a dozen others.

'Here we are,' said Wildgoose. 'If you seek my memorial, look around you.'

Pascoe bent and examined the furrowed ground. There were potatoes here still, some straggly carrot tops, something which could have been leaf spinach.

'What happened?' he asked.

'A couple of years ago it seemed a good idea. Self-sufficiency. Part of the male menopause.'

'You're a little young for that, surely?'

'Forty,' said Wildgoose. 'I just know a good couturier. And the male menopause has nothing to do with age or physical changes. It has to do with meanings.'

'And you found something more meaningful?'

'Still looking, Inspector.'

Pascoe too was looking. The rickety old shed in which June McCarthy's body had been found stood about twenty-five yards away. As he watched, the door opened and a man emerged. He had a bucket in one hand and a garden fork in the other. Carefully with the economic movements of age and experience he began to unearth some potatoes. This was Mr Ribble, the owner of the shed and the only one of the allotment holders that Pascoe had interviewed personally. A man in his late sixties, he had taken the discovery of the body with a phlegm which was to some extent explained when Pascoe found out that he had cancer of the bowel and had already outlived the surgeon's estimate by eighteen months.

Pascoe turned back to Wildgoose and coldly wondered how such a diagnosis would affect his search for meanings.

'I see you keep your greenhouse locked,' he said. 'Worried about your tomatoes?'

'I kept my tools in there,' said Wildgoose. 'I didn't really grow much. It came with the allotment. The old boy who had it before me died and it seemed a kindness to pay his missus a couple of quid for the thing. Would you like a look?'

He searched in his pocket for a key while Pascoe examined the greenhouse from the outside. It was very much a homemade affair, more of a converted garden shed than a proper greenhouse. It was glazed with panels of translucent plastic which had the advantage of not being so fragile as glass. In one or two places kids had hurled stones without doing more damage than denting and cracking, easily repaired with transparent tape.

Wildgoose found the key and unlocked the padlock which fastened the door. Pascoe let him go in first. Mrs Wildgoose had been wrong. While you could not see clearly through the plastic, you could certainly distinguish shapes and it would take either irresistible passion or brazen exhibitionism to persuade a couple to fornicate in here. Pascoe did not dismiss the possibility. But it was unlikely that one of the elderly gardeners would not have passed on details of this shadowy entertainment to Sergeant Brady.

The interior of the greenhouse smelt hot and stuffy. There was a rusty spade in one corner, a broken hoe in another. A few earthenware plant pots were stacked along a sagging shelf. Nothing was growing in here, though the mummified remains of some unidentifiable plants crowded together sadly in a propagating tray. The floor was wooden, beginning to rot in places. A couple of sacks were draped across a particularly decayed section. An almost empty plastic bag of some proprietary fertilizer lay alongside them. Pascoe's memory was stirred. Among many other things, the laboratory examination of June McCarthy's clothes had revealed the presence of traces of peat and other fibrous organic material associated with gardening, precisely the kind of thing you'd expect to find in a garden shed.

He wondered whether anyone had bothered to make sure they were definitely present in Mr Ribble's shed.

For Wildgoose to kill her in his greenhouse and then lug the body twenty-five yards across the allotment didn't seem likely. It had been early in the morning, but broad daylight.

Still, when you had nothing, anything was something.

He stooped to pick up the bag.

And smiled with incredulous delight as he saw the small adhesive price tag still clinging to the grubby plastic. The name of the retailer was still on it.

The Linden Garden Centre.

He picked it up carefully.

'You use a lot of this stuff?' he asked.

'In the first flush of enthusiasm, I used everything,' said Wildgoose. 'Soot, blood, horse-shit, sea-weed. Why?'

'And where did you buy your garden stuff, Mr Wildgoose?'

'Where? Hell, wherever I was. Garden shops, market stalls, Woolworth's even. They're very good in Woolworth's these days.'

'Garden centres? This price tag says *Linden Garden Centre.*'

'I don't remember that. Is it important?'

'It's on the East Coast Road,' said Pascoe. 'Four, five miles.'

'Sorry. I don't recall, for all I know that stuff was here when I took the allotment on. Don't tell me it's a clue!'

For someone who had seemed so bright and alert to every innuendo, he was being very dim about this, thought Pascoe.

'I'd like to take this if I may.'

'I'll need a receipt,' mocked Wildgoose. 'What about a few old plant pots into the bargain?'

The plastic bag was leaking, Pascoe discovered, and the remaining fertilizer was spilling out of it. Picking up one of the old sacks from the floor, he thrust the bag inside.

'Let's go,' he said.

'Where?'

'Why, back to your flat, of course, Mr Wildgoose. Unless I can drop you anywhere else?'

'No, that'll be fine.'

He managed not to sound relieved.

On the drive back, Pascoe stopped by a telephone kiosk, 'to check what my boss wants next,' he explained half grumblingly to Wildgoose.

He stopped a little later to get some cigarettes, then got stuck behind a slow double-decker bus.

'Sorry to have taken up so much of your time,' he said to Wildgoose as he got out of the car in front of the house which contained the flat.

'Always a pleasure,' said Wildgoose. 'Will I see you again?'

'Who knows? Nothing is impossible to coincidence.'

Pascoe watched Wildgoose walk jauntily up the steps to the front door. Then he looked across the street to make sure that there'd been time to carry out his telephoned instructions. Detective-Constable Preece sitting in a dilapidated VW Beetle raised a languid hand. He looked half asleep. Pascoe hoped it was an act.

He drove round the corner and waited. After a couple of minutes the door of the car opened and Preece slid in. He still looked tired.

'OK?' said Pascoe.

Preece passed him a film cartridge.

'I shot off half a dozen,' he said. 'One should be all right. You want me to hang about, sir?'

'Please,' said Pascoe. 'I want to know where he goes, who he talks to.'

'These houses have got a lane running down the back,' said Preece diffidently.

'Sorry,' said Pascoe. 'You're on your own. You'll just have to hope he comes out of the front. Or be in two places at the same time. Do your best. Which is to say, please don't lose him. And Preece. It doesn't bother me if you don't sleep in your own bed. But make bloody sure you sleep in your own time. OK? Enjoy yourself.'

Preece nodded and left. As he walked away he thought, *Christ! He may be politer than Dalziel but he's just as fucking impossible!*

Pascoe decided to short-circuit normal lines of communication and drive round to the police labs himself. These were a fairly recent acquisition, very up to date and a source of such pride to the Chief Constable that he tended to skirt round the fact that shortage of space in the congested city centre had obliged them to be built some considerable distance from the central police HQ. An efficient shuttle service had been devised and all officers were given strict instructions that this was the only channel to be used.

Thus Pascoe was greeted frostily by the duty officer, a fat, normally jolly man called Harry Hopper.

'You know this is against regulations,' he said.

'Oh Christ. Is it? I'm sorry, Harry,' said Pascoe. 'It's a fair cop then. You'd better complain to my boss. Andy Dalziel, that is. I'll take what's coming to me.'

'There's no need to threaten me,' grumbled the other. 'All right. What do you want?'

'This developed. A couple of prints of each,' said Pascoe, handing over the cartridge. Alongside it, he laid the sack containing the fertilizer. 'And this to be given the treatment. I'll hang on for the photos if it's not going to take too long, which I'm sure it's not. And if you could rustle me up a copy of the lab reports on June McCarthy and on the garden shed she was found in, it'll give me something to look at and stop me getting impatient.'

Hopper went away, returning some time later with the reports and a smile.

'Everyone's very busy,' he said. 'Some stuff had just come in from your Mr Dalziel—for urgent attention, it was marked, but I told 'em if he gets impatient we'll just have to explain that you have priority, was that all right?'

'Bastard,' said Pascoe.

He sat down and studied the reports. At first things looked hopeful. The fibres of fertilizer on June McCarthy's clothing were identified as probably belonging to one of three proprietary brands and one of these was the same as that found in Wildgoose's greenhouse. But a quick glance at the report on the examination of Mr Ribble's shed revealed that there was a bag of the mixture in question stored there. It was both reassuring and disappointing to find that the reports were models of thoroughness. It had been a long shot that such a discrepancy might exist and have gone unnoticed, but such things did happen.

Still, the reports didn't *disprove* that she *might* have been in the greenhouse, thought Pascoe, seeking a tortuous comfort.

And there *was* that odd air of a recent clear-out about it. Worth sending a team in to give it the full treatment? Not without Dalziel's say-so, he decided. The press would be on to it like a flash and who knows what kind of shit Wildgoose might be provoked into flinging about.

The photographs arrived. A couple of them, one side, one full face, were good enough to identify Wildgoose from.

'How's it going?' enquired Hopper. 'Getting anywhere?'

'If we are, it's too slow for human perception,' said Pascoe. 'Thanks a lot Harry.'

'A pleasure. But like sex at my age, not one to be repeated too frequently. Here, you might as well take this, it's marked for you. Final report on that last lot of clothes. Pauline Stanhope's.'

Pascoe took the sheet of paper and ran his eyes down it.

'Anything?' he asked.

'Bugger all,' said Hopper. 'It's all wrapped up for next-of-kin as soon as you care to release it.'

Pascoe thought a moment.

'All right,' he said. 'Look, I'm going to be seeing her aunt. I'll take it with me. Better than just having it pushed into her hands by some anonymous bobby.'

He signed for the small bundle of clothes and the box containing Pauline Stanhope's watch and other personal effects.

'Poor kid,' said Hopper. 'I've got one of my own, just turned twenty. They think they know it all, jobs, key of the door, getting engaged next month, but they're just kids still. I wouldn't dare tell her, but she's so bloody defenceless really. I mean, they need protection, Peter. Get this bastard and get him quick, will you?'

'We'll try,' said Pascoe. 'We'll try.' He glanced at his watch. 'But not till after lunch,' he added.

And wondered as he walked away how long it took for protective cynicism to seep to the deep heart's core.

CHAPTER 15

Pascoe didn't enjoy his lunch.

Using the justification that the road to the village of Shafton outside which the Linden Garden Centre was situated could (with a detour of a mere six or seven miles) be said to pass his door, he decided to surprise Ellie by eating at home.

His sense of injury at finding she was out intensified when he discovered the larder was almost bare.

A piece of antique cheese and a wrinkled apple later, he continued on his way. The deserted appearance of the Garden Centre did not improve his mood.

It was a medium-sized operation, centred upon an old stone-built farmhouse which looked to be in need of repair. There were two long greenhouses abutting on what had once been a byre but was now a garden shop. Two or three acres of land were under cultivation, mainly to rose-bushes plus a few rows of fruit trees and ornamental shrubs. Even the bright sunshine could not disguise the sense of neglect there was about the place.

Someone was moving behind the house and Pascoe headed in that direction. It was an old countryman with a wheelbarrow in which was a sackful of what looked like bonemeal. He walked slowly past Pascoe, saying out of the corner of his mouth, 'Place is closed.'

'So I see,' said Pascoe, falling into step beside him. 'Who are you?'

The old man didn't answer straightaway. He had a skin as hard, brown and cracked as the sun-baked earth he walked on, and his eyes which were the faded blue of hydrangea remained fixed unblinkingly on his load as though he were walking a high wire.

Impatiently Pascoe produced his warrant card and thrust it under the man's nose.

'Police,' he said.

'I know that.'

'You mean, you know me?' said Pascoe, nonplussed.

'The way you walk. Talk. I know that,' said the old man.

'Do you mind telling me who you are?' said Pascoe wearily. 'Please.'

The old man stopped, rested the barrow and sat on its edge between the shafts.

'Agar,' he said. 'Ted Agar.'

'And what's happened here, Mr Agar.'

'Since she got herself killed, you mean?'

'Yes, since then.'

Pascoe perched himself on a stack of ornamental slabs. He was, he realized with an amusement which helped dissipate his ill-humour, very much in the interviewee's seat—about six inches lower than Agar who had the sun at his back.

'Well, nothing rightly,' said the old man. 'Lawyers' business, nowt else.'

'What's the trouble?'

'In the first place, no will. In second place, no close relatives, though you can always find one or two who'll make a claim. She was a widow, you see, Mrs Dinwoodie. Husband got killed last summer at Agricultural Show. You likely read about it. Run down by a traction engine. It was in the papers. Then the lass. Alison her daughter. Just a few months later. Car accident. She was just a kid. Not a lucky woman, Mrs Dinwoodie.'

Pascoe of course knew most of this. Mary Dinwoodie's friends had been checked as a priority after the murder. But the family had been non-existent and she had apparently made a determined effort to cut herself off from her acquaintance. Her grief had been very private, rejecting offers of comfort or companionship. It was a sad irony that her first positive move in the direction of human society once more should have taken her into the Choker's hands.

The Shafton Players had been investigated so closely that Pascoe knew more about some of them than their spouses did. The possibility of a link between a drama group and the *Hamlet* calls had not gone unnoticed, but it had certainly remained undiscovered. Individually, the Players had neither motive nor opportunity. Collectively, they had never done *Hamlet*. So it looked as if Mary Dinwoodie had just had the misfortune to be available. Yet Pascoe could not forget Pottle's insistence that her death was, must be, the key.

'How long have you worked here, Mr Agar?' he asked.

'Six years. Since I left the farming.'

'What about other help?'

'No one else most of the time,' he said. 'Except I took a lad on when the missus went away after the lass died. Couldn't do it single-handed. Couldn't really do it proper with two of us. Before, me and Mr Dinwoodie looked after the trees and such. Planting, hoeing, all that. Mrs Dinwoodie helped with the greenhouses, and ran the shop. She'd been a teacher once or summat, so she was good with paperwork. The lass helped too. She'd just left school, didn't want to do anything else, an office job or such. She liked to be outside. Her lad was going to go into farming too.'

'Her lad?'

'Aye. Didn't you know? She'd just married him when they got killed. Same day. It doesn't bear thinking on. Well, after that, the heart went out of Mrs Dinwoodie. She went off. Just told me to look after things and went off. It were all right at first, but when spring got near, it starts getting busy, so I had to take a lad on, and my daughter-in-law came in to help with the shop. I saw the bank manager first. He weren't sure but I told him business would soon be knackered if I didn't and he soon changed his tune. Even then we were only open weekends. But we ticked over. And then she came back. I was that glad to see her! But, oh, she'd mebbe had done better to stay away for ever.'

There was a catch in the old man's voice. He really cares, thought Pascoe, and he said, 'You liked Mrs Dinwoodie?'

'I liked all on 'em, but her the best. She was a kind woman. She blamed herself for everything. She said it were her fault they were so close to that engine at the show. And blamed herself for letting the lass run off to Scotland to be wed. Well, that were daft, mebbe, and the girl's place was here by her mam's side with her dad only a few months dead. But at seventeen, what's to fill a lass's head but boys and such? Well, I never thought I'd see any one of them out, let alone all three. It doesn't bear thinking on, does it? It doesn't bear thinking.'

'No, it doesn't,' said Pascoe. 'So now you're in sole charge?'

'Oh aye. Till things is settled. Lawyers asked me to stay on. There's two relatives of his, half cousins or some such thing, down in the South. Likely they'll get it. Best I can do by myself is tend the roses and the fruit trees. We sold all the greenhouse stuff up. Market traders and the like. They got a bargain. But I couldn't have tended them and they'd not hire anyone else. Do you want to look in the house?'

'Yes, please,' said Pascoe, not knowing why. 'But first, I wonder if you've ever seen this chap around here?'

He passed over the two photographs of Wildgoose. Agar scrutinized them carefully.

'Nay,' said Agar. 'I don't recall him. Though that's not to say I've never seen him.'

'But would you say you might have seen him?'

'Not if there was money on it,' said the old man, adding shrewdly, 'and there'll likely be more than money on it, eh?'

'Likely,' said Pascoe, retrieving the photos.

The old man opened the house for him, then returned to his work. Pascoe went inside. Already the place smelt dank and unlived-in. One of the downstairs rooms had been turned into an office. He poked around for a while but found nothing but a chaos of neglected paperwork. He had no idea what he might be looking for. It was simply an exercise in serendipity. Abandoning the office, he went upstairs.

The girl's bedroom he found hard to bear. It was untidy, but with the untidiness of youth, as though its owner might be reappearing at any moment. He left it and went into the main bedroom. And here at last he made a find.

It was a cardboard box tucked away at the back of a crowded wardrobe. It was a sad box, full of memories which now lacked a mind to remember them. Christmas cards, birthday cards, many home-made, inscribed *To Mummy with lots of love from Alison* in a young round hand, some childish daubs. And a few secondary school reports. Alison it seemed had attended the Bishop Crump Comprehensive School.

Well, so had thousands of other kids. And Alison's death had nothing to do with the Choker. She had died in a car accident in the South of Scotland. The scrawled initials after the comments on her English and Drama lessons gave little clue to their author. Of course, mused Pascoe, if Wildgoose had taught this girl, then there were parent-teacher evenings, plenty of chance for him to have met the mother.

He dug deeper and for his pains made one more discovery. It was a programme on a brown card with scalloped edges to give a kind of parchment effect. On the front printed in

Gothic script were the words *Musik-und-Drama-Fest, Linden, Mai 1973*.

That Linden. The town in Germany. This was where the Centre's name came from. His schoolboy German was still sufficiently remembered to identify this as the general programme of a small amateur festival of music and drama (not difficult!) and get the gist of most of the promised goodies. Then an item caught and held his eye. *Scenes from Shakespeare*, he translated. *By members of a local drama society*, he guessed. *Plus staff from Devon School*. And there were two directors named, one German, the other Herr Peter Dinwoodie.

So here it was at last. Not *Hamlet*, but Shakespeare at least. *Unser Shakespeare*. He'd heard how the Germans admired him to the point of possessiveness. And Devon School? A touring party? Hardly. More likely a British Forces School. He'd known a girl who'd gone out there to teach and he seemed to recall the schools often had that kind of name, *Gloucester, Cornwall, Windsor*.

Linden, if his geography held as well as his German, was hard by Hanover. Lots of BAOR bases round there, so it made some sense.

He went downstairs and asked old Agar if Mary Dinwoodie and her husband had once been schoolteachers in Germany.

'Nay, I know nowt about that,' said the old man.

Well, it should be easy to check out, thought Pascoe pocketing the programme.

And at the same time it would be worth checking if Wildgoose had ever done any teaching abroad.

❋ ❋ ❋

At Rosetta Stanhope's flat he was admitted quickly, almost as though he were expected. I really must stop endowing her with supernatural powers, he told himself irritably. Certainly the room in which he found himself was ordinary enough. There was a lightly flowered paper on the walls, and the furniture consisted of a three-piece suite in imitation hide, a large colour TV and a small oak sideboard with a nest of matching tables. The only hint of the woman's background lay in a large glass-fronted cabinet almost filling one of the narrower walls and packed with what Pascoe had no doubt was fine china.

Rosetta Stanhope herself was dressed like any housewife doing her chores; she wore a blue cotton overall, moccasins on her feet, and her hair was tied back with a red silk bandanna. The only change was in her face where the flesh seemed more tightly drawn than ever over the fine thin bones.

'Will you have a cup of tea?' she asked very correctly. 'I can't offer you strong liquor. There's none in the place.'

'And I couldn't accept it anyway,' answered Pascoe even more correctly, though perhaps less accurately. 'You don't drink alcohol, Mrs Stanhope?'

'I can't afford to get confused, Mr Pascoe,' she said.

'And your niece? Did she drink?'

'Never here.'

'But elsewhere? A social drink with friends perhaps?'

She regarded him seriously but with no outward sign of distress. Pascoe congratulated himself on the subtlety of his introduction of the topic.

'Like at the Cheshire Cheese, you mean?' said Rosetta Stanhope.

Pascoe cancelled his congratulations.

'That might be significant,' he said. 'Did she?'

'Not that I know of,' said the woman. 'And I think I'd have known. It was funny. She was not my blood, not my flesh, but she grew to me like a daughter. Closer perhaps. Daughters grow up, turn away, despise their parents even. I've seen it many times. Trouble, misunderstanding, separation. Like poor Brenda Sorby and her father. But Pauline grew closer to me as she got older and when the time came for her to make her own choice of life, instead of turning away, she turned towards me. No one knew her father, but I sometimes think he could not have been *gorgio*.'

She nodded emphatically, for a moment every inch the gypsy queen.

'But she would have friends of her own age, a life of her own,' urged Pascoe.

'Of course she did,' said Mrs Stanhope. 'She was a nice ordinary attractive young lass. People liked her, she made friends easy...'

Her voice broke for a moment and the gypsy queen was gone and for the second time in an hour Pascoe felt the guilt of being embarrassed by the sight of grief.

It was over in a moment.

'You're barking up the wrong tree,' she resumed. 'No one who knew Pauline did this.'

Pascoe regarded her dubiously.

'Why so certain, Mrs Stanhope?' he asked.

'She told me,' she replied seriously. 'Last night.'

Pascoe had to make an effort to stop himself glancing uneasily around. The room suddenly felt much less ordinary and conventional and the bright sunlight falling through the broad window seemed to thicken and curdle.

'You communicated with her?' he said.

She suddenly smiled. It was not an unfriendly smile, but not the kind of smile much used between equals. There was something of exasperation in it, and of pity too.

'We didn't sit down and have a chat, Inspector,' she said. 'But she was here. I felt her. And if she'd known who it was that did it, she'd have let me know.'

'But,' objected Pascoe, 'even if she didn't know *then*, surely she knows *now*.'

'*Then* and *now*'s for the living,' she said dismissively. 'Anyway, I didn't mean she would have given me a name, though that's not impossible. All I meant was, I felt her here and she felt puzzled, uncertain, not like she'd have been if she knew who'd done it and why, when it was done, I mean.'

'Ah,' said Pascoe who found this picture of a puzzle-filled afterlife rather distressing. A lifetime as a policeman was enough; an eternity unthinkable. Dalziel with a golden truncheon and blue serge wings! The image thinned the light once more and the room returned to normal.

'It's quite unusual for a Romany to be a medium, isn't it?' he said, leaning back in his chair. 'Crystal balls, the tarot, that's the more usual area, isn't it?'

'It's how the *gorgios* have portrayed us,' said the woman. 'But I've known very few *chovihanis* who used a crystal as more than a prop. Or as something bright to act as a focus for self-hypnosis. Oh, I read the psychic journals, Mr Pascoe! I'm not an educated woman but I've lived a *gorgio* life long enough to pick up some of their knowledge too!'

'*Chovihani*. That's a sort of witch, isn't it?'

'You know a bit about our people?' she said. 'I felt it when we first met.'

'I once did a short study at college,' admitted Pascoe. 'It was social mainly, about education, fitting into the community, that sort of thing.'

'Looking for ways to change us, make us like you!' she said scornfully.

'Not really,' said Pascoe. 'Though some do change. You, for instance. You conformed.'

He didn't want an argument with this woman, but it seemed important to find out if there was really any more to her than a farrago of superstitions and self-delusions. He found out.

'Conformed? Me! What a bloody arrogant sod you are, just like the rest! I did anything but. I left my family and I left my people and I left my whole life behind me. That's conforming, is it? Conforming's being as daft and as dull and as stupid as you, is it?'

She was frightening in anger. Pascoe decided that on the whole he preferred the imminence of the other world to this.

'I'm sorry,' he said. 'It was stupid, you're quite right. Absolutely.'

Suddenly she was angry no more.

'It doesn't matter,' she said. 'It wasn't all that difficult, anyway. *Chovihanis* aren't expected to conform. They do odd, anti-social things. My grandma was one, too. It skipped my mother somehow. But my grandma foretold I would marry a *gorgio* when I was in my cradle. So it was expected in a way. Everyone knew the prophecy. It made for loneliness. From fourteen on, boys wanted me for their lusts. I was a good-looking girl, can you believe that?'

'Easily,' said Pascoe.

'But not for a wife,' she went on. 'If anyone married me, you see, the only way the prophecy could be fulfilled then would be for my husband to die! So I waited for Stanhope.'

She smiled, gently this time, reminiscently.

'He was worth the waiting. Now you would like to see Pauline's room.'

She rose abruptly, Pascoe more slowly, impressed again by her powers of anticipation.

She led him into a small bedroom. Pascoe regarded it with dismay. It looked as if an amateur burglar had been at it. Drawers hung out of the dressing-table and tallboy, all empty, as was the fitted wardrobe. Their contents seemed to have been stuffed into a variety of plastic rubbish bags which littered the floor. As he watched, Mrs Stanhope began to strip the blankets and linen off the bed and thrust these too into one of the bags.

'What on earth are you doing?' demanded Pascoe, bewildered.

'I thought you had studied the Romany,' she said. 'All these things of my dead niece must be destroyed. It is the custom.'

'But Pauline wasn't a gypsy,' protested Pascoe.

'She was my niece. She lived here. She is dead,' said the woman in a matter-of-fact tone. 'While her possessions remain, so must she. I did the same when my Bert died. Even a *chovihani* has a right to live among the living. I felt her last night. She was lost and puzzled. I may have been a comfort. But soon she may grow angry, resentful, bitter. Such a spirit is not good company. The gypsy way is to seek rest for both the living and the dead.'

There was no answer to this.

Pascoe said, 'You seem to have guessed we'd want to look through Pauline's things, so isn't this a bit premature?'

She picked up a shoe-box from the bedside table.

'Her letters, diary, address book,' she said. 'All that could be of interest to you. But none of it will be of use. I can tell you that. Take them anyway. Make copies and return them, please. They too must go. Also the things she was wearing when she died. Those especially must be destroyed. When can I have them?'

'They're in the car,' remembered Pascoe. 'I'll fetch them now.'

He returned a few moments later with the parcel of clothes and personal effects.

'Thank you,' she said. Then after a moment's hesitation, she added abruptly, 'I still want to help, you understand, like I told you. But it's harder now.'

'Because it's your own, you mean?'

She thought about this for a while, then agreed, 'Yes. Because it's my own.'

Pascoe puzzled over this remark as he went downstairs to his car. It seemed to him there might have been a rather strange emphasis in it, though at the same time he recognized that the whole ambience of the flat inclined him to suspicion of strangeness.

My own. In a way Pauline hadn't been her own, of course. For in a way, her own were the gypsies, particularly the Lees. And after Pauline's death she had been away on some unlikely family jaunt with Dave Lee.

Could family loyalty—or fear—persuade her to help cover

up Dave Lee's involvement in her niece's death? It hardly seemed likely. But there was something there, of that he was convinced.

As he was opening his car door he heard his name being called, and Rosetta Stanhope came running after him, breathless and agitated.

'What's the matter?' he asked.

'Where's the rest?' she demanded.

'Rest? Rest of what?'

'The rest of her clothes! The clothes she died in. Those I must have, those are the most important of all!'

'But you've got everything,' assured Pascoe. 'Jeans, suntop, underclothes, sandals. I checked them off myself as I signed for them.'

'Not those, you fool!' flashed the woman, all gypsy now. 'The headscarf, the shawl, the skirt. Where are they?'

'Oh God!' exclaimed Pascoe. Her theatricality was infectious for he found himself striking his forehead with his open hand. But he meant it.

'You bloody fool!' he said to himself. 'You fool!'

CHAPTER 16

Sergeant Wield was an expert typist, a skill he kept well concealed from less dextrous colleagues who would have been quick to attempt to abuse it. Alone in the CID room, he was able to finish his reports on his morning visits to the bank and the Pickersgill household in record time. Now his thoughts turned to Newcastle and Maurice. There was someone else, he was certain. Brief encounters he had suspected before. He avoided them himself, but was willing to tolerate them in Maurice, recognizing that the other lacked his own almost monastic self-discipline. But what he had felt last night was the imminence of someone more dangerous, more permanent.

He sipped at a cold cup of coffee and wondered what he would do. Something. He was not a man to sit back and do nothing.

'Penny for 'em,' said Dalziel who had entered the room unobserved. 'You must be solving at least six of the ten great mysteries of the century, the way you look. What've you decided—Jack the Ripper escaped on the *Mary Celeste*?'

The telephone rang. Wield raised it off the rest.

'Anything interesting?' said Dalziel.

'Not really, sir. Lee created merry hell for a bit after he was brought in. They could hear him at the desk. He was claiming assault. By you.'

'Oh aye. You didn't go near him, did you?'

'No, sir. The lad who brought him in was very clear about your instructions. He shut up after a bit.'

'Good. I'll get on to him by and by.' Dalziel belched generously. 'Answer your phone, lad. Don't keep the public waiting.'

It was Mulgan from the Northern Bank.

'Sergeant Wield? I got authority to do that check you asked for.'

'Oh good. I was going to call later, sir,' reminded Wield.

'Yes, I know. But something emerged which I thought you might like to know instantly. Did you find any money on Brenda's body?'

'Hang on,' said Wield. He left his desk and went to a filing cabinet. Dalziel raised his eyebrows but the sergeant ignored him.

'A little in her purse,' said Wield. 'Three pound notes, some coppers. Why do you ask?'

'It's just that among her other transactions, she drew a cheque for cash against her own account.'

'Oh,' said Wield. 'Is that normal?'

'It's not against the rules, if that's what you mean, as long as there are funds to cover it. But normally I would expect one of my staff to cash their own cheques at someone else's till. Safer, if you follow me.'

'I think so. But there were funds to cover Brenda Sorby's cheque?'

'Oh yes. She was a very provident girl. No, it was just the amount that interested me, particularly as I saw no reference to cash in any of the newspaper reports. That morning she drew out two hundred pounds. In five pound notes.'

Wield passed on the news to Dalziel who took the phone from him.

'Mr Mulgan, Superintendent Dalziel here. Listen, you wouldn't have the numbers of the notes that Miss Sorby received, would you?'

'I'm sorry, no. It's impossible to…'

'Yes, yes, I understand. But there might be some marks? I mean, often the things I get from my bank look as if they'd been left lying around in a kindergarten!'

'There might be the odd pencil mark left by a teller when counting them into bundles,' said Mulgan acidly.

'And these marks would be identifiable as coming from someone at your bank?'

'Possibly, but not necessarily,' said the manager.

'Right. Thanks a lot, Mr Mulgan. We'll get back to you.'

He replaced the receiver forcibly.

'Creepy sod,' he said.

'You know him, sir?'

'Hardly. He just sounds a creepy sod. Like he was chewing a ball-bearing to make himself sound like a chinless wonder. Two hundred pounds, Sergeant! We should have known about this sooner. Good job I sent you this morning.'

'Yes, sir,' said Wield. 'It was a good idea of yours to check through the girl's transactions.'

'All right, save the satire,' said Dalziel. 'You'll get the credit. Question is, who got the money?'

'You think this could have just been straight theft after all?' asked Wield.

'I think nowt,' said Dalziel. 'All I know is that this morning I found one hundred and five pounds hidden away in Dave Lee's caravan that he can't account for.'

He smacked a huge fist into a huge palm making a crack like a breaking bone.

'Let's go and have a chat with Mr Lee, shall we,' he said.

❀ ❀ ❀

It was the penultimate day of the High Fair and Pascoe found things booming everywhere at Charter Park except in the police caravan where Sergeant Brady, attempting to conceal his copy of *Penthouse*, confirmed that the public seemed to have run out of even the most useless and irrelevant bits of information.

'Dead as a doornail since I came on after lunch,' he said. 'Nothing at all.'

'Well, don't let it get you down,' said Pascoe.

He went into the fairground to talk with Ena Cooper. As he approached the penny-roll stall he had a sense of something not quite right. It took him a second or two to spot what was wrong. The fortune-teller's tent had disappeared!

'They came and took it down this morning,' said Mrs Cooper. 'Three or four gyppos. Didn't you know?'

Pascoe was non-committal and Mrs Cooper smiled maliciously. But the smile disappeared when she was questioned about Pauline Stanhope again.

No, she hadn't mentioned what she'd been wearing when she left the tent just before midday. Why should she?—nobody had asked. Yes, 'Pauline' had been wearing the headscarf, the shawl, and the full-length skirt which were the tools of her trade. No, there'd been nothing funny about the way she walked.

As for seeing anyone go into the tent *before* the 'girl' left, yes, like she'd said already, there'd been a few that morning, she couldn't say how many.

Pascoe knew there'd been four at least, two pairs of women who had come forward instantly to compete for the honour of a 'last sighting'. The winners, a pair of teenage girls, had attended at eleven-fifteen a.m. and had been very impressed by Madame Rashid's accuracy and optimism.

Pascoe thanked Mrs Cooper and turned away, taking one last look at the circle of anaemic grass which marked where the tent had been. His romantic imagination would have liked to see it as some kind of enchanted ring, haunted by a ghost pleading for the rest that only revenge could give her. But if anything it looked like a green on a miniature golf-course. People strolled across it, uncaring or unaware that their substance was intersecting whatever insubstantial re-run of a murdered girl's last moments might be taking place there. Perhaps one of them would have a vision like those women at Versailles. Certainly it was beginning to feel as if only some supernatural intervention could carry them any further forward. Could Dalziel be persuaded to cross Rosetta Stanhope's palm with silver?

Back at the caravan he dented Brady's phlegm by asking if he'd noticed the scene of the crime being removed. He then left the sergeant with the task of getting together some men to search the fairground for the missing clothes. Not that he had much hope. The Choker would have needed only a second to step out of the dress in the lee of one of the sideshows and the thin cotton fabric would have rolled up to almost nothing. Then, if he had his wits about him which in one sense at least he clearly did, he would have taken the dress far away from the park before dumping it, or even burning it.

And Brady made the prospect even less hopeful by telling him that the rubbish skips had been emptied the previous day by the cleansing department.

'After you've looked round here, you'd better get down to the dump, hadn't you?' suggested Pascoe amiably. 'Just the job for a hot day!'

❖ ❖ ❖

On his return to the station he was held up at the entrance to the car park by the emergence of an ambulance. He watched it move quietly down the service road, turn into the main traffic stream and was interested to note that only then did its lights start flashing and bells clanging.

Entering, he went straight up to Dalziel's room.

'Where the hell have you been hiding?' demanded the fat man.

'What's up? I saw an ambulance.'

'You don't know? God, you'll go far. Lily-white hands,' sneered Dalziel. 'They've just carted Lee off to hospital, all right?'

Pascoe was not offended by his superior's tone. He'd grown accustomed to his style and besides, he could see the fat man was worried.

'What happened?'

'Nothing. I had a few words with him. He just kept on moaning about this pain. I thought he was shooting the shit so I...'

'Yes, sir,' prompted Pascoe.

'I just yelled at him,' said Dalziel. 'What do you think I did? Next thing, he's lying on the floor. Well, then I called the quack. He says it could be appendix, he's not sure. Those bastards never are! So we got an ambulance.'

'You were alone when you questioned him, sir?'

'Yes,' said Dalziel.

Pascoe thought for a moment. He'd never seen his superior quite so ill at ease before.

'You'll have called the ACC, sir?' he said.

'That twat! Why should I want to call him?'

'Before someone else does,' said Pascoe. 'Excuse me.'

He went downstairs. Wield was ahead of him, studying the logged entries of the Lees' admission.

'Trouble?' said the sergeant.

'If we all do our duty, we'll come to no harm,' said Pascoe. 'Let's have a look at the chimney.'

He whistled when he saw the book.

'That's a long time.'

'And he was complaining from when he arrived. Said he'd been punched,' said Wield.

'The woman, she's still here?' asked Pascoe. 'Jesus! Get her out, get her down to the hospital, you go with her. And hang about there. Take a WPC to keep an eye on *her*, you watch *him*. They're both in police custody still, right?'

Back in Dalziel's office he found the fat man talking on the phone.

'Yes, sir,' he was saying. 'Both of them. She may be an accomplice.'

Pascoe scribbled on a bit of paper and passed it over. Dalziel glanced at it. His tone became injured.

'Of course, sir,' he said. 'She's at the hospital now. With one of my sergeants and a WPC. We're not without feelings, sir.'

He winked conspiratorially at Pascoe who felt at the same time relieved and uneasy. He was willing to close ranks a bit, but he had no intention of letting loyalty loom larger than legality. That was all right for the public schools, not so hot for the public service.

'That's all right then,' said Dalziel, replacing the receiver. 'Thanks, Peter.'

'For what? I was just tidying up,' said Pascoe.

He must have stressed the participle more than he intended.

'As opposed to *covering* up?' said Dalziel. 'Not to worry, lad. I won't drag you to the scaffold with me! Or mebbe that bugger Lee won't come out of the anaesthetic eh? They're mostly black buggers down there, operate with assegais!'

He roared with laughter.

'Or mebbe he'll be too busy answering charges to make them,' he continued.

'I hope you haven't got him lined up for the Stanhope killing, sir,' said Pascoe, glad to be back at the job in hand. 'I think you'll find he's about nine inches too tall.'

'Eh?'

Briefly Pascoe sketched his interview with Rosetta Stanhope.

'Christ, this should have been spotted earlier,' said Dalziel angrily. 'This has been bloody sloppy. And it's not the only thing either.'

In his turn he related the news about Brenda Sorby's money and the suspected tie-up with the notes found in Lee's caravan.

'What made you look in the flour jar, sir?'

'It was out of place up there with his valuables,' said Dalziel. 'Silly bugger probably didn't like to leave it in the kitchen where it'd have been inconspicuous but might have tempted his missus!'

'You don't think she knew about it?'

'Who knows?' said Dalziel. 'It'll be interesting to see whose prints are on the notes, if those idle buggers at the lab ever get round to looking at them! Whether she knows or not, Lee's got his own subtle methods to keep her mouth shut. Have you seen her face? By the way, talking of battered wives, I had lunch with yours today. Funny company she keeps.'

'It would seem so,' said Pascoe.

'Aye. That Lacewing. At the Aero Club. The fellow who runs it. Greenall, his name is, do you know owt about him?'

'Never heard of him,' said Pascoe. 'Why?'

'Nothing really. Just that while every other sod was saying how strange it was for an important fellow like me to be wasting his time on a tuppenny-halfpenny break-in, he just seemed to take it for granted. Still, the world's full of funny buggers and he pours a liberal Scotch. What else have you been up to that I ought to know about, Peter?'

Pascoe told him about Wildgoose and his visit to the Linden Garden Centre.

'Odd sod, is he?' said Dalziel.

'Not by contemporary standards,' protested Pascoe. 'In fact, of his type, almost conventional.'

'Abandons his family, screws young girls, dresses like a teenager, and spends his holidays on the golden fucking road to Samarkand? That's conventional, is it?' snarled Dalziel. 'God, give me the Dave Lees any time. At least he was *born* a bloody gyppo.'

This interesting sociological discussion was interrupted by a tap on the door. It was the desk sergeant.

'Sorry to interrupt, sir, but there's a young lady downstairs. Name of Pritchard. She's a solicitor, sir. Says she's come about Mr and Mrs Lee.'

'That Lacewing bitch!' roared Dalziel. 'Tell her to…no, just tell her the Lees are no longer being held here. If she doesn't go quietly, ask to see her authorization to represent them. And if she can't show you that, which she can't, boot her out.'

'I'm not to mention the hospital then, sir?' said the sergeant.

Dalziel clasped his huge grizzled head in his large spatulate hands.

'Oh God,' he said. 'No wonder murders get done! You mention the hospital, Sergeant, and you're likely to end in it. Get out!'

His bellow almost drowned the telephone bell. Pascoe picked up the receiver. It was Harry Hopper at the lab.

'That fertilizer you sent us. Well, that's what it is. Fertilizer. Proprietary brand, just like it says on the bag. No usable prints on the bag. Yes, the same stuff as they found on McCarthy's clothes. But as we know, that doesn't signify as there were bags of the same stuff in Mr Ribble's shed.'

'Thanks, Harry,' said Pascoe. 'I didn't expect any more.'

'Is that Hopper?' demanded Dalziel. 'Ask him if he's got owt for me yet.'

'I heard,' said Hopper before Pascoe could relay the message. 'There's a report on the way. Nothing startling, except that the money had been sodden wet, then dried out.'

'Wet?' echoed Dalziel who had brought his right ear close to the receiver. 'How wet?'

'The notes had been totally immersed in water and then dried out. Simple as that,' said Hopper. 'It's in the report.'

Pascoe and Dalziel looked at each other speculatively, then the fat man made a dismissive gesture towards the phone.

'Thanks, Harry,' said Pascoe.

'Hang about,' said Hopper. 'I hadn't finished with you when we were so rudely interrupted. We also had a look at the sack.'

'The sack?'

'The one you'd put the fertilizer bag in. We're very thorough despite the lack of proper appreciation.'

'And?' said Pascoe, aware of Dalziel's imminent impatience.

'Much more interesting. Dust, earth, the expectable stuff. Plus a few soft fibres. And a scattering of small globular achenes. He doesn't keep canaries, your man, does he?'

'What do you mean? And what's an achene?'

'A small hard plant-seed. In this case the plant is *cannabis sativa*. You'll often find its achenes in bird-food. But if you're not dealing with a bird-fancier, my boy, you're probably dealing with a hash-fancier. Someone's been growing Indian hemp on your patch!'

CHAPTER 17

This Friday seemed to have stretched out long enough to end the world, let alone the week. And it was still a long way from being over.

Dalziel set off for the lab. He liked to see people face to face when they were telling him something important and the report on the money he regarded as being of the essence. Not even Pascoe's awkwardly expressed opinion that the notes' erstwhile wetness was more likely to prove Lee's innocence than his guilt could deter the fat man.

'The girl was drowned, wasn't she? Near the fairground. Where the Stanhope girl was murdered. Your idea about the missing clothes is all right, Peter. But it's only a theory. Lee's mixed up in it somewhere. There's too many close connections for coincidence.'

'Close?' said Pascoe.

'Like I said, there's the fairground. And don't forget, Lee and the Stanhope girl were related,' said Dalziel triumphantly.

'By marriage. And very distantly!' protested Pascoe.

'There's no such thing as a distant relation by marriage,' said Dalziel coldly. 'If you don't know 'em, they're close. And if you do know 'em, they're here.'

And off he went, leaving Pascoe to meditate on the Wildgoose connection. When he found himself hypothesizing that the whole of the Linden Garden Centre had been given over to the growth of cannabis and that the murders were in reality a series of gangland killings triggered off by the Mafia's attempt to muscle in on the Mid-Yorkshire rackets, he shook his head, drank a cup of canteen coffee (the strongest anti-hallucinogen known to science) and got Control to raise DC Preece's car for him.

'Report,' he said.

Wildgoose had left the house shortly after Pascoe, Preece told him. He had walked about a quarter of a mile to Danby Row, a street of substantial Edwardian semis not yet overtaken by the spread of multiple occupation though on the fringe of the bed-sit area where Wildgoose's flat was situated. Here he had gone into No 73, where he had remained for forty-five minutes before returning to his flat.

'Was he carrying anything?' asked Pascoe.

A plastic carrier bag. Yes, he'd still got it when he left the house on Danby Row. On the way back he had gone into a bread shop and bought a loaf.

Pascoe said, 'All right, Preece. We can't tie up your valuable body like this for ever. Jack it in now. But on your way back here, find out what you can about who lives at 73 Danby Row. Pretend to be a Mormon missionary or something. On second thoughts, the way you look, a trainee window-cleaner touting for business would be more convincing. See me when you come in.'

Covering up for my superiors, putting down my subordinates, have I finally joined the establishment? wondered Pascoe uneasily.

He picked up his phone again and got through to the hospital to talk to Wield.

'Any word on Lee yet?' he asked.

'They reckon it's a perforated ulcer,' said Wield. 'His wife says he's been suffering with his guts for months. They're going to cut him open and take a look, but not till this evening. The silly sod grabbed a jugful of water and drank about half a gallon while he was lying around, so they won't touch him till that's safely out of the way.'

'Is he still going on about being assaulted?' asked Pascoe.

'I don't know. They won't let me near him. Do you want me to stay?'

'I think so,' said Pascoe after a moment's thought. 'I know it's a bore, but in the circumstances… And see if you can squeeze anything but abuse out of the wife.'

He told Wield about the lab report.

'Soaked? But why should the money have got wet?'

'Search me. It may not even be the same money, of course.'

'Perhaps not, sir. But I did have a thought about the other things. The ring and the watch. There's a jeweller's near the bank. *Conrad's*, I think. Locked up for the holidays, but he'd have been there on that Thursday.'

'Nice thinking,' complimented Pascoe. 'Let me know how things go. By the way, if a female solicitor called Pritchard shows up, be polite but firm. She's got no official standing. All right?'

'None politer, none firmer,' said Wield.

Next Pascoe got through to the Department of Education and Science in London, where after various delays and changes of personnel he was told that yes there was a Forces' school called Devon School near Linden, but for details of personnel he would need to get in touch with the Service Children's Education Authority at the Institute of Army Education. With a sigh Pascoe obeyed.

Things were no better here. Pascoe had to repeat himself several times and wonder audibly if there were some clause in the Official Secrets Act which covered Army education before he finally got someone who preferred to remain anonymous but who sounded sympathetic to promise to get back to him as soon as possible.

'Though it may be Monday morning,' concluded the voice, somewhat spoiling the good impression.

'I didn't think the Army recognized weekends,' said Pascoe.

'Things have changed. They run a course in weekend recognition at Sandhurst now,' said the voice. 'Bye.'

As Pascoe replaced the receiver, there was a perfunctory knock and Dicky Gladmann came in. 'They seemed pretty busy downstairs, so I just came on up,' he said, mouth a-beam above his spotted bow tie, and brightly bloodshoot eyes flickering inquisitively round the room.

'So much for security,' said Pascoe.

'Should I have been announced? I'm sorry,' said Gladmann with cheerful insincerity. 'But I carry my credentials with me.'

He held up a Sainsbury's carrier bag.

'The tapes? Oh good. So Mr Urquart is going to materialize also?'

'I think not,' said Gladmann, sitting down. 'We popped across to the University at lunch-time...'

'The University? I thought you said you had all you needed out at the College.'

'Not so. As you must know, being a sort of in-law of the place, the College is very small beer academically speaking, soon to evaporate completely. Our language lab is pretty OK but we felt we would really like to make sonograms of the tapes...'

'To make what?' interrupted Pascoe once more.

'Sonograms. Oh sorry. I thought the police were so technical these days. A sonogram is an analysis printed out by a machine called a sonograph and it displays the various distributions of energy across the frequency spectrum that occur for different sounds. OK?'

'If you say so. And there's one of these machines at the University?'

'Plus a rather delectable assistant professor who finds Drew's intellectual arrogance, social gaucheness and undamped body odour irresistible. God knows what noises they analyse together, but it's a wonder the machine hasn't exploded. So, while I have returned posthaste, he has remained. In the interests of science, naturally.'

'Naturally. *Is* there anything useful you can tell us, Mr Gladmann?' asked Pascoe.

'Well now. Here we go,' replied the linguist, upending the carrier bag so that the tapes and various bits and pieces of paper fell on to Pascoe's desk.

'This is our report,' said Gladmann, holding up a handful of sheets stapled together. 'It's pretty clear, I would say. I could take you through it if you like.'

'I'd be grateful.'

'OK. First, we're pretty well agreed there are four speakers involved here or a very high degree of mimicking. There was some resemblance in tempo and pitch range between (A) and (D), that is to say, *now get you to my lady's chamber* etc., and *the time is out of joint* etc. But there are several significant differences. They both use RP, Received Pronunciation, but it's fairly clear it's been received in rather different ways, ha ha.'

'Ha ha,' said Pascoe. 'Explain.'

'Well, if we look at the phonetic realization of those phonemes we find in both utterances, we can spot the following. In the word *to*, (A) uses a central vowel while (D) has a close back vowel. Like this.'

Gladmann demonstrated, Pascoe looked doubtful, Gladmann repeated the demonstration, Pascoe echoed the sounds, hesitantly at first, then with more certainty.

'By George, you've got it. I think you've got it,' said Gladmann.

'I could have danced all night,' rejoined Pascoe. 'Go on.'

'Next take (A)'s *now* and (D)'s *out*. (D) has the usual RP diphthong in which the glide begins with an unrounded open back vowel, whereas (A) has a diphthong in which the glide begins from much further forward and nearer a half open position.'

Again the demonstration.

'Note also,' continued Gladmann, the bit between his teeth now, 'that where (D)'s stressed-syllable-initial voiceless plosives (as in *time* and *cursed*) are aspirated, in (A) they are not.'

'Hang on. What does that mean?'

'Well, when they're aspirated, they're said with a little puff of air accompanying the release…'

'I know what *aspirated* means, also *exasperated*,' said Pascoe. 'But what does it *signify*?'

'Ah, always the policeman,' said Gladmann sadly. 'You could say that the aspiration is normal in RP, and its absence often occurs in Northern regional accents. Similarly, while the one final voiceless plosive we find in (D), that is, in *spite*, is unreleased, in (A) all the final voiceless plosives are glottalized.'

'You mean, spat out?'

'If you like,' said Gladmann, as if disheartened.

'So, conclusions please.'

'If you must,' said Gladmann, '(D) is fairly simple. He speaks RP of a kind he probably learned in a middle-class home and during the course of an education, not necessarily private, but certainly grammar school and probably in the Home Counties. There are a couple of relatively conservative features of his version of RP which underline these conclusions. When he says *O*, the glide of the diphthong begins with a centralized back vowel quality and in *born* his pronunciation of the vowel is diphthongal rather than the monophthongal one common among younger RP speakers.'

'Yes, yes,' said Pascoe impatiently. 'And (A)?'

'Here we would say there has been a fairly marked regional accent which has been changed, for whatever reason, towards a modified RP. Some regional features remain. Northern, certainly. Drew Urquhart did some field work in dialectology in north Derbyshire last summer and he claims he got an odd echo from those parts, but he tends to be a bit obsessive about his own interests.'

'OK,' said Pascoe. 'What about the others.'

'Well, they say rather less, but fortunately say it rather more revealingly in regional terms. *One may smile and smile, and be a villain.* Note the giveaway *one*, the diphthongal pronunciation of the vowel in *be* and the very close articulation of the first vowel in *villain.* West Midlands, certainly. Birmingham, very likely. And even you, I'm sure, Inspector, spotted that (C) was a Scot. The final 'r' in *or* tells all, though if you want further evidence, you could point to the use of a closer back vowel for *not* than an educated Englishman would employ.'

'That's excellent,' said Pascoe, not sure if it was or not. 'And these are the sonograms I suppose. What do they tell us?'

He picked up some lengths of thin paper printed with wavy varying vibration patterns above a scale.

'They help to confirm that four different speakers are involved,' said Gladmann. 'And if you're fortunate enough, or perhaps unfortunate enough, to get another message on tape, they'd help us work out which of these four it might have come from. Do you think that one of these is definitely this Choker chappie?'

'It's very likely,' said Pascoe.

'Well, I hope you get him. Though incidentally, young Drew asked me to be certain to reiterate his objection to the use of our findings in any but the most peripheral supportive role.'

'Did he?' said Pascoe. 'Well, thank him, and tell him we won't rush into anything, though over the next month we hope to arrest the entire population of Scotland and the West Midlands on suspicion.'

He stood up and held out his hand.

Gladmann took it and held it a little longer than convention required. Not all the spots on his bow tie were in the original pattern, Pascoe noticed. He got a sense that the man was rather lonely and glad of the contact involved in helping the police with their enquiries.

'Which part of the world are you from, Mr Gladmann?' he heard himself asking. It was not the most diplomatic of questions even to a duller mind than the linguist's.

'Surrey,' he answered with a half smile. 'Good solid bourgeois background. Old grammar school, nice class of kid. And I got my first degree in Eng. Lit., Renaissance drama a speciality. Good day to you, now, Inspector. Don't forget. Call on me at any time.'

Pascoe sat and ruminated on what Gladmann had told him for a few minutes, but then he put the report and the tapes away in a filing cabinet and got down to some overdue paperwork. Tomorrow, Saturday, should be his day off and he wanted to be as up to date as possible.

After half an hour he was interrupted by the return of DC Preece.

No 73 Danby Row, he reported, was the property of one Hubert Valentine, who worked in the Rates and Valuation department of the local council and who was presently on holiday in Minorca with his wife. His seventeen-year-old daughter, Andrea, was alone in the house.

'Very tasty,' said Preece, grinning salaciously. 'I told her I was on a consumer research survey for a big record company. What did she buy, what did her parents buy? It all came out. Very friendly girl.'

What had also come out was that Andrea was a sixth-form pupil at the Bishop Crump Comprehensive School. Preece's description fitted the girl Pascoe had seen leaving Wildgoose's flat that morning.

He dismissed Preece and got back to work, but a few minutes later, Dalziel burst in.

'Bloody lab,' he said. 'A few residuals, nothing. The watch is one of them digital things, new. Waterproof so they can't say if it's been in the water or not. No way of tracing where it was bought. The ring's nine carat gold. There's an inscription inside. *All my love all my life*. And there's a monogram on the signet. Too fancy to be clear with all them curlicues and things but it could be MLA or WTA. Neither of the things has been reported missing.'

Pascoe rose and went to his filing cabinet.

'What about TAM?' he said.

'What about it?'

'Tommy Maggs's middle name is Arthur.'

He passed on Wield's thought about the holidaymaking jeweller.

'That's possible. That'd explain a lot,' said Dalziel. 'There's a brain behind that ugly mask. When's this jeweller expected back?'

'Tomorrow, the notice on his door said, according to Wield.'

'Right. We'll be waiting for him. Meanwhile, let's assume that he did provide the ring and the watch. So, Brenda draws out the cash, spends some of it on the watch and the ring—which must have been ordered in advance, obviously, to get the inscription done. And somehow the whole bloody lot ends up in Lee's caravan. That bugger's got some explaining to do!'

'Not for a while yet,' said Pascoe, telling him about the operation.

'At least we know where he is. Do you know what time it is, lad?'

'Late,' said Pascoe.

'Nigh on opening time. Let's wash the day away.' Pascoe demurred, but Dalziel was not in a mood to be denied.

'It's your day off tomorrow, isn't it? Ellie will see quite enough of you then. It's being scarce that makes a thing valuable.'

'A quick one, then,' conceded Pascoe.

As he tidied up his desk, he told the fat man about Gladmann's findings. Dalziel was unimpressed.

'Linguists, psychiatrists, crap-merchants the lot of them.'

'Maybe,' said Pascoe. 'But Dave Lee doesn't fit into this phone-call pattern at all.'

'So mebbe it means nothing.'

'And Pottle's reading of the Choker doesn't fit Lee either.'

'Pottle! What's he know?'

'He's been right before.'

'So had Pontius Pilate. Are you going to be all night?' He clattered down the stairs ahead of Pascoe, but pulled up sharp at the swing-doors which opened into the main foyer of the station and peered cautiously through the central crack. When Pascoe joined him the fat man put a huge finger cautiously to his lips and motioned his subordinate to peep through.

At the desk a youngish woman in a grey dress was talking to the sergeant.

'If I am not to be allowed access to Mr and Mrs Lee wherever they are, then I insist on talking to the officer in charge of the case,' she said in a clear, angry voice.

'I'm not sure if he's in, Miss Pritchard,' said the sergeant.

'Then you'd better find out,' insisted the woman.

Reluctantly the sergeant picked up his telephone.

'Lacewing's solicitor?' whispered Pascoe.

'Aye. Come on, lad, before she starts searching the building.'

And chortling gleefully, Dalziel led the way to the rear exit.

CHAPTER 18

Shortly before seven p.m. Dave Lee was wheeled off to the operating theatre. Only the fact that it was Friday evening and the consultant treasured his Saturday morning golf prevented the gypsy from being put into storage overnight, or so the ward sister assured Wield. The sergeant was pleased to have the man anaesthetized so that he could relax his vigilance. He went down to the hospital canteen but changed his mind when he spotted Mrs Lee with her attendant WPC, both tucking into healthy portions of pie, peas and chips. Instead he went for a stroll outside to get the smell of medicine and illness out of his nostrils.

His perambulations took him past the entrance to Casualty as an ambulance drew up. He paused and watched with professional interest the unhurried efficiency with which the attendants got the incoming patient out of the vehicle and on to the trolley. As the man was wheeled by him, the sergeant looked down. There had been considerable violence here, he saw with a small shock. One eye was closed by a huge and purple swelling, the lips were cracked and bleeding, the nose looked as if it might be broken and the open mouth through which bloody spittle bubbled revealed at least two broken teeth.

The still-functioning eye touched Wield's face in passing and for a second registered something other than pain. The reaction suddenly brought the damaged individual features into a single focus and Wield felt a second shock, stronger than the first.

It was Ron Ludlam.

He followed the trolley through the automatic doors. One of the ambulance men was talking to the girl on reception.

'Excuse me,' interrupted Wield. 'What happened to him?'

When he reinforced his question with his warrant card, the ambulance man said, 'Fell down stairs.'

'Eh?'

'That's what he says, mate. And that's what his sister says. I just bring 'em in.'

'His sister. That'd be Mrs Pickersgill, right? Where's she?'

'Coming on later, she said. It was her that rang us. She was very upset.'

'Not upset enough to come with you, though?' said Wield.

'Mebbe she had things to do, baby to feed, old mother to look after. Like I said, I just bring 'em in.'

Wield now went after the trolley which, after a bit of trial and error, he found in one of the examination cubicles.

A nurse was talking to the second ambulance man and taking down details. It struck Wield that they seemed to spend rather a lot of time taking down details but he supposed it was necessary for them to know what they were dealing with.

Again his warrant card worked and he leaned over the recumbent figure.

'Ron,' he said.

The eye flickered recognition if not welcome.

'What happened, Ron?'

The tongue moved like a blind animal in the ruined mouth. He caught the word *stairs*.

'Ho ho. Come on, Ron, Frankie did this, didn't he?'

There was a vigorous shaking of the head which must have caused considerable pain and Ludlam even managed to raise himself up on his elbow and say with a hard-won clarity, 'I fell down stairs.'

'All right, take it easy. Let's have a look at you.'

The doctor had arrived. Wield found himself eased out into the corridor. Not that he resisted much. If Ron in this state was determined not to put the finger on his brother-in-law, his mind must have been very firmly made up. Presumably Janey had passed on the information Wield had left with her that morning. Presumably Frankie had blown his gasket. Presumably it was fear of more of the same that was keeping Ludlam's mouth shut.

Presumably...presumably...

He didn't like the feel of it, Wield realized. If Ron had shot his mouth off in his present state, then recanted like mad when wiser counsel returned with health, that might have made sense. This way, there had to be something else, some extra pressure. Something.

He thought of ringing George Headingley and suggesting he should send a man round to see Pickersgill. It was after all the Spinks's warehouse case that was likely to be involved here.

Instead, knowing he was ripe for an excuse to get away from the hospital but unable to resist the temptation, he checked Dave Lee's status, which was alive and well but unconscious, and headed for the car park. As he drove out, a taxi came in. There was a woman alone in the back and he thought he recognized Janey Pickersgill. That cleared the ground nicely, he thought.

It took a lot of ringing at the doorbell to get any reply. Finally Pickersgill's face scowled out through a span about six inches wide.

'What do you want?' he demanded.

'You,' said Wield promptly. 'Better let me in, Frankie.'

Grudgingly he was admitted. Pickersgill was a long wiry man with a narrow face and restless eyes. He was wearing his working clothes—jeans and a white sweat shirt. Wield guessed that he had arrived home just as Janey was confronting her brother with the accusation that he'd fingered Frankie for the whisky job. Given time, she might have decided not to tell her husband, but she'd have been unable to miss lashing out at her brother first. Once Frankie picked up what was going on, he would have been unstoppable.

'I've just been talking to Ron,' said Wield. 'Oh yes. No need to look surprised. They called us right away when they heard what had happened to him.'

'*Heard*? Heard what?'

'That's right, Frankie. I said *heard*. He's been chatting away as fast as he can through the broken teeth.'

'What's he say, then?' asked Pickersgill defiantly.

For answer Wield grabbed his wrists, turned the hands over and struck the bruised and swelling knuckles together.

'You'll find it hard to hold a steering-wheel,' he said. 'Still, you probably won't have to for a while.'

'What the hell are you on about?' demanded Pickersgill. 'What's all this about Ron, anyway? I've just got home this minute. I had a bit of an accident with my hands, that's all.'

'Fell down stairs as well, did you? It doesn't matter anyway, Frankie. Assault and battery's the least of your troubles, son.'

Pickersgill tried to pull his hands away but Wield's grip was unbreakable.

'That's right, Frankie. Ron's gone all the way. You didn't think he wouldn't, did you? I mean, he's done it once, hasn't he, so why not again? So now there's just our Janey to alibi you and you know what her word's worth after last time.'

Pickersgill's reaction was not what he'd expected. Incredulity first, then simple bewilderment, then something not far off amusement.

'You're telling me he says it was me that got into Spinks's warehouse?' he said. 'You want me to believe he's got the nerve to try that? You'll have to do a lot better than that, Mr Wield!'

I shall indeed, thought Wield, trying desperately to interpret this unforeseen turn. I shall indeed.

And he did. It was stupidly simple.

'It's the other way round, isn't it, Frankie?' he said softly. 'It's not been him alibi-ing you, but you alibi-ing him.'

He let go of the hands. He had no need of contact now. He had a stronger, better kind of grip on Pickersgill, the grip of a charge he could make stick.

'*You* lied about *him* being here that night. That's obstruction, Frankie. At the very least, we've got you for obstruction.'

The long thin face was sullen and uncertain.

'I don't know what you're on about,' he said.

It's Janey, thought Wield. Janey's told him the beating was enough. But it's a long way from being enough in Frankie's eyes.

'All right,' he said. 'You'd better come down to the nick with me, Frankie.'

'What the hell for?'

'Just to keep you out of the way, mainly,' said Wield. 'Though we'll think of something better for your brief. You'll need a brief, Frankie. You see, after I've shut you up, I'm going back to the hospital where I'll tell Ron you've shopped him for the Spinks job. Now, I reckon he's going to tell me you were the other man on that job.'

'Me! Do a job with that cowboy? You know that's not on, Mr Wield!'

'Mebbe I do, mebbe I don't. Who was the second man then, Frankie? Come on, lad. You know the watchman's dead. You don't want to be mixed up in this any more than you have to. Who was he?'

Again the unexpected reaction. A sort of triumphant amusement emerging in a raucous rush of laughter which almost drowned the noise of a door opening.

Almost.

Wield spun round and darted into the long narrow entrance hall. The front door was shut but at the other end the door which led into the kitchen was wide open and through it Wield could see a figure fumbling at the exit to the back yard.

It must have been locked. It was only half open when Wield reached him, hands flat and stiff like butcher's cleavers. The figure turned, his hands raised also. But one look at the pale and frightened face told Wield that the only intention here was a terrified defence.

Lowering his own arms, he smiled, the smile playing round his pitted face like a butterfly on a slag heap.

In response the other relaxed also and let his hands fall slowly from before his youthful anxious features.

'Hello, Tommy,' said Wield.

CHAPTER 19

Statement of Thomas Arthur Maggs made at Mid-Yorkshire Police HQ in the presence of Detective-Sergeant V. K. Wield.

'I'm sorry about all the trouble I've caused. I didn't mean it but there didn't seem much else to do. It was all on top of me and Ron said I'd be dropping him in the shit if I told the truth but likely I would have done if the watchman hadn't died. I want whoever killed Brenda to get caught even though whatever they do to him won't be enough. But I didn't want to go to prison myself not for murder which is what I knew I'd get done for even though I never touched the man. That was Ron. I know it doesn't make any difference because I was there anyway, but it was Ron not me that hit him.

'It was all Ron's idea really. Brenda should have met me in the Bay Tree at eight o'clock that night only she didn't turn up. I wasn't all that surprised because we'd had a big row the previous night. It was about how far we should go now we'd got engaged.

We'd just got engaged and I thought we could do it, I mean, go all the way now that it was fixed we were going to marry, but she wouldn't. Not inside her. Everything else, but not inside her and I got a bit annoyed and so did she. So when she didn't turn up, I thought she was just carrying on the row.

'Ron was there and we drank together till nearly nine. It was very crowded by then and I was a bit pissed off with being stood up so we went off to have a drive around and see what we could find to do. Ron had a bottle of whisky and we thought we might find some spare and go for a drive. We looked in a couple of places but there wasn't much on and we ended up parked alongside Spinks's warehouse having a drink when Ron said why shouldn't we do it? So we did. It was just a bit of fun till the watchman came. It was dead easy getting in and we'd found a box full of pocket transistors when this old fellow comes through the door, waving a torch. Ron hit him and pushed him over and we ran. We only had a couple of transistors apiece but it didn't matter because like I say it still seemed just a bit of fun.

'But when the car broke down on the way home, we got worried. So Ron stuffed all the transistors up his bomber jacket and he took off with them in case anyone should come along asking questions. The coppers rolled up just a few minutes later so I told them I'd been out with my girl-friend and she'd set off home by herself when the car broke down. Then they tested me and took me in for a blood test so I had to keep on lying especially as I heard they'd found out about the break-in while I was there and the watchman was badly hurt.

'Next morning I tried to ring Brenda at the bank to square things with her, but she wasn't there. And when the police came round to the garage later on and told me she'd disappeared, I was worried sick. Ron said I'd better stick to my story. It'd be daft to say something that incriminated us, then find that Brenda had just gone off somewhere in the huff. I didn't think she had, though. She wasn't that sort of girl. When they came round and told me they'd found her, I was so sick I thought I'd die. I didn't know what to do. I mean, I wasn't thinking at all. I just wanted to curl up. Ron said to keep quiet still because by now the watchman was critical. But it wasn't just that. I just couldn't think of doing anything because all I could think of was Brenda.

'Then the watchman died and I was a bit better by then and wondering what I should do. But when he died it was as bad as ever, so I took off in the car. It got me as far as Watford Gap, then it broke down. I sat around for a bit drinking tea and thinking of hitching a ride to London. But in the end I just crossed the motorway and got a lift back north. I've been living with Ron round at his sister's house since then. I didn't know what to do after the fight but Janey said it would be all right, Ron had had it coming to him, but it was over now and nothing more would happen. Then Mr Wield, Sergeant Wield that is, came round and I listened and I could see that he was on to us and I decided I'd better get away again.

'I'm really sorry about all this and I'm sorry the watchman's dead and I wish he wasn't but I want to do anything I can to help the police catch whoever it was that killed my Brenda.'

'That'll grab them in the gallery,' said Dalziel. 'There'll be more water in the jury box than on a test match wicket at Manchester.'

'I feel sorry for the lad,' said Wield quietly.

'That's a bad sign, Sergeant. Next thing you'll be putting stamps on your Christmas cards.'

Dalziel yawned. It was eight-thirty on Saturday morning. After Maggs had made his statement the previous night, Dalziel had talked to him earnestly for nearly two hours, going over everything again and again. His instinct had been to explore the new dimensions opened up by the statement instantly, but in the end he had decided to sleep on it, using as a soporific half a bottle of Scotch.

Now he was stretching himself, ready for action.

The news from the hospital was that Dave Lee had had a good night. Better still from Dalziel's point of view had been the confirmation of the hospital diagnosis of a perforated ulcer whose condition could hardly have been aggravated by a blow to the stomach. Ludlam too was doing well. He had refused to say anything when questioned briefly after Maggs's statement and the doctor had insisted that the interview be postponed till the morning. But Frankie Pickersgill had talked freely till Janey arrived on the scene and let her split loyalties tear her into hysterics.

'You see what this means, Sergeant,' continued Dalziel.

Wield, who had seen what it meant the minute Tommy had started talking, prepared himself to be amused at the fat man's analysis.

'We haven't got a single sighting of Brenda from the time she left the bank, that's what it means. We weren't bothered as long as we thought she'd met up with Tommy at half-eight. But now things look different. We're back to square one. Every man who's got anything to do with this case, I'll want him checked out again. Before, we were just asking what they were doing at eleven o'clock that night. Now I want to know what they were doing at six o'clock! That bank manager, for instance. Mulgan. You said he was reported to have a bit of a lech going for the girl. Mebbe he offered her a lift into town after work. That schoolteacher too. And Lee, of course. We'll need to get round the lot. I think I'll give Mr Pascoe a ring.'

'I thought it was his day off, sir,' said Wield neutrally. 'And with the Spinks job cleared up, won't we be able to use Mr Headingley's men?'

'There's a lot of loose ends there still. And what will they know about anything anyway?' said Dalziel irritably. 'No, we need men who've got this thing at their fingertips.'

He reached for the phone.

Pascoe answered with a sharp, suspicious *Yes?* and his tone did not change when he realized who it was.

He listened to Dalziel's digest of Maggs's statement and its implications without comment or question.

'You don't seem all that interested, Peter,' said Dalziel in an injured tone.

'Don't I, sir? I'm sorry. I'm not long up. Ellie hasn't been feeling too well and we had a rather disturbed night.'

'Nowt serious, I hope,' said Dalziel.

'I don't think so. But I reckon she ought to lie on in bed.'

'Best place for her,' said Dalziel expertly. 'These things always happen at weekends.'

'What things?'

'Anything,' said Dalziel. 'But I'm glad it's not serious. Look, I know it's your day off, but if Ellie's just going to be lying around, I'd appreciate it if you could pop in and lend a hand for a couple of hours. After you've taken her breakfast up, of course.'

'Now that's what I call big of you, Andy,' interrupted Ellie's voice.

'Ellie! You've got yourself up after all,' said Dalziel.

'No, I've been eavesdropping on the extension,' she said. 'Early morning calls on Peter's day off always fill me with suspicion.'

'Are you all right, lass? I told you yesterday, this flying wasn't for you in your condition.'

'Flying?' said Pascoe.

'I didn't go flying,' protested Ellie. 'Listen, Andy, I'll do a deal. Peter goes in today, he gets next Friday and Saturday off, no reservations, no conditions, earthquakes, wind and fire not excepted.'

'You have my personal guarantee,' said Dalziel.

'Now hold on,' began Pascoe.

'Soon as you can, Peter,' said Dalziel hastily. 'Ellie, brandy's the stuff, listen to an expert.'

'Brandy? The stuff for what?'

'Owt that Scotch can't cure. Take care!'

Pascoe went slowly up to the bedroom.

'Eavesdropping now, is it?'

'Certainly.'

'What's all this about next Friday?'

'Well, we've got to go down and see my mother sometime and I thought it'd be nice to stay overnight.'

'Jesus. And for this I give up my Saturday?'

'I could invite her up here for a while,' said Ellie.

'All right, you win. But listen, are you sure you feel OK?'

'Never better. I'll give Thelma a ring, maybe. Now what was it you said about breakfast?'

Later as he cleared away the tray, he said, 'Are you sure there's nothing else you want?'

She looked lugubriously down at her swelling breasts and belly.

'How about a nice big shiny egg we could take turns to sit on? And when it hatched, out would pop a nice little brat about six years old with your eyes and my nose all neatly dressed and talking and ready for school.'

He smiled so uncertainly that she laughed at him and pulled him down and kissed his mouth.

'OK,' she said. 'I'll say the right things and do the dewy-eyed bit, but not all the time. And whatever I have, I promise you I'm bringing the little sod up to be a transvestite.'

'Everyone'll be transvestite by the time he's old enough to enjoy it,' said Pascoe. 'Me, I sometimes wish I could spend my Saturdays lying in bed, contributing to the Life Force.'

'Get knotted,' she said amicably. 'It's the police force that's got you hooked. Now push off, or you might miss being in at the kill and you know how you'd hate that.'

He was on the landing when she called out, 'Peter!'

He rushed back in full of anxiety.

'Yes? What's wrong?'

'Nothing. Christ, you mustn't be so nervous. You'll never last another four months! No, it was just what Andy was saying about that boy's statement. I just thought.'

'All right, Sherlock. Shoot.'

'Well,' said Ellie, running her fingers through her hair. 'You know you laughed at me when I said that perhaps what the medium said in her trance might have come out of some time-slip caused by the violence of death?'

'Yes, I remember it well.'

'All right. But now there doesn't need to be a time-slip, does there? I mean, if she didn't meet her boyfriend, who knows what time she got killed? The sun could have been shining anyway. Perhaps that medium woman got some of it right after all.'

❀ ❀ ❀

Sergeant Wield had the perfect excuse for calling on Mulgan at home. He had promised to pick up the list of Brenda Sorby's transactions on the day of her death, but developments had prevented him from doing so the previous evening.

Mrs Mulgan, looking worried almost to the point of fear, admitted him first to the entrance hall of their ugly detached bungalow where he spoke with her in a low voice for several minutes, then to the lounge where Mulgan, reading the *Daily Mail* in his shirtsleeves, looked annoyed and made it clear he'd have preferred to deal with the sergeant on the doorstep. Unabashed, Wield accepted Mrs Mulgan's offer of a coffee.

'What use can this stuff be to you anyway?' asked Mulgan after his wife had gone out.

'The information about the money was very useful indeed, sir,' said Wield.

'Yes. Well, that was different. These other transactions can hardly be relevant. I hope you're not going to be bothering our customers.'

'I'm sure every one of them would want to help catch our man, sir. Every little helps. Someone somewhere knows something.'

'You mean, someone's protecting this lunatic?' said Mulgan incredulously.

'Maybe. Or perhaps someone doesn't realize what they know. Could be you, sir.'

'Me?' said Mulgan, thick lips pursed. 'Hardly. I gave you a comprehensive statement.'

'First statements aren't usually. Comprehensive, I mean. I mean, they can't be, really.'

'*First* statements.'

'Oh yes, sir. Often one's enough, but when we get a bit bogged down, we start crossing the t's and dotting the i's. We'll be going over everything again with everyone. For instance, sir, we know all about what you did that Thursday till the time the bank was closed, but nothing after that.'

'Oh yes you do,' said Mulgan sarcastically. 'You made sure, without, I may say, a great deal of subtlety, that I was at home that evening about the time that poor Brenda was killed.'

'What time was that, sir?'

'Between eleven and midnight the papers said. During the storm.'

'That's true, sir,' said Wield ambiguously. 'I'm sorry if we were heavy-handed, but we have to check everyone. No, it's the earlier bit of the evening I'm interested in. We're still trying to find someone who saw Brenda earlier, so those as would have recognized her are particularly interesting. Did you go straight home from the bank?'

'I think so. I may have popped into the shops along the parade. It's very handy; at least my wife thinks it so.'

He laughed and played with the square, black-rimmed spectacles he wore to read his paper.

'It was Thursday, sir,' prompted Wield gently. 'Half-day closing here. But late opening in the town centre. You didn't go into the centre, did you?'

'No. I very rarely do. And Thursday or not, Jennings', that's the newsagents, he's always open. I usually pick up an evening paper there.'

'Then you'd drive home?'

'Yes.'

'Arriving when?'

'Six at least. Often earlier.'

'Nice to have regular hours, sir,' said Wield appreciatively. 'I expect Mrs Mulgan likes it too. Do you eat at the same time most nights?'

'Yes. Half six, usually. It's our main meal of the day. If you want the details, Sergeant, though I can't imagine why, my wife and I will probably sit and have a sherry and talk about the day, then we eat, wash up, go out for a stroll perhaps if the weather's nice, or potter in the garden. Watch a bit of television, then bed. That's about it.'

'And that night was no different.'

'Very few of them are different enough to be distinguishable, Sergeant,' said Mulgan. 'Had it been, though, I would certainly recall.'

He put his spectacles back on and looked pointedly at his newspaper as though to indicate the interview was over.

Wield gave him a quarter-minute.

'It was a Thursday, though, sir,' he said.

Mulgan didn't look up.

'Yes?' he said.

'And your wife was saying that most Thursdays she goes to visit her mother in the afternoon. She often doesn't get back till eight. Or later.'

Now Mulgan looked up again.

'That's right,' he said. 'And as it was a Thursday, she probably wasn't in when I got home and probably didn't get back till late. What are you trying to say, Sergeant? And why didn't you tell me you'd been cross-examining my wife too.'

'No, honestly, I'm sorry,' said Wield, rearranging his features into a new chaos which his tone signalled meant distress. 'All I wondered was, did you maybe stop off, have a drink somewhere that night? I mean there'd be no rush to get home, would there? And if so, did you perhaps see anything of Brenda, just passing, I mean? Or talking to someone?'

The bait was a bit obvious, he thought. Guilty or innocent, Mulgan would see it dangling there.

'I'll tell you something, Sergeant,' said the manager with a sigh. 'Then perhaps you'll go away and leave me to get on with my weekend, and tell the world you're a liar if you try to use what I've told you. I fancied Brenda. Yes, it's clear someone's suggested this to you, and it's true. She was a nice girl, I felt relaxed with her and we could have a laugh and a joke together. If I'd had the slightest encouragement, well, who knows what any of us might not do with encouragement! But I didn't and when I realized our other junior Miss Brighouse, who no doubt is your source of information, was ready to make a joke of it, I became the soul of correctness. I have no desire to be a joke to empty-headed children, Sergeant. When I saw her engagement ring, I made sure my congratulations were formal and sincere, which indeed they were. I never saw her again after she said good night that Thursday evening. Now if that completes the inquisition, perhaps you'd like to cast your eye over these transactions in case there's anything you want to ask. I should prefer to have the rest of my weekend free from interruption.'

There was something not quite right about Mulgan's man-of-the-world confession and sarcastic dismissal, but it possibly had nothing to do with the case. As a long-established expert in putting up fronts, Wield had a sharp ear and eye for uncertainties of tone and manner. Mulgan, he decided, seemed to think that being an acting manager somehow meant *acting* like a manager. He was probably right too. Being a policeman certainly involved a lot of role-playing. Pascoe had once said that. Clever bugger. Too clever by half, according to Dalziel in his darker moments. Wield thought he'd got the pair of 'em worked out. Pay heed to what Pascoe says but do as Dalziel does. What would Dalziel do now?

Probably put his shark-like mouth to Mulgan's shell-like ear and enquire in a Force Ten murmur how many members of his staff an acting manager could expect to screw in an average week.

Instead Wield cast his eye down the list, not really seeing it, said, 'This looks fine, sir. I hope it won't be necessary to trouble you again. This morning, anyway.' And left.

When he signed back on watch through his car radio, a message was awaiting him.

He smiled sadly as he listened to the instructions for him to rendezvous with Inspector Pascoe at the Aero Club in fifteen minutes' time.

So much for the sanctity of a detective's day off.

Do as Dalziel does, was the golden rule.

And what does Dalziel do?

What he bloody well wants!

CHAPTER 20

Pascoe did not like what he was doing.

To him it seemed that Dalziel was becoming obsessed with Lee.

'But there's no real evidence,' he protested. 'OK, it's reasonable to expect him to account for the money and the ring and watch. But there's still no definite tie-in with Brenda Sorby.'

'Michael Conrad, Fine Jeweller and Watch Repairer, will give us that,' said Dalziel confidently. 'Due back from the sunny Med this afternoon.'

'Then shouldn't we wait?'

'Why? What do you want to do?' demanded Dalziel.

Mow my lawn and then cool off with a tube of lager, thought Pascoe.

'What about Wildgoose? Shouldn't we talk to him?' he said.

'Not home,' said Dalziel promptly. 'I sent Preece round there this morning. Paper, milk, no Wildgoose. He's probably shacked up with that little bird you mentioned, Andrea Valentine. We could bust in there, I suppose.'

'What?'

'Well, you think Wildgoose may have dumped his spare hash there for safekeeping, don't you? Suspicion of possession. We'd get a warrant easy.'

'No, but...' Pascoe began to protest, but Dalziel interrupted him with agreement.

'Quite right, lad. Can't do things like that. Girl on her own, parents away, it'd give us a bad name. Anyway, we want to get our hands on little Andrea while Wildgoose isn't around to feed her lines. If she's holding the hash, that should give us a nice little lever to squeeze what she knows about her boy-friend out of her!'

Dalziel rubbed his hands together like two sheets of emery paper.

'But what do you hope to find by searching the gypsy encampment?' demanded Pascoe.

'Probably enough stolen gear to put the whole bloody tribe away!' said the fat man. 'I don't know, Peter. But there'll be summat there. Perhaps other bits and pieces that went missing after the other killings and we never knew about them. Listen, that Pritchard cow, the solicitor, she's finally got to Lee's wife. We kept her at the hospital last night—still in custody, sort of, you understand. Well, not for long. We've precious little to hold her on, and Pritchard's raising merry hell. Once she gets back to the encampment, anything that might be evidence really will disappear, you can bet on that.'

'So you want me to search Lee's caravan like you did? But officially this time?'

'No!' roared Dalziel. 'The whole bloody site!'

'But you can't do that! It's provocative! These people have rights too. It's like searching every house on an estate because you suspect one householder of a crime! With what we've got, you'd never get a justice to issue such a general warrant!'

Dalziel grinned and reached into his inside pocket.

'Depends how you pick your justice. Bernard Middlefield didn't have to think twice,' he said, producing the document like a conjuror's rabbit and handing it over.

'Aren't you coming along, sir?' asked Pascoe unhappily.

'Me? No, I don't think so, Peter,' said Dalziel in a sanctimonious tone. 'You're dead right. These people may be dirty gyppos but they're entitled to all the usual consideration and protection of the law. You're the man to see things are done properly. Me, I'm too old fashioned, I suppose. But I'm not so old fashioned that I don't know when to take a back seat and let a younger, more liberal sort of man get on with the job.'

You cunning old bastard! thought Pascoe.

He glanced back as he left the office. The fat man was smiling and nodding his head as though in accord.

❀ ❀ ❀

If you have to do a job, do it properly, was a maxim which Pascoe believed in. The essence of search is surprise. For this reason he had devised the strategy of dividing his team, sending four round to the Industrial Estate entrance to the encampment while he and two other DC's drove into the Aero Club car park where Wield was already waiting.

With him was a rather puzzled-looking blond man who was introduced to Pascoe as Austin Greenall, the club secretary. He and Wield were looking towards the section of the old aerodrome where the gypsies were. Just over the picket fence a large bonfire had been lit. Its flames were scarcely more than a violet vibration of the air in the bright sunlight, but a plume of dark smoke curved up from the fire towards the clubhouse.

'What's going on?' asked Pascoe.

'Perhaps they feel the cold, sir,' suggested the shirt-sleeved Wield.

'Is it a hazard?' said Pascoe to Greenall, glancing up beyond the smoke to where five or six gliders wheeled slowly high in the sky.

'No, there's not enough for that,' said Greenall. 'If anything, it could be useful. Shows the wind drift and strength.'

'So, no complaints, sir?'

'Do you want me to complain?' wondered Greenall looking at Pascoe curiously. 'I mean, are you after an excuse to go in there?'

'Don't need an excuse, sir,' interjected Wield. 'Not if we've got a warrant.'

'Which we have,' said Pascoe. He spoke into his personal radio. 'Preece, you and the others ready? OK. Wait till you see us coming over the fence, then move in.'

'Are you expecting someone to run?' asked Wield as they set off across the grass.

'Not really,' said Pascoe. 'But if someone did run I don't want Mr Dalziel asking why I hadn't thought of it.'

In fact if anyone had wanted to run, there was plenty of time for it. The picket fence had been repaired so effectively that the policemen had to climb over it, a dangerous and undignified business that soon drew the attention of the crowd of gypsies standing just outside the circle of unbearable heat from the fire which seemed to be centred on a wooden pole rising out of the flames, gruesomely like a martyr's stake.

'It's the tent,' said Pascoe suddenly, and his guess was confirmed by the emergence from the spectators of Rosetta Stanhope. She looked all gypsy now in a dirndl skirt with a red and blue blouse and her hair tied back in a green and yellow bandanna. Her brow was smeared with ash, though whether by accident or by ritual design, Pascoe did not know.

'Mrs Stanhope,' he said. 'I'm sorry if we're disturbing a ceremony...'

'Don't let it bother you,' she said. 'Pauline will be getting a straightforward Anglican burial. This is just a cleaning up, for my benefit mainly. To most of these people, she was just a *gorgio*, hardly worth taking your hat off for.'

'But they're helping you,' said Pascoe. 'They took the tent away.'

She smiled grimly.

'When a *chovihani* asks you the time, you buy a clock,' she said. 'Have you come to bring me the clothes she died in?'

'I'm sorry. We haven't found them yet,' said Pascoe.

She looked worried.

'That's a pity. They should be burnt, above all things.'

'I wouldn't be surprised if they had been already,' said Pascoe.

'You think so? I hope you're right,' she said. 'What is it you're after, then?'

'Is there someone here who's in charge, some sort of leader?'

She left him and went to the main group of gypsies and talked to them for a moment. A short fat man emerged who might have been anything between fifty and seventy and returned with the woman. He was introduced as Silvester Herne and he enquired pleasantly of Pascoe, 'How can I help you, pal?'

Pascoe regarded him dubiously, wondering what his qualifications as leader were. He didn't look much like a gypsy king. Most likely he had been selected as a front man because of some qualities of glibness or shrewdness he possessed. Still, that was their business.

Briefly he explained that he and his men wanted to look around the camp site and talk to the people on it. They had a warrant which entitled them to enter any or all of the caravans and make a search but this might not be necessary.

Herne scratched his nose reflectively.

'Looking for anything special, pal?'

Pascoe thought for a moment, then said slowly and clearly, 'It's the Choker case I'm working on, Mr Herne. Anything relevant to that case is what I'm looking for. Nothing else interests me much. You might tell your people that.'

'OK,' said Herne.

He rejoined the others.

'Trying to keep the peace, Inspector?' said Rosetta Stanhope.

'That's what I'm paid for,' said Pascoe. 'Tell me, Mrs Stanhope, if any of them knew anything about the Choker, would they keep quiet? Out of loyalty, I mean?'

'Maybe,' she said. 'And maybe I'm not the person to ask. I'm one of them too, remember?'

'Yes, I know,' said Pascoe. 'I also know you came to me offering to help only last Wednesday morning, but since then you've been a lot less keen.'

There was a time to be subtle, a time to push. Dalziel was pushing forward like a traction engine at this moment. Pascoe suspected his direction but he knew he would have to get up a good head of steam himself to head him off.

'Since then my niece got killed,' said Mrs Stanhope sharply. 'Have you forgotten already?'

'No. But I'd have thought that would have sharpened your appetite to help, if anything,' answered Pascoe just as tartly. 'You know Dave Lee's in trouble?'

'I know he's in hospital,' said Rosetta. 'His missus told me that.'

'She's here?'

Mrs Pritchard must have worked even faster than Dalziel anticipated. This hardly boded well for the search.

'Over there, sir,' said Wield.

Pascoe looked and saw a thin, not bad-looking woman with a fading bruise on her left cheek crouching among a gaggle of children, talking to them. She rose as he watched and the children ran off, whooping excitedly at which noise others detached themselves from the group round the fire and galloped after them. Pascoe looked round to get his bearings. To the south was the Aero Club, to the north-west was the arterial road with the sprawl of the Avro Industrial Estate beyond, to the northeast was the suburb of Millhill, while due east would be the river, invisible in a heavily coppiced fold of land some fifty yards beyond the airfield boundary. That was the direction the children were taking. Pascoe envied them. The combination of sun and fire was bringing the sweat to his brow.

'Let's get to it,' he said to Wield.

Wield nodded and with calm efficiency set the men to work. He was a good man, thought Pascoe and wondered as he had done before why Wield had stuck at sergeant.

The gypsies seemed indifferent to the search though not so indifferent that there wasn't at least one member of each family present as the caravans were searched in turn.

Silvester Herne moved from one caravan to the next, then back to Pascoe with offers of help so solicitous that they bordered on parody.

It was hopeless, thought Pascoe. Dalziel had struck lucky because he had taken the Lees completely by surprise and because he didn't give much of a damn for the niceties of the law. No, that was too grudging an assessment. Dalziel like all good cops made his own luck and wasn't afraid of pursuing it no matter what unlikely direction it took him in.

He found himself quite close to Mrs Lee who was standing with arms folded and a twistedly cynical smile on her face.

Pascoe introduced himself.

'Well, ain't you a change from them other mumply old hedgecrawlers that keep talking to me,' she said, looking at him with mock admiration. 'A good-looking one at last. Theys'll try anything!'

'I'm pleased your husband is out of danger, Mrs Lee,' said Pascoe.

She looked at him with blank indifference.

'Unfortunately he's not out of trouble,' pursued Pascoe. 'Not unless he can explain how that money and the watch and ring came into his possession.'

'Which money? Which watch and ring?' she asked.

Pascoe sighed.

'Look, there's no one can hear us now, Mrs Lee,' he said. 'Dave's not a very good husband to you, is he? I mean, a fine-looking woman like you can't much enjoy being knocked around. Just a couple of words now, just a hint, and we could get him out of your life for a bit. No need to worry about the money, married woman with kids and a husband in gaol, you'd probably get more out of the social security than Dave makes in a moderate week. We'd see the forms were filled in properly, all that sort of thing. No one has to suffer these days!'

She didn't answer but fixed her gaze over his shoulder. Pascoe looked round and saw Rosetta Stanhope talking with a woman who didn't look like a gypsy.

'What's the matter?' asked Pascoe. 'Are you frightened of Mrs Stanhope? Frightened because she's a *chovihani*?'

'*Chovihani*? Her?' snorted the woman. 'She's nowt but a *didikoi*, a *posh-ratt*. Coming here from her little house and expecting us to treat her like a traveller still after fifty years. She even smells like a *gorgio*!'

Pascoe recognized the insulting terms for half-breed, but was less than convinced of the sincerity of this expression of fearless contempt. It seemed to him more based on deep resentment than genuine scorn.

'Mrs Lee?'

Pascoe turned and groaned inwardly as he recognized the woman who had joined them. This was Pritchard, the solicitor. The last thing he wanted at the moment was an antagonistic legal eye peering over his shoulder.

'You don't have to talk to this man, Mrs Lee,' continued Pritchard in clear tones resonant with upper-class certainty.

'Certainly you don't have to answer any questions he might put to you without benefit of legal advice.'

'Doesn't the Law Society have some convention about not touting for business?' wondered Pascoe aloud.

'You're Pascoe, aren't you?' she said. 'I've heard about you. If protecting women against the police means touting for business then I'll do it. And if the Law Society objects, then they can go and screw themselves.'

'It's your licence,' said Pascoe. 'Excuse me.'

He went away to urge Wield and his men to accelerate their search so that it could be completed before Ms Pritchard turned her crusading eye in their direction. Wield said thirty minutes and Pascoe, pointing out Pritchard, said that he was taking a stroll down to the river and that if the solicitor did start sticking her nose in, she should be met by a display of subordinate blankness and referred to him. By the time she found him, with luck their business would be over.

It was easy to find the exit hole in the boundary fence. During the hot weather the children's feet had beaten a distinct path towards it. Folding back the wire, Pascoe squeezed through and within a few paces had dropped out of sight of the encampment. He could hear the children at play—cries of delight, excitement, abuse and fear accompanied by much splashing of water. Forcing his way through a tight-knit clump of sallows, he reached the bank.

It wasn't much of a river, at its widest no more than fifty or sixty feet, though the farmer who owned the huge field of turnips which lay on the further bank must have been glad to have this barrier between him and the encampment. How many turnips could a swimming child carry? wondered Pascoe.

He sat down on the bank where the hungry water had eaten away a crescent of earth to form a small bay with a deep still pool. The children were playing a little further upstream, too absorbed in their games to take notice of Pascoe. He watched them with pleasure, delighting in their easy movements, their lithe brown bodies, their undiluted animal spirits, and tried to recall when last he had been capable of such total submersion in present joy. Not counting sex, that was; though even in the great gallop of sex there was all too often that little slave clinging to the back of the chariot and whispering in his ear, *remember you are you.*

A pair of small boys detached themselves from the other children and came running down the bank to peer speculatively into the pool above which Pascoe sat. They were young enough to be stark naked—gypsies have extremely rigid ideas about carnal exposure—and were urging each other to plunge in.

One of them looked up and saw Pascoe and spoke to the other. Pascoe smiled amiably at them and, convinced he was harmless, they returned to the debate till another older boy, spotting them from the river, floated on his back and shouted angrily at them. Pascoe caught the word *mokadi* repeated several times. This he knew was the Romany term for taboo or unclean, and at first he assumed, not without hurt, that the expression was meant for himself.

But observation of the two naked children told him he was wrong. It was not himself but the edge of the bank they were withdrawing from with expressions of uncertainty and trepidation. In fact their retreat brought them closer to Pascoe's position and he addressed them gently.

'Hey, *chavvies*,' he said. 'What's the matter? Don't you like to swim? Here, I'll give this to the one who makes the biggest splash!'

He held up a fifty-pence piece so that it glinted in the sun.

The boys chattered excitedly, then ran to the bank a little way upstream.

'No. Here,' commanded Pascoe, pointing to the pool.

They shook their heads.

'Oh all right,' said Pascoe, rising and strolling towards them. 'Here will do.'

He squatted down alongside them.

'But why's that pool *mokadi*?' he asked. 'It's a good place to swim. Why is it *mokadi*?'

He held up the coin as he spoke. One of the boys, the younger, took a step backwards, then turned and ran towards his friends. The other looked as if he might follow instantly.

Pascoe instinctively reached out and grasped his arm lightly.

'Do you not want the money, son?' he asked.

There was movement behind him.

'*Chikli muskro!*' screamed a furious voice. 'Sodding dirty old queer!'

Pascoe looked up. It was Mrs Lee. Behind her trailed Miss Pritchard and Sergeant Wield. He let go of the child and began to rise, but he was still at the crouch and unbalanced when the gypsy woman hit him. It wasn't really a blow, just a simple shove with both arms.

But it was enough to set him teetering on the edge of the river and it took hardly more than another gentle touch to send him plunging over.

The water was green and deep close by the bank. He came up and saw the children's heads craning over the edge to view this fascinating spectacle. He grabbed at the bank but his fingers slipped in the wet clay and down he went once more.

This time when he surfaced, he lay back and floated. The small brown faces were still there, big-eyed, watching. And beyond them, high in the summer blue sky, slowly wheeling like huge birds of prey, black crosses in the aureole of the sun, he saw the gliders.

The water was filling his clothes, pulling him down. But he was in no danger. Wield's strong grip was on his forearm. And as he was dragged gasping from the pool that was *mokadi*, he found himself looking up at Rosetta Stanhope and he wondered how an English judge would react to the production of a dead witness by proxy in a murder trial.

CHAPTER 21

Michael Conrad was at first puzzled, then rather frightened when, arriving home that Saturday lunch-time, he found a policeman waiting outside his shop. His relief was great when he realized that the policeman's presence did not mean a break-in, nor did it have anything to do with the three litres of cognac he had just smuggled in from Corfu.

But his shock on hearing of Brenda Sorby's death was deep and genuine. He had not heard the news before he left on Friday night and it was a point of honour with him not to read an English paper while on holiday abroad.

Yes, he knew her well. Didn't she often serve him in the bank? Yes, he had seen her that Thursday lunchtime, just before he closed. She had collected and paid for a gentleman's gold signet ring. That was the ring there on the Superintendent's desk, no doubt. And the watch too. A gift for her young man. A nice watch for the money and he had given her a good discount because he liked her. Her engagement ring he had admired. Not an expensive stone and the setting…well, he would have been ashamed to sell such a setting but it was no business of his to dull a young girl's happiness so he had admired it as the most perfect of rings and taken her to the door and waved goodbye to her.

And would never see her again.

His eyes filled with tears and he had to blow his nose before he could sign his statement.

'Grand,' said Dalziel rubbing his hands together. 'Now for Lee. Peter, we should put you back on the beat. I'd forgotten how pretty you looked in uniform.'

Pascoe had been provided with a blue shirt and a pair of uniform trousers while his own gear dried off. He had just escaped from a neighbouring interview room which Lee's wife, four of her children, Silvester Herne, two policemen and Ms Pritchard had turned into a Bedlam cell.

'And I'd forgotten how itchy these trousers were,' he answered, 'Look, sir, I haven't got much sense yet out of that lot. They keep jabbering away at each other in Anglo-Romany every time I think I'm getting somewhere, but here's how it's looking to me…'

Dalziel put a huge finger to his broad lips.

'Later,' he said. 'Lee'll tell us all or I'll personally undo his stitches. That Pritchard thing's still there, is she?'

Pascoe nodded.

'Right,' said Dalziel. 'We'll send Wield in, tell him to be a bit aggressive towards the woman and the kids. That should keep her busy while we do our spot of hospital visiting!'

On their way to the hospital Pascoe said, 'I don't think he did it, sir.'

Dalziel hushed him again, but with sufficient good humour to make Pascoe believe their conclusions were in accord till they stood by Lee's bedside and the fat man said without any preamble, 'Lee, we're here to charge you with murder.'

'You must be cracked? Who says I killed anyone?' demanded the recumbent man.

'Not a soul,' admitted Dalziel. 'Your wife, kids, mates, not one of 'em is telling us anything. That's your bad luck, lad. You'll need all the talking you can get on your behalf to pull you out of this. We can prove that the money, the watch and the ring were all in Brenda Sorby's handbag when she left the bank that night. They ended up in your caravan. That's what tells us you killed her, lad. We need nowt else.'

Lee twisted uneasily in his bed.

'Look, mister,' he said. 'If I tell yous what really happened, will you look out for me, like?'

Dalziel seized the man's hospital pyjamas lapel and pulled him a little way off the pillow.

'Listen, Lee,' he said viciously. 'I think I know what really happened. You killed her. If you want anyone to believe different, you'd better open your mouth and hope that what comes out flows like honey.'

A nurse came into the room and paused at the door as she took in the scene.

'Just rearranging his pillows, Sister,' assured Dalziel. 'There we are, Dave. That better? Grand. Off you go, dear. This is private.'

The nurse went out.

Lee said, 'I didn't kill her. She was dead.'

'If you're going to make up a story, at least give it a proper beginning, lad,' said Dalziel wearily. There was one armchair in the room. The fat man slumped into it while Pascoe perched on a hard plastic chair with his notebook on his knee.

'It were the kids,' said Lee. 'It were the kids that saw her.'

It had been round about seven o'clock. Lee had been answering a call of nature by the boundary fence when his four children who had just headed down to the river for a swim came running back, full of excitement, crying there was a woman in the water.

Lee had gone down to investigate. There she was, Brenda Sorby (as he found out later), floating face upwards. He pulled her out, tried what he knew of artificial respiration, but it was useless. Then he noticed the marks on her neck and realized it was not just a simple case of accident.

His eldest boy was sent to summon Silvester Herne, with strict instructions to tell no one else. Herne, as Pascoe had suspected, was not so much the gypsy leader as their cunning counsellor, the man who knew how to fix things. Lee then peered in the water again and saw the woman's handbag. He had fished this out and was just opening it as Herne arrived. Together they discovered the watch, the ring, the wad of notes.

This it was that tipped the scales.

Herne's first advice was to dump the woman back into the river. A *gorgio* woman, let the *gorgios* find her. It would do the gypsies in general and Lee, with his record, in particular no good to be mixed up in this. Not that merely returning the body to the water would prevent them from being involved, though. Centuries of experience have taught gypsies that proximity is guilt.

So, on second thoughts, Herne had suggested, it might be better to dump her somewhere more distant.

For the general good.

Also, that way, they could keep the money, the watch and the ring with impunity.

Lee had backed his van up to the hole in the wire and together he and Herne had loaded the body on to it. The children were frightened to silence with all the superstitious threats that arise naturally from Romany lore. And Lee had driven his van back to the fairground where he was working that night.

The intention had been to wait till after dark which came late in early July, and then to put the body back in the river somewhere further downstream beyond Charter Park. But when the storm broke and the fairground cleared, Herne had suggested they gild the lily a bit by transporting it across the river and dropping it into the canal. This served the double purpose of keeping it out of the river which after all ran by the gypsy encampment, and perhaps postponing discovery, as the canal was that much deeper and murkier.

It also provided a group of ready-made suspects in the form of the canal people who, in Herne's opinion, were capable of any crime known to man and some known only to fish.

And that's what they had done. The padlock on the hire-boats had presented no problems to Herne who emerged more and more in Lee's narrative as the moving force behind the whole sequence of events. Only when it came to the question of the money did Lee assert himself. *He'd* found it. *He* would keep it safe till the time seemed propitious for a split.

'Which was just as well,' said Dalziel. 'Herne wouldn't have hidden it somewhere so easy to spot.'

'You believe him then?'

'Why not?'

They were hanging around in the corridor outside Lee's room. The consultant surgeon, triumphant from his morning golf, had turned up a few moments earlier and Dalziel after a brief trial of strength had abandoned the field, acknowledging that only fools or heroes challenged consultants on their own ground.

'We haven't found out yet what happened on Wednesday, when he disappeared with Rosetta Stanhope,' said Pascoe.

'Simple. He read, if he can read, or was told what the papers said about that bloody message from the stars...'

'Which turned out to be pretty accurate,' observed Pascoe parenthetically.

'...and he checked with the girl, Pauline, in the morn-ing—you said you saw him chatting to her and because he's a superstitious pagan like the rest of his tribe and he reckoned it wouldn't be long before the spirits were being even more precise about time and place, and the subsequent travels of the dead body, he went round to see Rosetta.'

The door opened, the consultant emerged trailing clouds of interns, nodded distantly at Dalziel and went on his way.

'Very *grand seigneur,*' observed Pascoe.

'They'll find the bugger pissed in his Daimler one of these days and then it'll be *hello Andy!*' said Dalziel philosophically. 'Let's get back to it.'

The superintendent's forecast of Lee's actions on the Wednesday proved remarkably accurate. Rosetta Stanhope was summoned, still smelling of smoke. She largely substantiated the story, though in her version it became apparent that a minor form of kidnapping had taken place, in that she had been picked up by Lee in his van as she left her flat and driven north while in a roundabout way he explained his involvement with the Sorby case. At first she had thought he was confessing to the murder and that had kept her quiet. They had indeed ended up in a camp in Teesdale where the presence of some elderly relatives and some mechanical trouble with the van had persuaded her to spend the night. She had rung her flat, not been too bothered when she couldn't get Pauline at first, tried again much later, began to be concerned, and woken up the following morning to learn from the radio of her niece's death.

Loyalty to Lee had prevented her from attempting to use her gifts to help the police as she had volunteered to Pascoe, but now the truth about Brenda Sorby was out, she repeated her offer vehemently.

Dalziel shrugged when Pascoe told him.

'You want to cross her palm with silver, that's up to you, lad. But don't let it get into the papers. And don't make a claim on your expenses sheet!'

The children, after being absolved from their vow of silence by their father who was now only too eager for them to talk, had chattered away merrily to Wield who lubricated their vocal cords with cream cake and ginger beer from the canteen. They had heard someone moving away through the shallows along the river bank just before they found the lady. Pressed for more details they had indicated to Wield, who was now a great favourite, that whatever he wanted them to have seen—large, small, fair, dark, man, woman, orangutan—was OK with them. Mrs Lee and Ms Pritchard were present throughout the questioning, the former indifferent now that the men had given their approval, the latter vociferously alert to any hint of police pressure. Finally Wield pointed at her and said to the children, 'Was this figure anything like that lady.'

'Yes,' said the eldest after close scrutiny. 'I think it was her, mister.'

'No,' shouted the littlest carried away by this imaginative game. 'She's the lady that was in the water!'

And burst into sobs of terror which rapidly spread and could not be stemmed till Ms Pritchard reluctantly left the room.

Silvester Herne too supported Lee's story with some slight modification which reduced his role to that of innocent dupe, unwittingly involved through misplaced loyalty.

And finally the pathologist with the hindsight which is the basis of all great expertise confirmed that the circumstances described by Lee accounted precisely for the state of the body as described in his report and even managed to suggest that they were so clearly implied by his findings that he could not imagine how the police had overlooked them.

'Where's it leave us?' wondered Wield.

'Up shit creek,' said Dalziel.

'No,' argued Pascoe. 'We're a lot further forward. We must be. We now know very precisely where and when Brenda Sorby was killed. Someone strangled her on that river bank and was probably going to leave her nicely laid out like the others when he heard the kids coming. So he tipped her body, not quite dead as it happened, into the water and made off. So, question: did he force Brenda to go with him? Answer, unlikely, the final attack must have been so unexpected she didn't have time to scream, else the kids would have heard her. Conclusion: she knew the man, and trusted him.'

'Question,' said Wield. 'Even if she knew the man and trusted him, what was she doing strolling along the river bank with him when she should have been out shopping prior to meeting Tommy?'

'There's an obvious answer to that,' said Dalziel.

'Hardly!' protested Pascoe. 'She doesn't sound like a two-timer. And she'd just got engaged and bought the ring for Tommy, not to mention the watch.'

'Who said the watch was for Tommy?' asked Dalziel cynically. 'She wouldn't have been the first girl to run two men at the same time—one her own age, one a bit more mature, maybe, bit more exotic.'

'Like a tall, dark, handsome gypsy, you mean, sir?' said Wield.

'Why not?' said Dalziel.

Pascoe snorted in disgust, a noise which Ellie had taught him.

'You're not back to Lee. Is he *that* cunning?'

'It would be bloody clever,' admitted Dalziel. 'I mean, the double alibi. And them buggers are all cunning enough, Peter. They're born with the art. Besides, if not Lee, there's plenty of others of his tribe. Come Fair fortnight and there's enough golden earrings about the place to hang the Grand Theatre curtain on.'

'No,' said Pascoe vehemently. 'I don't see it. Not this girl, not at this time.'

'All right,' said Dalziel. 'If a bit of nooky's the most likely reason for being along that river bank on a summer evening, and if you think she was too bloody upright for a bit on the side, what's wrong with the legal tenant?'

'You mean Maggs, sir?' said Wield, incredulous.

'Why not? Has anyone asked him yet precisely what he was doing between six and seven that night?'

'No!' protested Pascoe. 'I'd find it easier to believe in Lee than that Tommy could carry something like this off!'

'Racial prejudice,' said Dalziel smugly.

'No, not just that,' said Pascoe, grinning. 'Some of my best friends are Yorkshiremen. But it's just that while I go along with the personal connection, I don't think we should confuse this with the personal motive. Now, Tommy or a secret lover might both have very good motives for murdering Brenda—jealousy, or fear of revealment for instance—but they're not Choker motives, if you follow me.'

'And what's a Choker motive?' demanded Dalziel. 'What that trick-cyclist—whatsisname?—Potty, says?'

'Pottle,' said Pascoe. 'Perhaps. Something like that. But not personal, not in the strict sense. You know what I mean, sir.'

'Do I?'

'Oh yes. You were very sure, I recall, that Brenda was a Choker victim even though she was found in the water, just as you had doubts about Pauline Stanhope, even though she was laid out in the classic style.'

'I can change my mind, can't I?' said Dalziel. 'I mean, a man gets fed up of being right all the time.'

'It must be painful,' said Pascoe and tried not to respond to Wield's grin behind the fat man's shoulder.

He continued. 'I just wondered if you were thinking what I've been thinking. Perhaps Dave Lee wasn't the only one to get worried when Rosetta Stanhope got so near the mark. Perhaps someone went to the fairground on Wednesday to shut Madame Rashid up and didn't know enough to know that Pauline wasn't Rosetta.'

'Perhaps, perhaps,' said Dalziel irritably. 'But why should anyone but a pig-ignorant gyppo get so upset by this mumbo-jumbo? I mean, what did that newspaper report say?'

The offending paper was produced.

'Blue sky, golden sun, big birds, black faces,' itemized Dalziel. 'Makes it sound like a travel brochure.'

'That's what I thought,' said Pascoe.

'So what's to be scared of?' grumbled Dalziel. 'This was that Duxbury woman, the neighbour? Oh yes, here she's mentioned. She says it was definitely the girl's voice.'

'The mother thought so too,' said Pascoe. 'But of course the situation was hysterical.'

'Aye. I bet old Wield here was falling about, pissing himself,' grunted Dalziel in the sergeant's direction.

'Perhaps I should have let that pair of linguists have a listen,' said Pascoe.

'For what? Experts, I've shit 'em,' announced Dalziel. 'What have they done for us so far, tell me that?'

'They've analysed those phone voices. Why don't we get every man connected with the case on tape and pass them over for comparison?' suggested Pascoe.

'That implies that (a) you trust that pair of Midsummer Night Dreams and (b) you're certain the Choker made one of those calls. It wouldn't be admissible evidence in any case.'

'No, but it's surely worth a try,' urged Pascoe.

Dalziel continued to look doubtful. He glanced at his watch.

'Christ, it's after two o'clock,' he said. 'And I haven't had my dinner. Peter, I think we may have gone as far as we can today. Why don't you push off home, take your rest day as scheduled? You've earned it.'

'Oh no,' said Pascoe firmly. 'The bargain was, I get next Friday and Saturday, guaranteed. Try to wriggle out of that and Ellie'll twist your arm off and hit you with the soggy end. I'll just give her a ring and see how she is, though.'

But the phone rang before he could reach it.

He picked it up and listened.

'For you,' he said, handing it over to Dalziel.

'Of course I wouldn't try to wriggle out of anything,' said Dalziel, aggrieved. 'I was saying you could take the afternoon off as a bonus, but seeing as you don't want it... *Hello*!'

He bellowed into the receiver from which a tinny voice had been emerging unregarded as he spoke.

'Jesus!' said the voice. 'Why don't you just open the window and forget about the phone.'

'Who's that?' demanded Dalziel.

'Sammy Locke, *Evening News*. How's business?'

'Quiet,' said Dalziel suspiciously. 'What've you heard?'

'Well, one of our contributors has phoned in a piece about strange goings-on among the gypsies. Police raids, brutality, interference with traditional funeral rites.'

'What? Who the hell was that? You print that and you won't get within spitting distance of another crime story in this town.' promised Dalziel.

'We'll see,' said Locke indifferently. 'And nothing else has been happening?'

'No. Why? Should it?'

'You tell me. Listen to this.'

There was a click, a pause, then a voice said wearily, '*Oh God! I could be bounded in a nut-shell and count myself a king of infinite space, were it not that I have bad dreams.*'

'There,' said Sammy Locke, 'Perhaps you'd better start looking for a body.'

CHAPTER 22

Interestingly, a message without a body seemed to stir up Dalziel much more than a message with a body.

'Got them linguists yet?' he demanded of Pascoe for the third time.

'I've sent cars out, told the lads to pick them up as soon as they come home,' said Pascoe. 'But really, all they can tell us is which of the other four, if any, this is. Sounds like (A) to me.'

'Me too,' said Wield. 'Though it's hard to be sure. He sounds different somehow. You know, not so certain of himself. Unhappy.'

'Hell's bells,' said Dalziel. '*He's* unhappy! Wait till this hits the papers. They'll give us stick, and not having had the advantage of a public school education, I don't care for stick.'

'No, sir. But the sergeant's right. I've sent for Dr Pottle as well to see what he thinks,' said Pascoe.

Dalziel's shrug, like Atlas getting a bit restless, indicated his opinion of Dr Pottle.

Sergeant Brady came into the Murder Room. He had been checking the missing persons reports. Weekend nights always brought in a good crop of non-returning youngsters.

'Seven lasses,' said Brady. 'Three turned up very late, looking satisfied, likely. Another two are back as well, only the parents didn't bother to tell us. That leaves two. They sound like they've just taken off to the Smoke. Classic backgrounds, like Mr Pascoe says.'

'Keep after them all the same,' ordered Dalziel, adding when the sergeant left, 'Christ, Peter, what're you doing to Brady? *Classic backgrounds*! He'll be spelling psychology with two p's and only one k next!'

On cue, the sergeant returned to announce that Dr Pottle was here.

'Hasn't he got a golf-course to go to?' muttered Dalziel. In fact whatever it was that Pottle did on Saturday afternoons he seemed only too pleased to have been invited away from it. He took the new tape into a neighbouring room and played it through several times.

'You have no body?' he enquired when he had finished.

'No. You think we're likely to get one?' said Dalziel.

'That I can't say. But whether this is your man or not, he certainly sounds to me very disturbed. If we assume that he is the (A) of the previous set of tapes, the change is marked.'

'That's what I thought,' said Wield. 'Unhappier, sort of.'

Pottle looked at him approvingly.

'You have a sensitive ear,' he said.

Wield coughed almost noiselessly into his fist. Pascoe who was beginning to be a keen student of Wieldology noted this down as the equivalent of a flush of pleasure.

'Last time his tone was regretful but resolved, as though he were performing a painful necessity,' continued Pottle.

'This is hurting me as much as it hurts you, you mean?' said Dalziel. 'We had an old sod at school used to say that as he thumped you.'

'Partly that. More being cruel to be kind. Compassionate, almost,' said the doctor. 'As I said in my written report, these are just impressions, but supported, I think, by the treatment of his victims and the tone and content of the telephone calls. Now, here there are two distinct changes. His voice sounds much more distressed, there's not the same authority there as before. And the words he speaks are concerned with himself, not with his victim. *Oh God! I could be bounded in a nut-shell and count myself a king of infinite space, were it not that I have bad dreams.* He's beginning to find it hard to live with himself, I would say.'

'Would this show in his outer behaviour?' wondered Pascoe.

'Not necessarily. Not yet anyway.'

'More important, does it mean he's less or more dangerous?' demanded Dalziel.

'I can't answer that,' said Pottle.

Dalziel gave an expressive pout of his thick lips and putting his hand into his waistband began to scratch his stomach audibly.

'One last thing,' said Pascoe. 'Suppose that his last killing, that is the last we definitely knew about, had been motivated not by whatever it is that's bugging him deep down, but by a simple desire not to be caught. How would this affect him?'

Pottle lit a cigarette from the one he was already smoking.

'This is a hypothesis, or do you know something?' he asked.

'An educated guess,' replied Pascoe.

'Then I would guess also that his own survival might not be sufficient justification to himself for taking life. Not unless it was definitely a one-off once-for-all-time act.'

'In other words, he might do it, resolved that after this there would be no more killings.'

'Yes.'

'And then if he found there were going to be other killings, that the compulsion was still there...?'

'I see what you're getting at, Mr Pascoe,' said Pottle. 'Yes, that could explain the change of tone here in this message. If he has killed again because of his compulsion, he now knows he may be tempted to kill again for his survival. And that is what he finds it hard to contemplate.'

'Hold on, now,' said Dalziel. 'If he killed that girl on the fairground just to protect himself, surely it's the call that followed that murder which should be full of this unhappiness your sensitive ears are picking up.'

'Oh no,' said Pottle. 'His motivation would have been sufficient at the time to justify himself thoroughly. Therefore he would be most meticulous about his cover-up.'

'Cover-up?'

'That's right. By laying the girl out as he did and by making the phone-call in the same tone and terms as before, he was attempting to misdirect you into pursuing him as the motiveless Choker still.'

'Which is what you hinted at in the first place, sir,' reminded Pascoe.

'Aye, I know,' muttered Dalziel. 'But I always get suspicious of my good ideas when clever buggers start supporting them. Well, thank you, Doctor. You've been very helpful.'

Pottle closed his notebook so firmly that an ashy emanation puffed out of his hands like fumes from a censer. He is after all our society's high-priest, thought Pascoe. The ungodly Dalziel had already turned away.

'He doesn't care for "clever buggers", I see,' murmured Pottle. 'And yet…how clever is he himself? Of the other, I have no doubts.'

'Oh, he knows a hawk from a handsaw,' said Pascoe lightly. 'Any more thoughts on why *Hamlet*, Doctor?'

'The first lady is the key, I believe,' said Pottle, making for the door. 'Had she been a little older, and had she remarried after her husband's death, and had she got a son who was a thirty-five-year-old adolescent…'

'She had a daughter who died,' said Pascoe.

'That might be significant. But you'll need powers other than mine to establish *that* connection, Inspector. Good day to you.'

'Inspector Pascoe,' bellowed Dalziel as the door closed behind the psychiatrist.

Pascoe went to the table behind which the fat man was sitting, viewing with distaste its paper-strewn surface.

'There's too many people just hanging around here,' he said fretfully. 'It's like just after pub closing-time in a brothel.'

'Some brothel,' said Pascoe. 'The girl we're all waiting for is dead.'

'I'll believe that when I see it,' said Dalziel. 'Meanwhile, there's things to be done. The fair finishes tonight. They'll be packing up in the morning, so I'm sending a team down there just in case there's any last-minute memories or anything turns up when the council start raking in the rubbish. Next, I'm fed up with all these wiseacres farting about with these tapes. Let's get something really useful out of 'em. Every man connected with this case, I want his voice on tape. It can be by agreement or by stealth, I don't mind. Sergeant Wield's a dab hand at working with a microphone up his nostrils aren't you, Sergeant? Then we'll see if these sodding experts can actually say if it was one of this lot on the telephone, right?'

He glared at Pascoe as if defying him to recall that this had been his own suggestion only an hour earlier.

'Excellent idea, sir,' said Pascoe. 'I'll do Wildgoose. I want another word with that sod anyway.'

'And I'll have another chat with Mr Mulgan,' said Sergeant Wield who had been studying the linguists' report with great interest.

'Talking of Mulgan, was there anything on that list of the Sorby girl's transactions?' enquired Dalziel.

Guiltily, Wield took it out of his pocket and handed it over.

'Forgot all about it, sir,' he confessed. 'What with the bother at the encampment and all.'

Dalziel grunted and glanced down the list. Because it was half-day closing, a lot of the local traders had been putting their takings in during the afternoon, including M. Conrad, the jeweller. Also, he noticed, there had been a deposit made on behalf of the Aero Club account and a large sum withdrawn from the Middlefield Electronic account.

He frowned.

'She was wearing her engagement ring that day, wasn't she?' he said.

Pascoe and Wield exchanged glances.

'I think so,' said Wield. 'Why, sir?'

'Nothing. You're getting me as loopy as the rest of you. Go on, bugger off and get some work done, will you?'

❀ ❀ ❀

Before he left the station, Pascoe put a copy of the latest tape in an envelope and addressed it to Gladmann or Urquhart in case either should surface before his return. Then, as an afterthought, he dropped in the Rosetta Stanhope cassette with a copy of Wield's transcription and a note with the vague query, 'What do you make of this?'

Wildgoose's milk and paper still remained uncollected. Pascoe contemplated burglary but was deterred by the appearance of a neighbour, a hairy young man apparently dying of consumption, who told him in a series of wheezy grunts that he'd heard Wildgoose go out last night but hadn't heard him return. Deterred from his criminal intents by the young man's presence, if not his information, Pascoe left.

He thought of going round to see Lorraine Wildgoose. But it didn't seem likely that the man would be there and he felt he ought to be careful about feeding the woman's obsession.

No, the girl, Andrea Valentine, seemed the best bet. Preece had gathered that the parents were due back this weekend, so perhaps Wildgoose was having a last fling round there. He got in his car and headed for Danby Row.

He spotted the house and drove slowly past. There was no sign of life. The milk was on the doorstep here too, which meant that the parents almost certainly had not returned and the happy couple if they were indeed inside were still probably making each other happy.

He turned at the end of the street and drove back. Dalziel, he thought, wouldn't have driven past the first time. Young girl screwing around with her middle-aged and married schoolteacher—her parents had a right to know. Pascoe's softness wasn't doing anyone any good, least of all the girl.

To some extent Pascoe had to agree. Certainly he'd been as kind as he could. Theoretically, suspecting that Wildgoose might have dumped the remains of his cannabis crop in Danby Row, he ought to have gone in there the previous day, searching it out and slapping a possession charge so hard on the girl that she'd try to ease the pain by agreeing to witness the more serious charge of cultivation and distribution against Wildgoose.

That's what he should have done. But he hadn't. Still, don't get uptight about it, he told himself philosophically as he leaned on the doorbell. It was impossible to be a cop and not break the rules. And in the great scheme of things perhaps his being soft on cannabis compensated for the readiness of some of his colleagues to drive home their arguments with a fist in the gut.

There was no answer here either. He didn't want to attract the neighbour's attention, so he went round the side of the house. At the front there had only been a paved rectangle with a home-sick magnolia in the middle of it. Behind, however, a long narrow garden, made private and well-nigh impenetrable by profusion of competing shrubs, stretched down to a wall with a green-shrouded door in it, presumably leading into a back lane.

Pascoe rapped on the rear door. There was no response, so he tried the handle. It turned and the unlocked door swung creakingly open.

He stepped into an old-fashioned kitchen—marble sink, solid fuel stove, a wooden clothes pulley hanging from the ceiling, blue and white lavatorial tiles everywhere. The Valentines obviously didn't spend their money on home improvements. If the parents' attitudes were like their home, they'd have a fit when they found out what little Andrea had been getting up to.

'Hello!' called Pascoe opening the interior door. 'Anyone home?'

His voice echoed up the stairwell, gloomy with brown paint and dark green flocked wall paper.

'Hello,' he called again, but more softly now, not expecting an answer.

Yet there was someone or something here, he felt it, and his heart was suddenly tight with dread. He found himself thinking of Wield pulling back the tent-flap and stepping inside. What he had found there had taken him completely by surprise. But perhaps the anticipated horror is even worse.

Oddly, it wasn't. It was anti-climactic, a relief almost. He pushed open another door. It led into a shadowy sitting-room. There on a threadbare chaise-longue lay Andrea Valentine. She was wearing only a short towelling wrap, but it had been decently arranged to effect maximum coverage. Her slippered feet were together and her hands were crossed on her breast. On the third finger of her left hand glowed a bright red stone set in a circlet of silver.

Pascoe touched the hand. It was quite cold. He looked for a moment at the blood-suffused face and knew the regrets and self-accusations that the sight was stirring up for him.

It was no time for them now.

Ignoring the telephone in the hallway he went out of the house the way he had come in and spoke rapidly and urgently into his car radio.

Then he returned inside to wait.

CHAPTER 23

It was the story as before.

The girl had been strangled and then laid out with limbs and features arranged to conceal the violence of her death as much as possible. She had been killed between midnight and two a.m.

A unique feature was that this girl had had sex shortly before dying. There were no signs of force.

In a shoe-box at the back of her wardrobe they found what they took to be the remnants of Wildgoose's Indian hemp harvest.

All over the house, they found his fingerprints or at least prints which corresponded with those they found all over his flat.

But these were the only trace of the man they found.

Pascoe went to see Lorraine Wildgoose.

'What's happened?' she said.

He tried to by-pass the question, but she was not easy to by-pass, so he told her.

'You'll want to look around,' she said. 'To make sure I'm not hiding him. Jesus!'

Feeling foolish, Pascoe looked. Fortunately the children were both out.

'You don't seem very surprised. Or shocked,' he suggested.

'What do you want, hypocrisy?' she asked fiercely. 'Who put you on to him in the first place?'

'It's still only surmise,' he urged gently. 'We just want to talk to him.'

'What do you mean, surmise?'

'All right, the evidence points that way, but we've got to talk to him first. If he does get in touch, you'll let us know?'

'If possible I'll crack the bastard's skull and bring him in personally,' she said.

Pascoe regarded her uneasily. Was she fit to be left alone?

'Is there anyone you could go to? Parents perhaps. You and the children,' he began.

'Go? Why?'

'For the children's sake, I mean,' he said quickly. 'Once the press get on to it, they'll be round here straightaway. And they have the same notions of delicacy as a pack of wolves.'

'I'm beyond sensitivity, Mr Pascoe,' she said.

'But not your children, perhaps.'

'You may be right,' she said more soberly. 'Thanks for the advice.'

'If you do go, let us have an address,' said Pascoe. 'Goodbye, Mrs Wildgoose.'

He was glad to get away, less glad when he returned to Danby Row and found the Valentines had just returned from their holiday. They were a tiny couple, at first fragile in grief, but then growing fierce in anger and inclined to talk as if the police were the perpetrators rather than the investigators of the crime. Neighbours were summoned to placate them, neighbours who had already been questioned and had heard nothing unusual from inside the house the previous night though one thought she may have heard a rustling in the garden as she summoned her cat shortly after midnight.

The same woman had seen Wildgoose visit the house a couple of times, but only in daylight and never staying long enough for 'anything to happen'. Sin, she clearly thought, needed working at.

So Wildgoose had been most discreet, a sensible trait in a man of his profession. The sedated Valentines knew him only as one of Andrea's teachers. The suggestion that he might have been having an affair with their daughter seemed to take them aback almost as much as the murder.

Pascoe sneaked away now to ring Ellie. It was six o'clock already and he could see a long night unwinding before him.

There was a worrying delay before she answered the phone, but she assured him she'd just been sunbathing in the garden.

'People used to hire light aeroplanes to fly overhead in the hope of glimpsing my naked flesh,' she said in self-mockery. 'Now they use radar to avoid hitting it. What's new with you, darling?'

He was reluctant to puncture her light mood, but he couldn't stop her listening to the news on the radio.

'Oh Peter,' she said after he had told her. 'How old do you say? Oh Jesus. And Mark Wildgoose is definitely your man?'

'He's certainly top of the list at the moment!'

'Poor Lorraine. I must ring her.'

'Don't use up too much sympathy. I've just seen her. She's got a bad case of the I-told-you-so's.'

'She has to cover up somehow. Peter, listen, I don't know if you've found out yet or if it's useful, but I can tell you where Mark Wildgoose was last night. Presumably that poor girl too.'

'You can? Well, come on, Sherlock!'

'It was Thelma. She was round here today. We were talking about Lorraine and she said that last night she'd seen Lorraine's husband at the disco at the Aero Club. There's one every Friday and Saturday night, evidently.'

'And Thelma goes to discos!' said Pascoe disbelievingly.

'Why not? But no, not really. This was different. There's been a bit of trouble recently, suggestions that kids under eighteen were buying the hard stuff, that sort of thing. Well, Bernard Middlefield JP, you probably know him, he's on the Club committee and he took it on himself to conduct a personal investigation. Thelma heard about this and she doesn't much care for Middlefield or his attitudes, so she took it on herself to turn up too and provide an objective check on his conclusions.'

'Objective!' snorted Pascoe. 'And Wildgoose?'

'She noticed him late on. He didn't do much dancing. In fact she said he didn't seem too happy. Well, surrounded by sixteen-year-olds mainly from his own school, who'd blame him?'

'He could have stayed at home with a good book. Anyway, thanks, love. We'd have got there soon enough, but this saves a bit of leg-work. Now look, just take me when I come, OK? Don't wait up if you get tired. You're sure you're all right now?'

'Yes, I'm fine,' she said irritably. 'Take care, Peter. Don't beat up anyone I wouldn't beat up.'

'Ha ha,' said Pascoe. 'Bye.'

❋ ❋ ❋

The technicians were finished with the house in Danby Row now and soon it was left to grief and silence. It was a relief to be back in the busy, functional Murder Room.

Dalziel had put the full national machinery of pursuit into motion. Locally, bus stations, railway stations, taxi and car-hire firms were checked thoroughly as were hotels and lodging-houses. Descriptions were issued to the media and, despite the fact that Wildgoose's passport, all visa'd for his approaching Asian tour, was found in his flat, seaports and airports were alerted too.

'You're sure he's our man?' said Pascoe uneasily.

'I'm sure I want to talk to him,' said Dalziel, belching. 'Christ. It's after eight o'clock and I've not had a proper meal today. Why shouldn't he be our man?'

'Well, no reason. Except, maybe, the sex. I mean, before there's never been...'

'Before he's never killed anyone he's been screwing,' interrupted Dalziel. 'All right, he's not a sex killer, the killing and the screwing don't go together. But that's no reason why he shouldn't enjoy it. I mean, he's having an affair with this kid, with the others he wasn't.'

'Then why kill her at this moment?'

'For fuck's sake, Peter, you know a better moment, you show me it!'

'There was the ring,' stuck in Wield.

'The ring?'

'Yes, sir. On her engagement finger. Mr Pascoe said that Dr Pottle said...'

'Pottle snottle!' snarled Dalziel. 'What the hell can a ring have to do with it? Look, let's just find the sod and pull bits off him till he gives us a few answers.'

'Don't let it bother you,' said Pascoe as Dalziel moved away. 'It's the time of the month.'

'Or he's not so sure,' said Wield.

'He's right about the ring, though. I mean, if Wildgoose gave it to her, then he's not likely to kill her for wearing it!'

'And if he did give it to her, he was jumping the gun a bit, wasn't he?' added Wield.

'We'll probably find out at the Aero Club,' said Pascoe. 'Preece! Come here. I want to take you to a disco.'

As he explained in the car, his reasons for choosing Preece were that the DC could pass for a dissolute twelve-year-old in the dusk with the strobe behind him. But in the event, such diplomatic considerations proved unnecessary. As Pascoe had observed before, this younger generation who were supposed to hold the police in greater fear and distrust than any previous age certainly had strange ways of showing it. Though it was still relatively early, the Aero Club was crowded, the curtains drawn so that evening sunlight should not interfere with the electronic glories within, and the whole place throbbing to a violent beat. Once identified as the fuzz, they were rapidly surrounded by a throng of enthusiastic potential witnesses whose demeanour was far from fearful.

'Sergeant, you and Preece pick the bones out of this lot and I'll join my own age group,' said Pascoe.

'Not many bones here, sir,' said Preece, unambiguously enjoying the pressure of a pair of fourteen-year-old breasts whose fullness bore splendid testimony to the benefits of the National Health Service.

Pascoe's 'own age group' consisted of Bernard Middlefield, Thelma Lacewing and Austin Greenall, the secretary, who were standing together looking far more distressed than any of the dead girl's contemporaries. The first two had both heard the news on the radio, recognized its relevance to their own whereabouts the previous night, and been drawn here again by motives which were not yet clear.

'You know Mark Wildgoose, sir?' Pascoe asked Middlefield.

'Not at all. But I noticed him last night. He stuck out, that much older than the rest. I asked who he was.'

'And you know him, sir?' Pascoe addressed Greenall.

'No,' said the secretary. 'He hadn't been here before. But Thelma, Miss Lacewing, she knew him.'

'I'm a friend of his wife. As you probably know,' said Thelma Lacewing.

'Yes. How was he behaving?' asked Pascoe. 'Anything unusual?'

'What's usual at something like this?' asked Middlefield. 'I'm going to be suggesting to the committee that we put a stop to this kind of thing. This is a flying club, supposed to be, not a sex-maniacs' kindergarten!'

'Most of their parents are members, *they* are all potential members, and it subsidizes your cheap gin-and-tonics the rest of the week,' flashed the woman.

'He was a bit unusual,' said Greenall, ignoring the other two. 'You sometimes get an older man in. Usually he's trying to show that he's as good as any of the youngsters. Wildgoose hardly danced at all. They came late. I got the impression it was the girl's idea and it came as a bit of a shock to him to see who was here. I heard one or two of the kids calling him "sir". They must have been pupils at the school he taught at.'

'And what about the ring?'

'Ring?'

'The girl was wearing an engagement ring. A large red stone.'

'No, I didn't notice anything of that,' said Greenall. 'Excuse me. The barman's looking a bit distressed. Ages are a bit difficult. I'd better go to the rescue.'

'A bit difficult!' said Middlefield. 'Inspector, you ought to bring some of your squad down here one weekend just to check this lot!'

'Perhaps I will, sir,' said Pascoe mildly. 'Any irregularities could, as you must know, mean that the club's licence might be completely revoked.'

'I saw the ring,' said Thelma Lacewing. 'It looked like a piece of costume jewellery. I noticed the girl showing it to a group of other girls.'

'And was Wildgoose with her?'

'No. He was at the bar. He didn't seem to want to know.'

The picture that emerged when he cross-checked with Preece and Wield confirmed Thelma Lacewing's impression.

Andrea Valentine had been dropping large hints for some time to her contemporaries about her conquest of Wildgoose. More recently she had been talking in terms of a permanent liaison when he finally unshipped his wife. Last night she had clearly set out to demonstrate in public the truth of the present closeness and the hoped-for permanence of their relationship.

'Yeah,' one girl had said to Preece. 'I thought she were just trying it on, like. I mean she could've bought the ring herself, couldn't she? And Wildgoose, he didn't seem all that pleased, did he?'

'Mebbe that's why he killed her?' suggested another girl.

'Yeah,' said the first, bright-eyed, pressing close against Preece. 'Is that why he killed her, mister! And how did he do it, mister? What did he do to her?'

Preece had retreated in disarray.

Before they left the Aero Club, Pascoe got Thelma Lacewing to herself and asked, 'Why did you come back here tonight?'

She answered. 'Another woman killed, this is probably the last place where she was seen alive, where else should I go, Peter? I should have said something to him last night. Perhaps if I had...'

'Forget it,' said Pascoe gently. 'You've got enough worries that aren't yours resting on your shoulders without looking for more. Thanks for looking in on Ellie, by the way. She needs company, I think, and I'm very tied up at the moment.'

'So's she,' said Lacewing. 'So's she.'

❀ ❀ ❀

At midnight there was still no trace of Wildgoose and in the Murder Room they were running out of jokes about his name.

'Let's wrap it up,' said Dalziel wearily. 'He'll have to show soon. Penny gets you a pound he's spotted in the morning.'

No one took him up, which was as well for the taker would have lost his penny.

Not that Dalziel was precisely right either. Wildgoose was certainly spotted, but not quite as he had implied in his forecast.

Ted Agar cycled slowly into the forecourt of the Linden Garden Centre early on Sunday morning. The dew still sparkled along the lines of rose-bushes and the church bells had not yet begun to summon the good people of Shafton to their Sabbath duties of car-washing, lawn-mowing and the like.

Agar was only paid to keep the place ticking over for half a day five days a week, but he liked to keep a closer eye on things, especially at weekends when potential customers, on discovering the Centre was closed, were not above excavating a couple of young bushes and tossing them into the boot before driving off. The previous day, Saturday, he had been otherwise engaged, watching Yorkshire prod their way to a draw in a County Championship match. Today however there was only a one-day game on offer and Agar believed that if God had wanted cricket to end in a day, He'd have rested on Tuesday instead of waiting till the end of the week.

As he propped his bike against the side of the house, his eyes were already checking the rose-plantation. So familiar was he with the silhouette of each row that he instantly spotted someone had been mucking about. Not that there was a gap, but out there in the middle where the orange-vermilion of his Super-Stars ran alongside the dappled apricot of his Sutter's Golds something was awry, the line had somehow altered.

Perhaps just a couple of stray dogs who imagined that no one would disturb the earth except to bury bones.

Dogs, however, didn't put the earth back after digging it out. Nor did they scatter earth regularly and evenly between the rows as though disposing of a surplus.

Four of the Super-Stars were looking a bit the worse for wear compared with their neighbours, a bit askew. A bit raised up.

He prodded the earth with the hoe he had instinctively picked up from the lean-to behind the house. He saw something small and white just alongside the union of one of the bushes. Like the end of a freshly pruned sucker.

He stooped and looked closer. Looked for a long time. Touched. Let out a long breath.

It was a little finger.

He backed slowly away for five or six paces before turning and hobbling rapidly towards the house.

CHAPTER 24

It didn't take long to identify the body. The name in the wallet was Wildgoose, Pascoe recognized the face instantly, and finally in the interests of bureaucracy Lorraine Wildgoose was asked to make it official.

'Was it suicide?' she asked afterwards, almost casually.

Not unless he could knock himself unconscious, strangle and bury himself, thought Pascoe.

He shook his head.

'No,' he said and when that produced no response, added gently, 'He was killed, I'm afraid, Mrs Wildgoose. But it does mean he probably wasn't the Choker.'

'Does it?' she said indifferently. 'I don't see why.' Then as though making an effort to find a more acceptable response, she added, 'But I'm glad for the children's sake.'

'Well, she's not going to toss herself on to her old man's pyre,' commented Dalziel after a WPC had taken Mrs Wildgoose out to the awaiting car.

'I think she's really broken up inside,' said Pascoe.

'Like my guts,' said Dalziel, beating his belly and belching. 'You didn't find out what she was doing early yesterday morning, between say midnight and four a.m.?'

'No,' said Pascoe. 'You don't really believe that...no, I'm sorry, sir. I didn't think.'

'You're probably right. Any road, I've told that lass with her to check as best she can, talk to the kids, that sort of thing. Better safe than sorry. She did hate the poor sod and she looks tough enough. That'd be the best solution too. He's the Choker, runs home for solace after killing the Valentine girl, wife bumps him off and buries him. End of case.'

'And who phones the *Evening Post* on Saturday afternoon?' wondered Pascoe.

'Who knows? Mebbe we've got a Joker as well as a Choker,' said Dalziel. 'We've got at least four voices on tape so far according to Laurel and Hardy, haven't we?'

'Urquhart and Gladmann,' said Pascoe. 'Yes. But yesterday afternoon only the Choker knew the girl was dead.'

'The Choker and anyone he might have told before he got himself killed,' urged Dalziel gently. 'What do your experts say about yesterday's voice anyway?'

'Nothing,' said Pascoe who had checked that the envelope was still at the desk. 'They must both be away for the weekend.'

Dalziel snorted his derision for people who had weekends away, a derision which included Wield whose day off it was and who had been heading north on his motorbike too early for even the long arm of Dalziel to haul him in.

Wildgoose had been knocked unconscious by a single blow at the top of the spine, either a very lucky or a very expert punch. Then he had been strangled. The only other point of significance was that he had had sexual intercourse not long before death.

'If we assume that he himself is not the Choker,' said Pascoe in deference to what he felt was probably a merely provocative theory on Dalziel's part, 'then it seems likely that after he left the girl, the Choker, who was perhaps waiting outside, moves swiftly in and kills her. As he leaves in his turn, he runs into Wildgoose who has returned for some reason.'

'Seconds,' said Dalziel ghoulishly.

'The Choker kills him. Carts him away. Presumably he has transport.'

'But why?' interrupted Dalziel. 'Why not leave the body in the house? I mean, why not lug the guts into the kitchen and take off rather than risk meeting someone in the back lane?'

Pascoe started inwardly. Dalziel was full of surprises. *Lug the guts*. Despite his mockery, had he too been studying *Hamlet* closely for whatever clues it might contain? Or was it just coincidence? There was no art to read Dalziel's mind in his ten-acre face.

'Perhaps he felt it would spoil the set-up there.' he answered. 'Girl neatly laid out, all decent and proper. Religious almost.'

'Or perhaps he just wanted to trail a red herring,' said Dalziel. 'Make us think that Wildgoose did it.'

'It's another link anyway,' said Pascoe. 'Burying him at the Garden Centre, I mean.'

'Aye, but what's it signify?'

'That's what we're paid to find out, sir,' said Pascoe sententiously.

If that were so, they did not earn their money that Sunday.

In hospital Dave Lee was well enough to work out that perhaps he could trade off his allegations of brutality against Dalziel's accusations of complicity. Ms Pritchard accompanied Mrs Lee during visiting hours and later to the station.

Dalziel, encountering them in the vestibule, refused a private audience, listened impatiently for a couple of minutes, got the drift and bellowed, 'You do what you bloody well like, my girl. Me, I've got more important things to occupy myself with. Like murder. Like the Choker.'

'You don't seem to be doing so well in that field either,' said the solicitor coolly.

'No, I'm not,' snarled Dalziel. 'And one reason why I'm not is that your client, if that's what he is, came as near as damn to catching this man in the act. And instead of getting hold of the police, he robbed the victim. And hid the body. And misled the police. And delayed the investigation. And probably made a large contribution to at least two more women and one man getting killed in the past five days. You tell him that, love. And if you don't care to, mebbe I'll come in and shout it down his ear-hole till his stitches pop!'

'There's no need to get excited,' said Ms Pritchard.

'You couldn't excite me on a desert island, love,' said Dalziel.

'That wasn't exactly conciliatory,' said Pascoe as they moved rapidly away.

'You don't conciliate that sort,' said Dalziel. 'Make 'em think you're a thick, racist, sexist pig. Then they underestimate you and overreach themselves.'

'Ah,' said Pascoe and wondered privately what strange self-image Dalziel kept locked away in his heart.

Thereafter it was a day of routine. Plain-clothes men going from house to house in Shafton village, checking whereabouts, taking statements; lines of men in dark blue moving slowly through the bands of red and yellow and pink and orange and white in the rose field, stooping and searching like gleaners after the harvest; Pascoe sitting in the Murder Room going painstakingly through every statement as it came in; Dalziel moving slowly around in threatening anger, like a tornado distantly glimpsed in a mid-West landscape and fled by all who saw it.

The taxi-driver who had taken Wildgoose and Andrea Valentine to the Aero Club was finally found.

The man who had taken them from the Club had been easier to track because his company was known. He had already made a statement saying that, after first directing him to Danby Row, they had changed their minds and asked to be dropped in Bright Avenue which ran at right-angles to Danby Row. As this gave access to the lane which ran behind the girl's house, it was presumed they had used the back entrance to avoid attracting attention.

The earlier driver had picked them up from Wildgoose's flat about nine-forty-five. They were both quite high, but he got the impression that it was the girl who wanted to be going out while the man was less enthusiastic. The girl had instructed him to drive to the Aero Club.

Dalziel now insisted on a check being made on the alleged whereabouts of every man concerned with the case between midnight and two a.m. on Saturday morning. He even got the man on duty at the hospital to confirm that Lee and Ron Ludlam were safely tucked up in bed all night. He himself did the check on Alistair Mulgan and Bernard Middlefield. The bank manager had watched the midnight movie on television by himself. His wife had gone to bed to read, had heard the television noise as she lay there and was able to confirm that her husband had come to bed as soon as the film finished at one-thirty.

'Good film, was it?' said Dalziel.

Mulgan cleared his throat and then gave a detailed résumé of the plot. Dalziel was not impressed. The picture had been shown at least twice before. But, while Danby Row was within walking distance, just, to get Wildgoose's body to the Garden Centre needed a car and Mrs Mulgan was adamant that the car had not left the garage which was next door to her bedroom in the bungalow.

Bernard Middlefield was approached rather less directly. Dalziel couldn't see him as a killer, certainly not of the kind described by Dr Pottle. But he was a customer at Brenda Sorby's bank, his company works were next to the Eden Park Canning Plant where June McCarthy had been employed, and he had been at the Aero Club the night Andrea Valentine was killed. So Dalziel treated him as a witness and only obliquely enquired about his own movements that night.

It emerged that he had stayed on after the disco finished. He hadn't noticed Wildgoose and the girl leave in particular, though he had said goodnight to Thelma Lacewing.

'What time would that be?' wondered Dalziel.

'Eleven. Eleven-fifteen. I don't know exactly.'

Middlefield was even vaguer about the time of his own departure. He'd had a couple of drinks with Greenall while the bar-helpers cleared up. Then, after they had gone, he had finally called it a night. He had then driven home, a distance of about three miles, arriving in time to join his wife in watching the last part of the same film that Mulgan was so well acquainted with.

Greenall whom Dalziel consulted later was able to be more precise. It had been nearly a quarter to one before Middlefield had left.

'I offered to drive him myself,' said Greenall. 'He was OK, you understand, but he'd put away quite a lot of Scotch. He got a bit huffy at that and I had to make a joke of it. But he drove away very steadily, I noticed. I remember thinking he was more likely to attract attention going at that rate than speeding!'

So, a sedate three miles—say ten minutes at the outside. It fitted, thought Dalziel not without relief. If there'd been any doubt, the next step would have been an examination of the boot of the JP's Jaguar, which would have meant coming into the open. Dalziel didn't give a bugger for anyone, but he knew who he wanted his friends to be.

In the middle of the afternoon Wield appeared. Quizzed about this devotion to duty on his day off, he shrugged, said he'd heard about the discovery of Wildgoose's body on the radio and thought he'd better check in to see if he could help.

'What a bloody miserable existence the poor sod must have,' commented Sergeant Brady to anyone who cared to listen.

'Nothing better to do than come in here on his Sunday off. What he needs is a short-sighted woman!'

Wield did not hear this, would not have reacted if he had. All his emotion for that day had been spent in a stormy scene in Maurice's Newcastle flat. Their usual roles had been reversed. Maurice, the more effervescent extrovert of the two, had tried to play it cool. Yes, there was somebody else, an interesting young chap who worked in the Borough Surveyor's office. Wield would like him. He was coming to lunch. Why didn't Wield stay on and have a drink and meet him?

And Wield, the calm, controlled, inscrutable Wield, had exploded in a wild, near hysterical fury which had amazed and frightened himself almost as much as it did his friend. He had left and made the normally two-hour journey back in seventy-five minutes. For two hours he had sat in his room examining the new vistas of violence his morning's experience had opened up for him. And finally he poured the tumblerful of whisky which had been standing before him back into the bottle untouched and went to work.

But there was little to do, just routine, nothing happening, no leads developing.

And when at six o'clock Gladmann appeared, full of the marvellous couple of days he had spent with rich and generous friends in their cottage on the coast, Pascoe thrust the envelope with the tape into his hands, said 'Sod it!' out loud, and went home, feeling, as he told Ellie, as if he'd spent the entire Sabbath at a very long and very tedious church service where the preacher's text had been *It is vain for you to rise up early, to sit up late, to eat the bread of sorrows.*

❊ ❊ ❊

It still felt pretty vain the next morning. Monday mornings normally don't mean much to policemen. If anything, they bring a sense of relief. The incidence of crime shoots up at weekends, much of it petty, it's true, but all of it time-consuming. But this

Monday, all the Monday morning feelings they had skipped for so long seemed to be lying in wait for those working on the Choker case.

The papers were full of comment, nearly all critical. An editorial in the *Yorkshire Post* wondered heretically if it might not be time to ask the Yard for assistance. Dr Pottle telephoned first thing to say that he had been invited to take part in a chat show on television and he wanted to be clear about what he should and shouldn't say.

'He thinks he knows something important?' queried Dalziel incredulously. 'Why hasn't the silly bugger told us, then?'

Pascoe removed the hand which he had pressed very firmly over the mouthpiece and said, 'Mr Dalziel says he can see no reason not to rely on your professional discretion, Doctor.'

'That's kind of him. By the way, have the papers got it right? This man, Wildgoose—you believe the Choker killed him to cover up his latest murder?'

'More or less. How does that fit with your profile?' asked Pascoe.

'Very well,' said Pottle. 'The killing of the girls he can clearly justify to himself. Even a one-off cover-up killing. But a *second* opens up the possibilities of a third, a fourth, indeed an infinitude. And that, if, as I posit, he is a man of conscience, must be very distressing.'

'What's he say?' asked Dalziel when Pascoe replaced the receiver.

'He says the Choker's probably sorry about killing Wildgoose.'

'Je-sus,' said Dalziel.

At ten a.m. the phone rang.

Wield took it. He looked unusually pale this morning and there were deeper shadows than usual in the canyons of his eyes.

'For you, sir,' he said to Pascoe. 'The Service Children's Education Authority.'

'Probably want their degree back,' muttered Dalziel. 'Obtaining by fraud.'

It was a woman, friendly, apologetic. She introduced herself as Captain Casey.

'Sorry this wasn't dealt with more promptly,' she said. 'But like most government offices, it's difficult to find anyone but half-wits round the place after lunch-time on Friday. I expect it's the same in the police.'

'All the time,' said Pascoe. 'What can you tell me, please?'

'Everything. Or at least all you asked for. Yes, there was a Peter Dinwoodie on the staff of Devon School. He resigned at the end of Summer Term, 1973. He hasn't been employed in any of our schools since. Nor does he seem to have had a job in the public sector in this country. I rang the DES to check. Thought you might like to know.'

'That was kind of you,' said Pascoe.

'Amends for the delay,' said Captain Casey. 'Now, you also asked whether his wife was employed at the same school, Mr Pascoe. No, she wasn't. In fact, according to our records, Mr Dinwoodie was a bachelor when last he worked for us.'

'Bachelor? Not married, you mean?' said Pascoe foolishly.

'I often do mean that when I say bachelor,' she said pleasantly.

'You're certain?'

'Our records are.'

'Well, thank you very much, Captain.'

'Hang on,' she said. 'You also wanted to know if a Mark Wildgoose had ever taught in Germany. The answer is no, definitely not. By the way, I saw that name in the newspaper this morning. A man murdered. Is it anything to do...'

'Thank you, Captain Casey,' said Pascoe firmly. 'Thanks a lot.'

'Oh well. Any time,' she said. 'Before lunch on Friday that is. Cheerio!'

'What was all that about?' asked Dalziel who had been watching Pascoe's reactions.

'More mystery,' said Pascoe.

When he had outlined the call, Dalziel said, 'Yes, well, all right. So he got married later, when he got back to the UK. What about it?'

'There was a daughter,' said Pascoe. 'She was killed in a car crash early this year. She was seventeen.'

He watched as Dalziel deliberately counted—on his fingers.

'I'm with you,' said the fat man. 'But so what? He married a widow.'

'I don't think so,' said Pascoe. 'Something the old man said. Agar. It struck me at the time, but I didn't know why. I think I'll have another word with him, if that's OK, sir.'

'It's better than having you wandering around here, being cryptic,' said Dalziel. 'But when the blinding flash comes, I'd like to be among the first to know.'

As though it had been specially ordered for Fair Fortnight, the fine weather which had begun to break up the day before was now definitely at an end. It was still warm, but in the eastern sky great ridges of violet-tinged cloud blocked out the sun and as he drove slowly by the empty expanse of Charter Park, seagulls driven inland by the still distant storm floated covetously over the heads of the council workmen clearing up the debris. There would be a couple of policemen hovering too in case anything relevant was discovered, but Pascoe reckoned that the seagulls had a better chance.

Heading for Shafton took him directly towards the storm and the air was quite dark by the time he reached the Garden Centre. He had Agar's home address, but he slowed as he approached the Centre and saw that his judgement had been right. There in the rose field was a solitary figure with a hoe, carefully repairing the damage done by yesterday's line of searching coppers.

The old man glanced up as Pascoe approached but did not pause in his work.

'Big feet some of you lads have,' he said, heeling a loosened root into the earth.

'They had to look,' said Pascoe.

'I dare say.'

'Looks like rain,' said Pascoe, falling into slow step alongside him.

'We can do with it,' said Agar. 'But that lot looks like it's going to come down cats and dogs, and any of these plants that're not firmly set can easy be toppled.'

'Well, I won't keep you back,' said Pascoe. 'It was just that last Friday when we talked you said something that didn't really register till later. You said that Mrs Dinwoodie blamed herself for letting her daughter run off to Scotland to be married. Now Mrs Dinwoodie as a widow would be solely responsible for her daughter while she was still a minor. If she agreed to the wedding, why did the girl have to go to Scotland?'

The old man paused.

'I said that? Well, mebbe I shouldn't have. But there's no harm to be done now. The lass, Alison, she weren't Mr Dinwoodie's daughter. No, she used the name, but she weren't his daughter. I knew, but only at the end when there was trouble and I heard 'em talking. Mrs Dinwoodie knew she could trust me.'

Pascoe put his hand on the old man's shoulder and brought him to a halt.

'Please, Mr Agar. Tell me everything you know,' he said.

It wasn't much. Shortly before Dinwoodie's death, Alison had met a boy, a nice lad, just eighteen, down from the Borders to do a six-month course at the Yorkshire Agricultural Institute. Their relationship had intensified after and probably as a result of her stepfather's death and they had been eager to get married. But somehow Alison's real father had emerged on the scene just about now. Still legally the girl's guardian, his permission was needed for an under-age marriage in England, and he was making a fuss about giving it. So Mary Dinwoodie had not raised any objection when her prospective son-in-law proposed taking Alison back to Scotland with him and marrying her there after she had the necessary residential qualifications.

She had gone up to the wedding, taken a train back to Yorkshire after the ceremony and was met at her house by the news that the honeymooners' car had skidded on the wintry roads only twenty miles after setting out and the young couple were both killed.

'Like I said, she went off after that. To stay with friends, she said, but I reckon she was off by herself and it wouldn't have surprised me if she'd killed herself. But I took care of the place as best I could, and the bank helped to keep the accounts straight, and then, lo and behold, last month she comes back, and it looks as if we can mebbe get things on a proper basis. Well, you know the rest, mister. Better if she'd stayed away forever. Better mebbe if she had killed herself even.'

The sky was completely veiled in cloud now and Pascoe felt the first splashes on his cheek, big warm drops that burst ripely as they struck.

'You should have told someone this before, Mr Agar,' he said.

'Should I? I never thought. It seemed of no account somehow, what with her dead. No account.'

'And the man's name? Mrs Dinwoodie's first husband. Alison's father.'

'Nay, I know nothing of that, mister,' said Agar, 'nothing more than what I've told you. Nothing more.'

❀ ❀ ❀

Back at the station he found that Dalziel was out. This suited him very well. There was a driving urgency in him which rendered him impatient of diversions for explanations and hypotheses.

Ignoring Wield's curious glances, he went to his own office, picked up the telephone and asked to be connected with the SCEA in London.

It took a few minutes to track down Captain Casey.

'Hello again,' she said. 'I didn't expect you so soon.'

'Me neither. Look, that school in Linden, the *Devon*—do you have a complete list of staff? What I'm particularly interested in is other people who resigned in 1973.'

'You're lucky, I haven't sent the file back yet,' she said. 'Hold on a sec. Here we are. You want the lot?'

'Just the resignations to start with,' he said.

Besides Dinwoodie there were only another two, and only one of these a woman.

'Now, do you want the whole list?'

'No thanks,' he said slowly. 'I think this'll do.'

He replaced the receiver and carefully drew a ring round the woman's name.

Mary Greenall.

Then he picked up the telephone again.

'I want the Air Ministry,' he said. 'I want the section that deals with personnel records.'

❀ ❀ ❀

Twenty minutes later he came out of his room, the sense of urgency pulsing stronger than ever. He found Wield and asked, 'Mr Dalziel back yet?'

'Not yet,' said the sergeant.

'Damn.'

'Are you on to something, sir?' asked Wield.

Pascoe hesitated, then said firmly. 'Yes. It may open up the whole damn thing. I'm almost certain. Listen, I'm going out now. Tell Mr Dalziel I'll be at the Aero Club. That's it. The Aero Club.'

It was silly. There was no need for all this rushing. But he felt impelled to it. Perhaps if there'd been a bit more rushing early on and a little less painstaking, step-by-stepping...

As he went through the door that led into the car park, he almost collided with Dicky Gladmann, clad in a streaming plastic mac.

'Hello there!' said the linguist. 'I say, I've had a listen. Most interesting.'

'Fine,' said Pascoe, turning his collar against the rain. 'I'm in a bit of a rush. We'll talk later.'

'Well, it's all written down,' said Gladmann, producing the buff envelope. 'Really, it's been terribly interesting. I'm not sure how significant it might be...'

'I'll let you know,' said Pascoe, taking the envelope and thrusting it into his jacket pocket. 'Many thanks. We'll be in touch.'

He dashed out into the storm and was well dampened in the short time it took to get into his car. The light was so bad now that he switched his headlights on before moving off. Behind him through the rear-view mirror he could see Gladmann standing forlornly in the doorway looking with his old-young-man's face and his plastic mac like the nucleus of a queue outside a porno-cinema.

The storm was at its height as he drove into the old aerodrome. There was no wind and the orange wind-sock hung heavily from its pole, its fluorescence dulled by the torrential rain. Sheet lightning flickered through canyons of cloud and thunder cracked and rolled like an artillery barrage. There would be no flying today, and precious little drinking either if the absence of cars was anything to go by.

Pascoe glanced at his watch. Nearly twelve-thirty.

He parked as close to the club-house door as he could get and dashed in, realized he'd left his lights on, dashed out again, switched them off and was sodden wet by the time he made his second entrance.

'Thought you'd changed your mind,' said Austin Greenall. 'Welcome. We were just beginning to think the weather had robbed us of all custom today.'

He was sitting on a stool at the bar. Behind it, a barmaid was arranging bottles and glasses.

Glancing significantly at her, Pascoe said, 'May we talk, Mr Greenall?'

'Of course,' said the secretary. 'Come into my office. Would you care for a drink en route? No? All right, this way.'

He led Pascoe into a small airless room with a desk, a filing cabinet and a couple of hard chairs.

'Sit down, Inspector,' he said. 'Now what is it you want to talk about?'

Pascoe sat.

'We could start with your ex-wife, Mary Dinwoodie,' he said. 'And go on from there.'

The telephone began to ring. It rang thirteen times. Both men ignored it. Finally it stopped, leaving its tone hanging on the air almost as long again.

'My wife, Mr Pascoe,' said Greenall. 'We are Roman Catholics. There was no divorce.'

Both men sighed gently, almost inaudibly, out of a sort of relief in both cases and, as if recognizing this, they exchanged shy smiles, glimmers fading almost as soon as they showed, but establishing a tenuous link for all that.

'Talking of wives, was it yours that talked you down here in the end?' said Greenall. His tone was light, cocktail-partyish, but with a harmonic of strain.

'I'm sorry?'

'She was talking about that seance when she was here last week. She had all kinds of daft ideas about it. But I saw the transcript on the table and I wondered if in the end... That's why of course I had to...'

The phone started ringing again. This time Greenall turned his attention to it, not touching it but staring fixedly at it as though the ceasing of the noise would be the signal of a beginning.

Pascoe took from his pocket the envelope which Gladmann had given him. As expected, it contained the short tape of the Choker's last call and the cassette of Rosetta Stanhope's interrupted seance. There were also several sheets in the linguist's rather self-consciously ornate handwriting.

Pascoe looked, selected, read.

'The poor quality of this recording makes accurate transcription difficult. Still it seems to me at least possible that the opening passage of the tape could be rendered as follows.

'It was Greenall, Greenall, over me, choking. The water then, boiling at first, and roaring, and seething...'

The phone stopped ringing.

CHAPTER 25

Greenall said, 'We were happy enough, not deliriously happy, but when does that ever last past the first few months? I was probably more content than Mary. Well, I'd done more, achieved more, relatively speaking. Whenever I felt dissatisfied I just had to look back to when I was a scruffy half-educated kid running round the back streets of Derby. God knows how I even got qualified enough to get into the RAF at the lowest level. But I did. And I did well. I learn fast. Barely ten years later I was commissioned, I was married to Mary. And of course, above all, I was flying.'

He smiled to himself, like a man who remembers glory.

Pascoe said casually, 'This is interesting. You needn't say anything you realize that? It may be used as evidence. I'll keep a record of it unless you prefer to write it yourself.'

It was a pretty feeble version of the correct procedure. And he ought to get Greenall to sign a declaration saying that he had been cautioned and still wanted to make a statement and have someone else write it down for him. But his instinct told him that he must take the minimum risk of fracturing this fragile mood. For a moment he thought he'd gone too far already but after a brief pause the man continued as though Pascoe had not spoken.

'I'd met Mary when I was stationed on Cyprus. She was teaching at the military school there. We liked each other from the first. Marriage might have come eventually, but when she found she was pregnant, it had to come at once. That might have been the trouble. Rushing things is never good. I know that now. But Alison was born and we were happy. Very happy. Once Alison got to school age, though, Mary got restless. She wanted to work again. I didn't like it too much and with me moving around from time to time, it wasn't all that easy anyway. But she insisted on it and when, twice within the space of four or five years, she had to give it up, you'd have thought she was the breadwinner and I was earning the pin-money.'

He shook his head at the incredibility of the thought.

'The second time was when I was posted to Hanover. She even suggested it might be better for Alison's schooling if she and the girl stayed in England for a while. I didn't think it was Alison she was really thinking of. Anyway, she came. And a few months later it looked as if things were turning right for her. One of the teachers at the local British School in Linden fell seriously ill. Mary was ideal for the post. On the spot, fully qualified, with just the right kind of experience. Things seemed to get back together for us for a while after that. There'd been a lot of rowing. She'd even managed to get the girl turned against me. Well, I expect there were faults on both sides. But now, for a time, everything seemed OK.'

He sighed deeply.

'Are you sure you won't have a drink?' he asked suddenly.

'No, thanks. But if you want one...'

'No,' he said emphatically. 'I can take it or leave it. She met Dinwoodie there, you know. He was deputy head, or some such thing. There was also some kind of drama group he was involved in and soon Mary was mixed up in it too. I got a bit concerned about how much of her time it was taking up, but I didn't want to rock the boat, things seemed to be going so well. So I didn't say much. But other people were saying things. Not directly to me. But after a bit you begin to notice silences, intonations. So I started going along myself. I couldn't do it regularly; but I thought if I took an interest, made myself useful with lights and so on...well, I don't know what I thought. Mary wasn't all that enthusiastic, but she didn't seem to mind. They were rehearsing for some local festival; Shakespeare. The Krauts love Shakespeare, God knows why. I didn't want to appear pig-ignorant, so I set out to read a bit myself. They were just doing scenes. Mary and Dinwoodie were doing a bit from *Hamlet*, the scene when he tells Gertrude what a whore she's been, then kills old Polonius behind the curtain. I read that play through a dozen times. I reckon I knew as much about it as anyone in that damned drama group. I just wanted to impress, you understand. I wasn't really suspicious, not any more. If they'd been doing a scene from *Romeo and Juliet* perhaps, but somehow with Mary acting as his mother, it didn't seem that there was anything to worry about. Stupid, really, isn't it?'

Pascoe nodded, not quite sure what he was acquiescing to.

'Even when I caught them at it, I didn't do anything rash. I told myself it was just a once-off thing, quickly over. I wasn't going to let her get away with it, of course. She deserved to be punished. I made that quite clear to her. I thought I might send the girl back to England to boarding-school, get her out of the way later. Meanwhile, though, I wanted to keep a low profile. I thought of the scandal it would cause in the mess, I could see all my hard work to get on over the years coming to nothing and, in any case, it was nearly the end of the school year and I knew that Dinwoodie's contract was up and he was returning to the UK. So I let things slide for a while. And the end of term came. And Dinwoodie went. And I came home from a few days on an exercise and found that Mary had disappeared and Alison with her. And after that, well, things went into a spin.'

As he talked now, first hesitations, then often lengthy gaps, began to appear in his speech, but Pascoe was able to fill it in from his long telephone conversation with an RAF records officer who had been extremely cooperative when the Choker case was mentioned.

Greenall had at first attempted to cover up, pretending that his wife and child had gone back to England for a holiday, though clearly not another person at the school or on the station believed this. He himself had returned to the UK on a fortnight's leave which he overstayed when his efforts to track them down were unavailing. This was the first stage in the long downhill slide his career now began to take. It didn't all happen at once. There were plunges and recoveries. He received a letter from his wife, explaining her motives, wanting to put everything on a civilized level. They met in a London hotel lounge to talk things over. The meeting ended with him striking her across the face and rushing across to the reception desk where a young girl, just arrived with her parents, was terrified to be embraced by this demented stranger and dragged towards the door.

That was the last contact for some time. Mary clearly decided, probably for a combination of religious and personal reasons, that disappearance was a better bet than any remedy of the law. Perhaps to keep their heads down, perhaps because the mid-seventies was a very bad time for expatriate teachers to try to filter back into the home system, they decided to abandon education for cultivation and went into the Garden Centre business. Certainly if they maintained any contact with the RAF world at all, reports of Greenall's condition would not have encouraged them to let him know their whereabouts. Drink and a growing oddness of behaviour patterns had resulted in first the loss of his flying status, then, after a period of breakdown, discharge on medical grounds.

All this over a period of nearly three years.

'So,' said Greenall, 'I woke up one morning and found I was back in civvy street. No wife, no daughter, no commission, no career. And no flying. I had to get that back to start with. Do you understand? Down here even when I was on the crest of the wave, I always felt there was something, I don't know, sort of pulling me back to where I started. Up there, it was different. Still is. Up there I was…am…'

'King of infinite space?' offered Pascoe.

'Yes. Right. That's it. King of infinite space. So I did an instructor's course. Just basic stuff. Work on trainers, that kind of thing. I knew I would never get back in the big boys again, but this way at least I got my feet off the ground. And there was work in it. I got a job down at a flying club in Surrey. Twice the size of this. I really enjoyed it, all of it, even the ground staff side.'

His speech, mirroring his mental recovery, had begun to flow freely again. Pottle would explain this, thought Pascoe. And probably advise me to listen carefully for the return of disjunction.

'And did you see your wife again in this time?'

'Neither saw nor heard from her,' said Greenall. 'When I got myself together, I started looking. I played your game, detective that is. Not an easy business, is it? I went to the address on that one letter, but it was a boardinghouse, no forwarding address. I tried local schools, then the Department of Education. They couldn't or wouldn't help. No, it wasn't easy.'

'Police?' suggested Pascoe. 'Did you try them?'

'Why?' said Greenall, surprised. 'It had nothing to do with the police. In the end, I stopped trying. I didn't give up, you understand. Just settled to play a waiting game. I knew that somehow, one day, something…well, I was right. There in the paper, just a paragraph. Tragic accident. Man chewed to death by machine at Agricultural Show. Mr Peter Dinwoodie. Leaving wife, Mary; daughter, Alison. Pure chance. But more than chance. The paper I saw it in was months out of date. I'd rented a small cottage. There was a coal fire. I used newspaper to light it and during the summer the papers just piled up. I'd missed the item when it first appeared, last summer. But one cold January morning this year I was making spills of paper to use as kindling, and there it was. Pure chance? I didn't think so.

'I was better at detective work this time. I thought about it for a week or two. All I had was one paragraph. Agricultural Show. So I came up to Yorkshire and started a search via the press. It was very easy. There were more details in the *Yorkshire Post*. I got the town and the name of the Garden Centre. *Linden*. That made me almost certain. But I had a look through back numbers of the local evening paper when I got here, and there was a photograph. Dinwoodie. I should have felt triumphant but I didn't. Sick almost. I nearly headed back south there and then. But I'd come this far...this far...

'That night I went out to the Garden Centre.

'Mary was alone. She was surprised to see me, but not too surprised. We sat and talked. I told her about myself, put her at her ease, told her I bore no grudges. It got late. Alison wasn't home. Mary said perhaps I should come back the next day, but I was getting a bit concerned. She was barely seventeen, a child still. I didn't like the idea that she was being kept out till all hours. Then we heard a car. I looked out of the window. I could see her in the passenger seat. She and the driver were in a pretty tight clinch you know, hands everywhere. I wanted to go out, but Mary wouldn't let me. A bit later Alison came in. God, what a change! I mean, all right, it was six years since I'd seen her, but she was still my girl, still just a child. But the clothes she had on, the hair-do, the makeup! And on her hand, on her left hand, a ring. She didn't notice me at first, she was so excited, waving this ring at her mother, saying she was engaged.

'I had to say something. I didn't want to spoil our reunion, but I had to say something. She was quiet at first, much more surprised than Mary. Pleased to see me, I thought, but also accusing. As if it had all been my fault. And wilful. Like her mother. She said she wanted to get married soon. Married? What did she know of life? A child. She said this boy was down here doing some kind of agricultural course. They'd met at the show where Dinwoodie had been killed. Irony. Even dying, he did me a bad turn. Soon he'd be finished, going back up to the Borders somewhere, and he wanted Alison to go with him. I said it was absurd. Legally she was still my daughter. I had my rights still. They let them choose for themselves when they're eighteen now. Stupid, isn't it? But there was still a year to go. And there was no way she was going to get my permission!'

But she didn't need it, thought Pascoe. One parent's agreement was enough now. Christ, why didn't people check what the latest state of the law was?

'Well, there was a row, of course,' resumed Greenall. 'Alison flew out of the room. Mary, however, seemed to be much more sensible about the situation. We talked and in the end I went away, satisfied that an understanding had been reached. It was far too early to talk about a reconciliation, but at least I felt we understood each other. How wrong can you be?'

Pascoe's pen was flying over the sheets of his notebook, yet he was making a great effort to keep it legible. This was an iron to strike while hot. This was not going to be a statement which would easily bear the delays of careful typing. Greenall's signature at the bottom of each handwritten page was going to be the first consideration.

'I couldn't get back for nearly a fortnight, and then just an overnight stay. Alison wasn't there. Staying with friends, said Mary. A long-standing commitment. I accepted it. Why not? We all had our own lives, we weren't a family again. Not yet. But I had hopes. I'd seen an advert in one of the journals. They wanted a secretary/instructor at the local Aero Club. It wasn't—*isn't*—a patch on the place I was at in Surrey and the job was much more of a general dogsbody from the sound of it, but I thought it might be worth a look. I said nothing to Mary, but I sent off for details.

'Then next time I came, there was no one at the house. There'd been heavy snow, you recall. It was a foot deep or more. The Garden Centre was closed, of course. And the house was empty. I went back to Surrey, not knowing what to do. I was worried sick. I'd not told a soul anything about this, so I couldn't even talk things over with anyone. I was in a dream for a couple of days. Then the phone rang. I'd given Mary my number and it was her. I knew it was her before I picked it up, and I knew it was bad news. Well, she was almost matter of fact about it. Against my will, against my rights, she'd encouraged Alison to run off with this boy. They'd been married in Scotland. And now they were dead.

'I don't know what I said. I don't know how long she listened. She was to blame, I knew that. Yet I could understand how utterly her life must have been destroyed. And Alison's death was the worst thing that had ever happened to me. Yet in a way it might be a sort of blessing, it seemed, for when I thought of all the agony and disillusion being married so young must have piled up for her, or being married at all for that matter, in a way this quick, sudden death...'

He took a deep breath.

'I thought of *Hamlet* again, suddenly, the first time in six years. What women could be, what they let themselves be, what they make of us... I tried to get in touch with Mary again. I wanted to explain, reprove, convince, I wanted to show her what she was, make her recognize—well, I wanted all kinds of things. But she wasn't there. And when I came up again, the Centre was still piled high with snow and she still wasn't there.

'So I applied for the job here. Don't ask me why. Just to be close, I suppose. To be ready. I got it, of course. In March I started. I kept away from Shafton. I guessed that Mary might be frightened of seeing me. If she came back and found there'd been someone around asking after her, she might take off again. But once or twice a week I'd ring the house in the evening, just to see if there was an answer. There never was. Meanwhile I got down to the job of putting this place on its feet. It was hard work, but I enjoy hard work. And I get on with people. I like people, Mr Pascoe. I like them a lot. That's why it's been so…hard.'

He passed his hand over his face.

Pascoe said gently, 'And did your wife answer the phone, Mr Greenall? Did you see her again before…'

'Before the Cheshire Cheese, you mean? No, I didn't. She had been back a couple of weeks, I gather. But either she wasn't in, or didn't answer when I rang. So it was quite unexpected. I like to keep fit, Mr Pascoe. A stroll last thing at night and a run first thing in the morning, that's my regime. I don't need more than five hours' sleep. I'd have been good in the Battle of Britain. God, what days those must have been!

'It was quiet here that night, I recall. So I went for my walk a bit earlier than usual and it wasn't quite closing time as I passed the Cheese. I suddenly had a fancy for a half of beer so I went in. I looked through the lounge-bar door to see how crowded it was, and there she was, Mary. A bit pale, a bit thinner, but with a glass in her hand, laughing, with a gang of people.

'I didn't go in. I went out to the edge of the car park and waited. People started to come out. Cars revved up and took off. Soon there was only a handful left. Then Mary came out with some people. They all shouted goodnight. The others all got into one car and drove off. Mary came over to a mini parked quite close to where I was standing. For a moment the car park was empty of people. I called her name as she reached the car. She said *Who's that?* puzzled, not frightened. *It's me, Austin*, I said. She came towards me, into the shadows under the trees just off the edge of the car park. She asked me what I wanted. *To talk*, I said. Someone else came out of the pub. I took her hand and drew her a little further away beneath the trees. She didn't resist. I said, *I want to talk about us. And about Alison.* And she said, so quiet I could hardly hear her, *I've been so frightened and so unhappy*, and she leaned against me. Somehow all the things I intended to say seemed irrelevant. Somehow there was nothing to be said at all.'

He paused again. The flow had been constant, thought Pascoe, with none of the anticipated disjointed incoherence as the crisis moment was reached.

He said, 'So you killed her.'

'Yes,' he said in a voice faintly surprised, as though at a quite unnecessary question. 'There was nothing else for her, you see. It's quick. I studied the manuals during my combat training. Then I carried her out of the way a bit and laid her down and made her look as peaceful as I could. I didn't want anyone to think that she'd been savagely attacked and molested, you know what I mean.'

'And then?'

'And then I walked home. It was a fine night, very clear, very still. Perfect for night flying, I remember thinking. I saw some navigation lights moving very high. Something big and fast. I envied the pilot a little. But I felt very much at peace. I thought it was all over, of course.'

'But it wasn't?'

'Oh no. You don't get experiences like I'd been through out of your system overnight. Ever since Alison's death, I'd been noticing girls. Kids, I mean. Standing at bus stops on wet mornings, going to work in some steamy office with loud-mouthed men. So young, so forlorn. You know what I mean. It really broke my heart to see them. We don't let them be kids long enough. We force them to grow up, and there's nothing there when they get there, and they have to change and turn into...well, that's how I felt. I'd started the disco nights at the Club. We had them in Surrey and I remembered how the kids used to enjoy them, just being kids if you follow me. There was no harm in it, despite what the fuddy-duddies like Middlefield said. And they brought in a bit of cash. We needed all the cash we could get if we were to make something decent out of this place. Oh I've got plans, Inspector, such plans... I had plans...

'Anyway, there was this youngster at the discos. I'd seen her a couple of times, I didn't know her name but she was so full of life and fun. Then suddenly she was there one Friday night, flashing an engagement ring. Her boy-friend was a soldier, serving in Belfast. They were to be married on his next leave. I thought of married life in the services. I thought of me and Mary. I thought of Alison. And I felt sick.'

'This was June McCarthy?' interposed Pascoe.

'Yes. I found out later. She wasn't there the next night. She had to go to work.'

'You knew this?' said Pascoe. 'You planned what happened?'

'Oh no,' said Greenall, shocked. 'No plan. It was fate. I hadn't been able to get her out of my mind, but I knew nothing about her. On the Sunday morning I went out for my usual run. Just after five. It's the best time of the day in summer. I felt so strong, I went further than usual. I usually stick to the airport and to the river, but on a Sunday the streets are so quiet, it's pleasant just to run along the pavement for a change. I ended up in Pump Street. To tell the truth I was a bit lost. And as I jogged past the allotments, I saw a girl there, kneeling down. She looked familiar. I went up to her. She gave quite a start when I spoke. What she was doing, I found out, was "borrowing" some sprigs of mint for the roast lamb she'd be cooking for her dad later in the day. She got quite chatty when she realized who I was, told me how busy they were at the canning plant in the fruit season, shifts every night, but she didn't mind as she was saving hard to get married. I'd recognized her by then, of course. The soldier's fiancée. She looked about thirteen, kneeling there with the mint. I couldn't bear the thought of it. Being spoilt so young. So I put her to rest.'

'You killed her? You strangled her?'

Greenall didn't reply. It was not an uneasy or guilty silence, rather a contemplative one, as though he were carefully examining the proposition.

'Yes,' he said just as Pascoe opened his mouth to prod again. 'Killed her. Strangled her. Saved her.'

'From *what*?'

'Disappointment. Disillusionment. Dismay. I felt nothing but love and pity. The girl in the bank was the same. I saw her that afternoon. She'd often served me since I took this job on. Only this time, I saw the ring. She saw me looking at it and smiled. You know, proudly. A child. I felt sick but I said "Congratulations." She said, "Thank you, Mr Greenall," And I left. But I knew I'd see her again.'

'You planned it, you mean?' asked Pascoe once more.

'Oh no. Nothing like that, though I had the feeling there was a plan. But it wasn't mine. No, about half-six the evening rush was over. It's always the same in summer when it's fine. Out of work, down to the Club, can't wait to get into the air. Well, who's to blame them? I went for a stroll, out through the boundary fence, across the waste ground till I reached the path along the river. It was a lovely evening but I didn't see a soul. It's a bit out of the way and eventually it brings you back to the main road just on the edge of the Industrial Estate. And if you follow that you get into Millhill.'

'Yes, I know,' said Pascoe impatiently.

'There she was,' said Greenall. 'It had to be planned. She was standing where the buses that come through the estate turn. There was no one else there. I said hello. She was annoyed, I could see. She told me she'd been having her hair done after work quite near the bank, had come out, just missed her bus, knew there wouldn't be another for twenty-five minutes, so thought that she'd be better off taking the ten-minute walk here and catching the estate bus. But it had just pulled off as she arrived. There wouldn't be another of those for at least half an hour. There was all kinds of shopping she had to do in the town centre. I gathered that on Thursdays a lot of the big shops stay open till eight o'clock, but it was now quarter to seven. So I offered her a lift. I explained it meant walking back to the Aero Club, but we could still get there and be in the town centre before the next bus arrived. She said OK and off we set.

'She chattered away. She was having a proper wedding, she said. That was one of the places she wanted to go this evening. She'd made up her mind about her wedding gown and she was going to put the money down. There were other things to get, too. She didn't want a long engagement, she said. There would be too much aggro at home from her father. He didn't understand.

'I understood,' said Greenall. 'Suddenly she stopped and looked up and said, "Are those your gliders? Aren't they beautiful? Like huge birds. It must be lovely to fly, but I don't think my Tommy would fancy it. It's all cars with him." That was when I took her throat. She fell backwards, hardly resisting, just staring at me in surprise. I thought she must have died very quickly, but when I let her go, suddenly she jerked and twisted, more a convulsion than anything. We were right at the edge of the river bank, and next thing she was over and in. At the very same moment I heard voices. Children. I knew we were close to the encampment and guessed it would be the gypsy kids. I hated to leave her, but there was nothing else to do. She was deep under the water. I turned and went on my way.'

'You must have expected an outcry immediately,' said Pascoe.

'I suppose so. I never really thought about it,' said Greenall. 'I just got back to the Club, went on as normal. And when I read in the *Evening Post* the next day about the girl being found in the canal, I was puzzled but somehow not surprised. And I was worried in case people wouldn't understand. So I phoned the paper again.'

'I meant to ask, why did you phone the first time?'

'Just to explain in a way,' said Greenall. 'Just so that it would be understood that these killings weren't meaningless. It seemed important.'

'And *Hamlet*?'

'It seemed apt. It just came to mind.'

'Why not just go to see the reporters, talk to them, tell your story?' wondered Pascoe ingenuously.

'But that would have meant giving myself up!' exclaimed Greenall. 'I wasn't ready for that.'

'No,' said Pascoe. 'You were quite determined not to be caught. As Pauline Stanhope could testify. If she were alive.'

'Yes,' said Greenall. 'Yes. Her. And the man, Wildgoose; it happened so quickly...both of them...a pilot's trained to make quick decisions you see...but afterwards time isn't so quick...not when you think...'

Now his narration once more lost its complacent, reasonable rhythm. Now once more the hesitation and uncertainties became apparent. Pottle had been right. It was here he felt the guilt, here where he had killed to protect himself rather than, as his delusion asserted, to protect the girls. His justification was the immediacy of the need. He had seen the transcript of the seance tape, read in the paper that the medium was Madame Rashid at the Charter Park Fair, driven there instantly with no plan, gone into the tent, asked Pauline if she were Madame Rashid, punched her in the belly and killed her. Now self-preservation had at last made him cunning. Seeing the Back Soon sign, he had put it on the chair and pushed it through the flap before removing and putting on the gypsy skirt, shawl and headscarf.

'You also laid the girl out like the others. And made a phone-call,' observed Pascoe.

'Yes, I thought it might confuse things...and I felt I *should* say something...I wasn't happy...and then it turned out she wasn't the woman at all...Christ. I felt ill.'

'But you didn't try to do anything about the real Madame Rashid after that, did you?' queried Pascoe.

Greenall shook his head almost indignantly.

'I couldn't...not *plan* it...not cold-bloodedly...'

Dalziel's going to love this, thought Pascoe.

Greenall recovered some of his composure to talk about Andrea Valentine whom he had overheard boasting to her friends at the disco that as soon as Wildgoose got rid of his wife, he was going to marry her.

'Did you follow them back to Danby Row?' asked Pascoe.

'No. I cleared up here and then went later. I had no plan, you understand. Just to look.'

'How did you know where to go?'

'I rang for their taxi,' said Greenall. 'Wildgoose gave me the address.'

That simple. No wonder he felt that he was merely an instrument of some benevolent and protective force. His path must have seemed to be smoothed out before him all the way.

He had driven by the house, round the block, spotted the back lane, found the rear entrance to number 73 and stepped inside just in time to meet Wildgoose coming out. The man had grabbed him. Brokenly, Greenall disclaimed any wish to hurt him.

'But he saw my face...it was dark but not that dark...I could see he recognized me...so I had to...again...'

Distressed though he was by this unlooked-for killing, it did not deter him from his main purpose. He went up to the house. There was still a light on in the kitchen. He tapped at the back door. 'Who's there?' asked the girl but was so sure that it must be Wildgoose returning for some reason that a muttered 'It's me,' had her turning the key.

'And then you killed her,' said Pascoe. 'But why? I mean she couldn't be going to get married, could she? Not when you'd just killed the man she was going to marry!'

Greenall hid his face in his hands.

'Don't you think I haven't thought of that?' he said. 'Even as she died, I thought of it. But I had to kill the man, you see. He knew me. I *had* to kill him.'

He spoke pleadingly as if seeking approval, or absolution. Pascoe was very willing to give him whatever he sought as long as he got his signature at the bottom of every page of the statement he was scribbling.

'Yes, I see that,' he said. 'I quite see that.'

'Do you? Do you really?' asked Greenall.

'I do,' assured Pascoe. 'I really do. Then you took the body to your car?'

The maniac's luck had held. No one had interrupted him. The idea of burying Wildgoose in the rose field of the Garden Centre had seemed like a triumph of logical thinking. He had driven past it from time to time since his wife's death and observed that it was no longer open. It was ideal.

'I didn't want him found. I thought he might get blamed, you see. It was going wrong. There was too much killing, too much *unnecessary* killing. I thought if you were looking for Wildgoose I might get a bit of peace and quiet to do some thinking in.'

Pascoe regarded the small, slight man who returned his gaze trustingly and hopefully.

'I think we might arrange that, sir,' he said gently. 'What I would like you to do now is...'

There was a perfunctory tap at the door and it burst open to reveal Sergeant Wield.

'Mr Pascoe,' he began.

'Later,' said Pascoe trying to combine the casual and the imperious in his tone.

'I'm sorry, sir, but...'

'I said *later*, Sergeant!' snapped Pascoe, abandoning his attempt at the casual.

But Wield stood his ground. 'We tried to ring, sir, but there was no answer,' he said. 'It's your wife.'

'What about her?' said Pascoe, standing up now and facing the sergeant. Wield's features, he noticed with a tightening of the heart, were softened to a recognizable anxiety.

'She's had to go to hospital, sir. They rang not long after you'd left. Like I say, we tried to telephone here...'

'What's happened to her?' demanded Pascoe.

'I don't know, sir. But I knew how worried you'd been, so I thought I'd better...'

Pascoe glanced from the sergeant to Greenall, who was looking musingly out of the window, as though none of this had impinged upon him. Perhaps it hadn't. Perhaps...but this was no time to be perhapsing around here. Not with Ellie...oh Christ!

'Excuse me, Mr Greenall,' he said and pushed Wield through the door, closing it behind them.

'Listen,' he said, putting the notebook into the sergeant's hands. 'It's him. It's all there. Get him to read it. Get him to sign it. Every last bloody page. That first. That most certainly first. No pressing. No taking him down town. Do you follow me?'

'Yes, sir,' said Wield. 'And then?'

'Get his name on that and then you can put him in irons for all I care,' snapped Pascoe. 'Do it. I'm off.'

'I hope Mrs Pascoe's OK,' called Wield after him but he doubted if the Inspector heard.

Slowly he turned and quietly opened the door.

'Hello, Mr Greenall,' he said.

CHAPTER 26

'And is that the verdict of you all?'

'It is,' said the foreman of the jury.

The Judge nodded and turned towards the figure in the dock. 'Austin Frederick Greenall,' he began.

Outside the sun still looked down from clear skies but it was no longer the burning orange of midsummer but the pale lemon of autumn. There were dry brown leaves from the municipal plane trees patterning the steps of the court building as Pascoe emerged. He thrust his hands deep into his pockets and stared moodily at the medieval guildhall across the way.

Wield came out behind him.

'I'm sorry, sir,' he said.

'Not your fault, sergeant,' said Pascoe. 'Even if he'd signed that statement, it would probably have been tossed out as inadmissible.'

'All the same…'

'Lawyers, I've shit 'em!' proclaimed Dalziel's voice. Pascoe looked round. The fat man looked as if he'd just emerged from a battle. In a way he probably had.

'I had a word with that fellow prosecuting. Told him I'd seen better cases presented at the left luggage.'

'What did he say, sir?'

'Threatened to report me. I said if he made complaints like he cross-examined, I'd likely get promoted.'

'It was all circumstantial, sir,' defended Pascoe. 'When you got down to it, there was precious little hard evidence.'

'There was enough, rightly put over,' said Dalziel. 'And I'd have cracked the bugger wide open if we'd got another postponement.'

Pascoe and Wield exchanged glances.

Four months had passed. Dalziel had used every delaying tactic in the book. There had been remands before the committal proceedings. Here there had been reporting restrictions imposed, not (as the general public believed) to conceal horrors which should not be allowed to fall twice on human ears but (as Wield cynically asserted) to conceal from the general public the flimsiness of the case. Fortunately (or not), examining justices are swayed as much by police certainties as police evidence, particularly where crimes like the Choker's are involved, and Greenall had been committed for trial, which should have commenced within eight weeks according to law. Two postponements had been achieved, but even justice gets impatient and on the threat of a writ of *habeas corpus* from the defence counsel, the trial had gone ahead.

There had been only one charge—the wilful murder of Mary Greenall also known as Mary Dinwoodie. This was where the prosecutors felt at their strongest. They could prove motive and opportunity. They could point to Greenall's record of breakdown, they could make great play of his odd behaviour in not coming forward after the death. They could do many things except prove that he was outside the Cheshire Cheese on the night in question.

Defence challenged the admissibility of medical records, pointed out that Greenall had been performing a responsible and demanding job in civilian life for more than three years without exciting any adverse comment, and tried to explain his silence after his wife's murder by getting their client to admit freely that he was dismayed and numbed by the news and in any case had no reason to believe the police wouldn't rapidly track down his connection with the dead woman. 'In the event, he overestimated their speed and efficiency, but that is a fault we must lay at the door of the investigating officers, not of my client,' said counsel for the defence blandly.

Desperately the prosecution had tried to bring the linguistic evidence forward. Gladmann had put on his best suit ('the one stained with Beluga caviare,' said Pascoe) but his hopes of fame were dashed.

The *first* telephone call had not been made till after the death of June McCarthy, argued defence. The first *recorded* telephone calls had not been made till after the death of Pauline Stanhope. To prove that any of those four voices was the same as the earlier voice would be difficult. But that was beside the case anyway. Their client was not accused of any of the subsequent killings. Indeed, although the subsequent killings had some *prima facie* connection in that they all involved young women, the murder of Mary Greenall or Dinwoodie must be taken as distinct and separate, unless the police had concrete proof of a connection.

The disposition of the body, suggested prosecution.

Very slight, replied defence, and explicable in terms of straightforward imitation. The Cheshire Cheese killing had been widely reported, after all.

The Judge before whom this argument had been conducted in the absence of the jury agreed with the defence. He wondered whether he should make his sternly rebuking speech about the waste of the court's time now or save it up till after the acquittal he now anticipated. In the event he never made it. After all, it was the kind of thing that the papers would quote gleefully if this fellow went out of court free and then was found in the act of strangling some other poor girl. You couldn't be too careful. Judges were not accorded the respect that was once their due, not even in obituaries.

In fact, he was surprised by how long the jury took. Five hours. Prosecution hopes had begun to rise. But then they had filed back in, twelve good men and true, and Austin Greenall had stood and regarded them neither defiantly nor fearfully, and nodded in quiet agreement as he heard the words *Not Guilty*.

'There he is,' said Wield suddenly.

Greenall emerged into the pale sunlight surrounded by reporters. They pressed and jostled around him but he moved steadily forward, the calm centre of their turbulence. He glanced across towards the group of policemen on the steps but did not pause. Pascoe caught the words '...get back to work...' and then the slight, dapper figure passed out of earshot and, soon after, out of sight.

A reporter detached himself from the group as they passed and said, 'Any reaction, Super?'

Pascoe said quickly, 'No comment.'

The reporter said, 'How's the Choker hunt going on? Is it true you're calling in the Yard? Or is it back to the crystal ball?'

'Same thing,' grunted Dalziel. 'They'll none of 'em work without their palms being crossed with silver.'

'Can I quote that,' grinned the reporter.

'Quote what?' said Pascoe. 'Who said anything? On your bike, Beaverbrook.'

'They love it,' said Dalziel as the man moved away. 'Seeing us look stupid. Bastards.'

'We won't look so stupid if he starts up again,' said Pascoe.

'Is that likely, sir?' asked Wield.

'Pottle says that his motivation is unique in his experience. He reacted to the idea of a young girl being spoilt by marriage, with the engagement ring acting as a kind of trigger. It's quite possible, he says, that being held in custody for so long will have effected a cure, given him time to think the thing through and come to terms with it.'

'You don't see many young girls with engagement rings in the nick,' said Dalziel.

'If he does that, perhaps it'll get to his conscience and he'll be ready to confess again,' said Wield.

'Pottle thinks not,' said Pascoe. 'He wanted to confess in the first place because of the unnecessary killings—that is, those that were motivated by simple self-preservation. It was a confession in the religious sense. He's a Catholic, remember. Pottle says I was the priest, but I turned out to be fraudulent. Real priests don't duck out of the confessional and send a curate in to finish things off. So, end of confession.'

'Fuck Pottle,' said Dalziel. 'I'll tell you one thing. That bugger won't pick his nose without me knowing about it from now on.'

'What?'

'Aye. Young Preece is on him now.'

'But he knows Preece,' said Pascoe.

'He'll know a lot of us before we're done,' said Dalziel. 'Day and night.'

'He'll be after us for harassment,' protested Pascoe.

'You reckon?' Dalziel looked at Pascoe curiously. 'Bothers you, does it?'

'A lot of things bother me, sir,' said Pascoe.

'I'll tell you something, Peter,' said Dalziel seriously. 'When I started this job, there was *us* and *them* and *their* weapons were brutality and deceit and not-giving-a-sod and *our* weapon was the law. Now the law's their weapon too, or haven't you noticed? So me, I'll use whatever I can lay my hands on.'

'Even if it's something *they* have discarded?' wondered Pascoe.

'Dog turds, if necessary,' said Dalziel. 'I'm off. If I see them lawyers coming out, all arm in arm and friendly, I may thump their bloody wigs together.'

Pascoe and Sergeant Wield watched as the fat man stumped down the steps.

'He's not happy,' said Wield.

'I'm not happy,' said Pascoe. 'But what the hell?'

'Mr Pascoe,' said a woman's voice.

They turned. Rosetta Stanhope was standing on the step above them.

'Hello,' said Pascoe. 'I noticed you in court. You know Sergeant Wield, I think.'

'Yes,' said the woman. 'We were talking earlier.'

'I'd best be off,' said Wield. 'See you later, sir. Goodbye, Mrs Stanhope.'

They watched him go.

'Nice man,' said the woman. 'He's been very unhappy lately, I think.'

'Has he?' said Pascoe. Somehow the states of happiness and unhappiness did not seem to relate to Wield.

'You haven't noticed? No, he wouldn't show much. He'll be happy again, eventually, I think. But you've got a lot to be happy about now, so he was telling me, Inspector. Congratulations.'

Pascoe returned the woman's warm smile and suddenly felt a surge of delight rising in him which drove out all the post-trial despondency.

'Yes,' he said. 'Thank you. Last week. It's been very worrying. Ellie, that's my wife, was ill for a long time. We thought she was going to lose it. She spent weeks in hospital. And it came a couple of weeks early.'

'It?'

'*She*,' said Pascoe. 'I haven't got used yet. She wasn't very heavy, but she's fine. She's OK. Perfect, I mean.'

'And your wife?'

'Fine too. She'll be all right soon. It's been very hard for her. Very hard.'

Pascoe frowned as he spoke and Rosetta Stanhope put a thin brown hand on his arm.

'Don't worry,' she said. 'It'll be all right. I feel it.'

'Yes. Well, thanks,' said Pascoe. 'And you? How are you? Look, I'm sorry. About all this, all being for nothing, I mean.'

'Don't worry,' she repeated, smiling. 'That will be all right too. I feel it. It will be as Pauline would have wanted it. I visited Dave the other day.'

'Lee? How is he? He should be out early next year if he's been behaving himself. He might even have got away with probation if it hadn't been for his record.'

'Yes, you were very gentle with him in the end. Perhaps the fat man has a bit of a conscience, eh? I explained this to Dave when he asked me to curse him.'

'Curse Mr Dalziel?' said Pascoe, amused.

'All of you, but especially Mr Dalziel,' said Rosetta Stanhope without amusement.

'But you wouldn't do it?'

'With your troubles, who needs curses?'

'Thanks anyway,' grinned Pascoe.

This time she smiled back. She was very smart in a tweed coat and elegant brogues.

'You're right not to be frightened of an ordinary old woman like me,' she said. 'But don't forget I'm purebred Romany under this outfit. I've been away a long time but you can't be away for ever.'

'You're not really thinking of going back?'

'To end my days sitting on the *vardo* steps puffing away at an old pipe to keep off the flies, you mean? Well, it may not seem a bad option when the spring's back in the air and the green's among the trees. I'd be someone there, at least. Here...well, I miss her, Mr Pascoe. She stopped me missing him and now she's gone, I miss them both.'

'I'm sorry,' said Pascoe helplessly. 'About everything.'

'It's going to be all right,' said Rosetta Stanhope. 'It's taken care of. Let me have your little girl's date and time of birth, if you like. I'll cast her horoscope. It'll be a fortunate one, I feel it. Everything's going to be all right. Everything.'

'Yes,' said Pascoe.

CHAPTER 27

Austin Greenall went straight to the Aero Club from the courtroom, but news of his acquittal had preceded him. Bernard Middlefield had been in court too and had had no lawyers and journalists to delay his departure.

It was late afternoon and the shadows were long. The only glider in the sky was making its approach, but in the club house were a dozen or so members who had presumably managed to organize their work so that they could enjoy their flight earlier in the afternoon. Perhaps not coincidentally they included three other committee members besides Middlefield. A quorum.

There was silence as he entered, then someone said, 'Congratulations, Austin.' This started a small spatter of *yes, well done, never doubted for a minute*, hardly felt before quickly drying up.

Middlefield said, 'Can we go into the office?'

'By all means,' said Greenall. 'Go ahead.'

'No; with you, I mean,' said Middlefield exasperatedly. 'There's business to do. We've had a committee meeting...'

'A very brief one, surely?'

'Not just now. Earlier this week. We had to make decisions.'

'Contingency plans? In case I got acquitted?'

'All we want is to find out what you plan to do.'

'I thought, first, a little flight. Just to clear the mind, stretch the muscles. Roger. Peter. Would you give me a hand?'

'It's a bit late, Austin,' protested the first man addressed, Roger Minstrel, his assistant, who had been running the Club single-handed for the past few months.

'I'll give you a hand,' said Thelma Lacewing from the doorway. She looked very fetching in boots, pink cords and a light blue anorak. 'Assistance is getting hard to find round here. I thought I'd hit the deserted village when I came down just now.'

'Thelma, I'm sorry,' apologized Minstrel. 'Honestly, I was out there watching you, but...'

He tailed off.

'You came inside for the welcome home party,' concluded Lacewing. 'You'd better get a move on, Austin. The lights are going out all over Yorkshire. Starting here, as usual.'

'Yes,' said Greenall making for the door. 'Roger?'

'All right, but it *is* late,' said Minstrel.

'We'll talk later,' called Middlefield after them in an attempt to re-affirm his authority.

By the time Greenall had got himself ready, Minstrel and Lacewing had manoeuvred the glider into position and the man went off to the towing winch.

Greenall climbed into the cockpit and strapped himself in.

'I gather you were acquitted,' said the woman.

He nodded.

'How do you feel about it?' she asked.

'I'm not sure,' he said.

'Do the police still think you're guilty?'

'I don't know. You'd better ask your friend.'

'Ellie Pascoe?' said Lacewing, frowning. 'She's had—still has—other things to worry her apart from whether you're guilty or not. What about you? What do you think?'

'About being guilty?' he said with a faint smile. 'I'm not very clear yet.'

'I should try to be clear before you land,' she said. 'For everyone's sake.'

She turned away and retreated to the wing tip which she grasped and raised. The signal was given to Minstrel. The winch engine bellowed into life. The glider began to move.

It was a perfect launch. The skills were too deeply grafted into Greenall's sinews and nerves for his enforced lay-off to have damaged them. Released from the towline, the glider soared as he expertly used the wind to carry him over the industrial estate where there was a complex of thermal activity he could read like a contour map.

Why had he chosen the glider? he wondered. The Cub would have taken him higher and further, given him more control. But he knew why, he realized. In the small aeroplane he was always aware of what it had once felt like to have at his fingertips control of such speed and power as most men could hardly dream of. A king of infinite space. Soaring in the glider brought no such memories. This was something different, not mastery of a kingdom by force of conquest, but more like acceptance as a citizen by a kind of naturalization process. Citizen of infinite space. Not quite the same ring about it but at this moment, at this time, the experience brought a peace and sense of belonging which he desperately needed.

What were his plans? Middlefield had asked.

What did he think about his guilt or innocence? Thelma Lacewing had wondered.

Stupid questions. Guilt, innocence, the future; these were not things to be decided or even usefully contemplated. He had felt guilty, it was true, else why had he talked at such length to that fellow Pascoe? But with the talking the guilt had lessened, was already going as he talked to the man, and had gone completely by the time that sergeant with a face like a hangman's labourer had come in.

Guilt might return, though it had not returned since then. And even if it did return, he now knew from experience that innocence returned too. So the future must take care of itself, whatever it brought. It was written. He knew it.

He hadn't told Pascoe everything, not quite everything. When he had slipped into Madame Rashid's tent at Charter Park, he hadn't killed the girl straightaway. He had given her his palm to read. She had examined it, murmuring a few well-worn platitudes, then she had gone very quiet, and looked at his hand quite fixedly, and slowly risen, pushing his hand away and raising her own to her mouth. He had punched her then, very hard, in the stomach, and killed her. She had seen he was going to kill her, he was sure of that. And what was going to happen had to happen. Guilt he had felt then, and again, still stronger, after the slaying of Wildgoose. But he was an evil man, a debaucher of youth. He saw that now. There was no more guilt to be felt there.

The flight was doing him good. He had known it would. He felt ready for the earth again, ready to go back and take his place once more and do whatever had to be done.

He looked down to get his bearings. Up here it was still bright but the height made a lot of difference. At ground level the sun was now dipping below the horizon, but it made no difference, not to a citizen of infinite space. He dipped across the airfield in a long descending run with the light wind behind him and turned for his landing approach. To his surprise he realized he was still rather high. Perhaps he was more out of practice than he imagined. To compensate and to reassure himself of his touch, he applied full airbrake and side-slipped to lose height till he was satisfied he was approaching at the optimum angle.

He was now low enough to be out of the full orb of the sun and the gloom of early evening visibly thickened beneath him, but not enough to cause concern. He was coming down parallel to the picket fence which the council had erected to keep the gypsies away from the airfield. To his right he could see the club house quite clearly. The flagpole, brilliant white and exactly thirty feet high, gave him a precise point of reference for his round-out, even though the ground surface itself seemed far from clear. It was rushing beneath him, vague and shadowy. And the shadows were uneven too. Some seemed to be moving *across* the line of his approach, and these had a look of shape and substance.

'Jesus!' he muttered suddenly, realizing what they were.

No shadows these, but ponies, a whole bloody herd by the look of it, wheeling and swerving beneath him as though driven in panic by the sound of his descent.

The picket fence must be broken again. The bloody things were everywhere. He shouted, knowing they couldn't hear and that it would make no difference if they could; but still he shouted. And still they thundered directly beneath him. Christ, they must be moving! He was doing almost fifty knots and he wasn't outrunning them.

It was time for decisions. Continue the landing as planned and hope the blasted things got out of the way. Or overshoot. He visualized what lay behind that section of the boundary fence directly ahead. Rough ground. Some gorse bushes, very substantial. And then the belt of trees beyond which curved the river.

Perilous country even if he could see it. But black as it was now, certain disaster.

So it had to be the landing as planned. He hadn't got enough speed to gain enough height for another turn on to a different line from the stampeding herd. Only the crassest of novices would try that, a fool, an idiot.

Yet that was what his hands and feet were trying to do. He cursed them and fought back, held the glider level, straight and level, the animals weren't stupid, they would get out of his way.

And suddenly he had won. He felt relaxed, looked out through the perspex. There seemed to be rather more light now. Everything was quite clear. And he could no longer see the ponies.

Suddenly he knew what was happening.

❀ ❀ ❀

By the time Dalziel and Pascoe reached the airfield, the ambulance had gone and the excited and horror-struck members were busy exchanging notes in the club house. Preece who met them in the car park was equally excited and eager for an audience.

'I saw it,' he said. 'I was just sitting in my car, waiting. I saw him coming in to land. It looked fine, but he just kept on going and going, made no attempt to touch down or lose speed. Just going and going. Right into the boundary fence. I couldn't believe it, I was watching and I couldn't believe it!'

'Dead?' said Dalziel.

'Oh yes. I was first across there. It was a mess. Broken neck, it looked like. I called an ambulance, but I might as well have called a dust-cart.'

'Let's take a look,' said Dalziel.

The three policemen walked across to the wreckage. The glider had hit the wire mesh of the boundary fence, flipped over and landed upside down with considerable fracturing of metal and fibreglass.

And bone.

'What do you think?' asked Dalziel. 'Suicide?'

'He just flew straight into it,' repeated Preece. 'He made no attempt to avoid it.'

'OK, lad,' said Dalziel. 'Peter, what do you think?'

'Guilty conscience, you mean? It'll be a popular theory with half the Great British Public.'

'And the other half?'

'Innocent man driven to extremes by false accusation and police harassment.'

'Yes, but what do *you* think?'

Pascoe walked a little further along the boundary fence till through the dusk he could see the line of picket-stakes which marched at right angles to it.

'The gypsies have gone,' he said, looking over the empty patch of land beyond.

'Oh aye. We're shot of them buggers till next year, thank God,' said Dalziel. 'How many times do I have to ask. *What do you think?*'

'I think it's mysterious and sad,' said Pascoe. 'That's it. A sorrow and a mystery. Like life.'

'Jesus bloody wept,' said Dalziel.